WARRIORS

MORITURI TE SALUTAMUS

We, who are about to die, salute you

KINGFISHER

NEW YORK

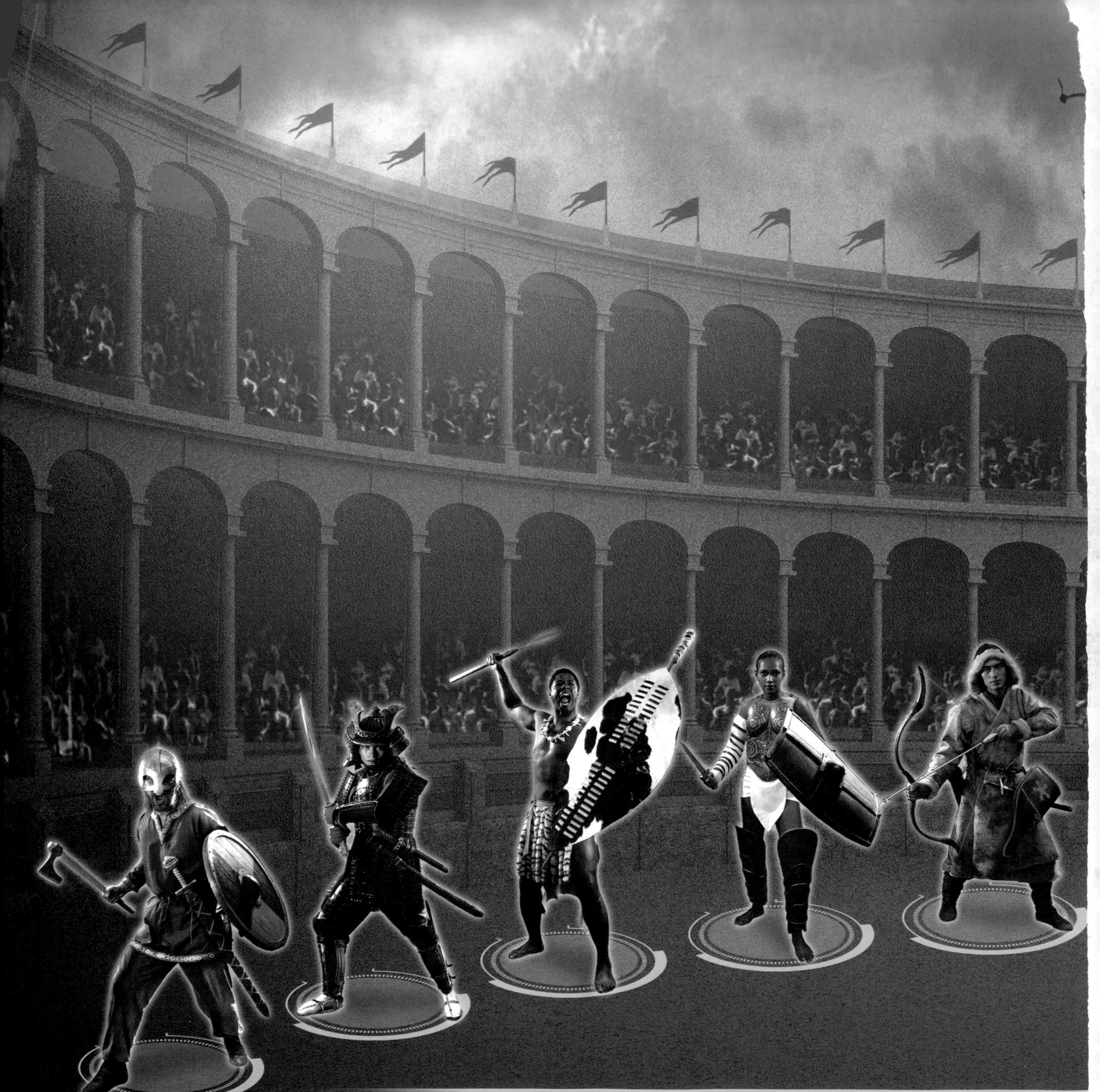

WELCOME TO VS, WHERE THE STAGE IS SET FOR AN EXTRAVAGANZA OF THE FIERCEST, BLOODIEST, AND MOST AMAZING CONTESTS OF ALL TIME.

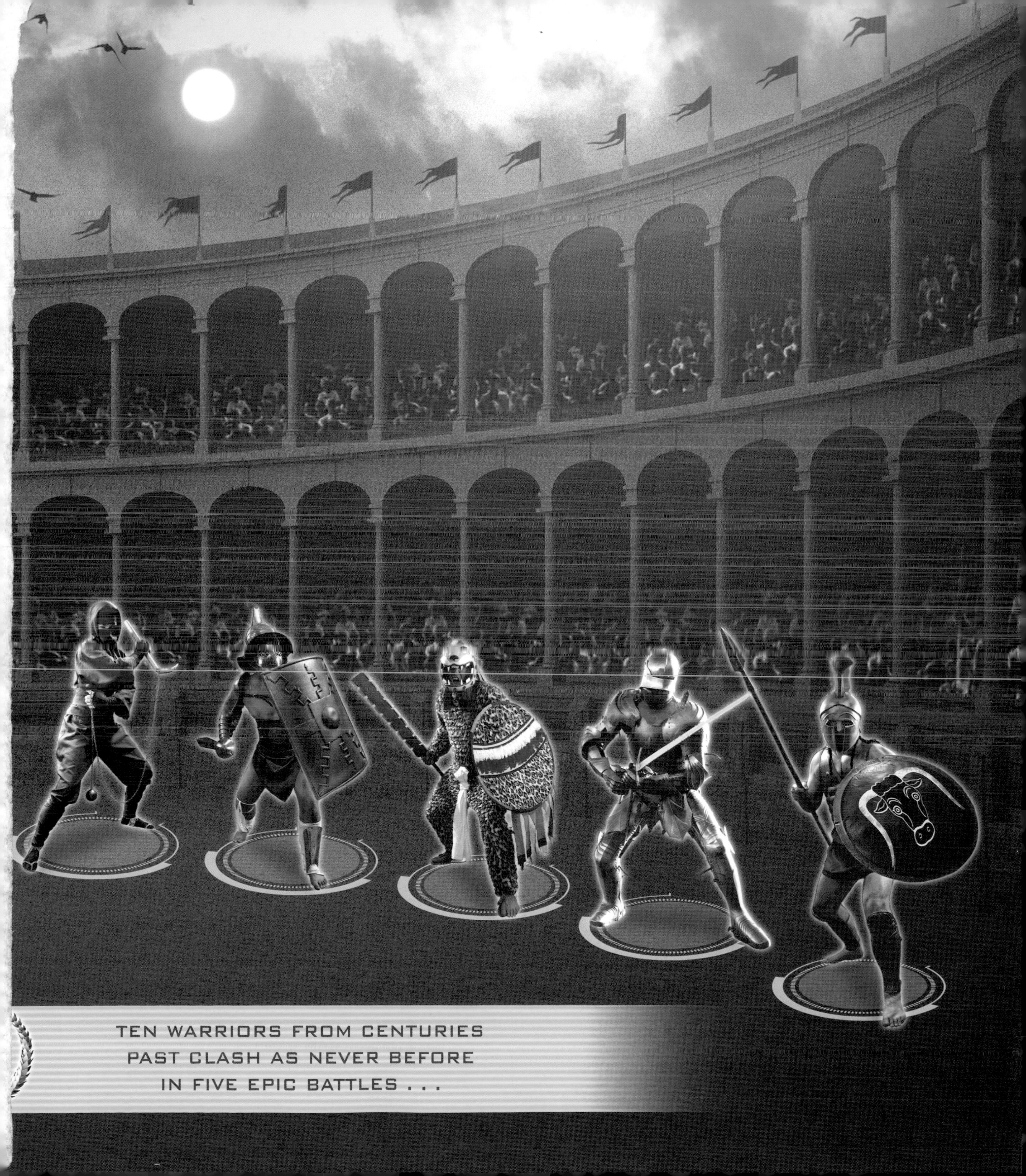

TEN WARRIORS FROM CENTURIES
PAST CLASH AS NEVER BEFORE
IN FIVE EPIC BATTLES . . .

THE ARENAS

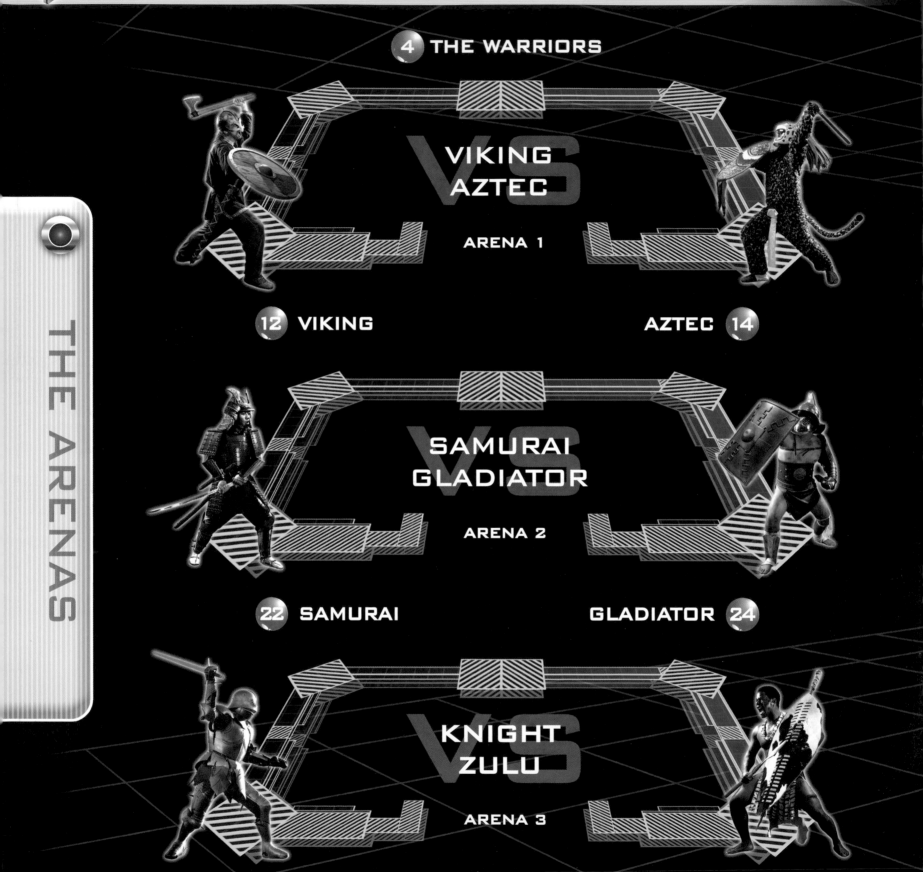

4 THE WARRIORS

VIKING VS AZTEC

ARENA 1

12 VIKING

AZTEC 14

SAMURAI VS GLADIATOR

ARENA 2

22 SAMURAI

GLADIATOR 24

KNIGHT VS ZULU

ARENA 3

32 KNIGHT

ZULU 34

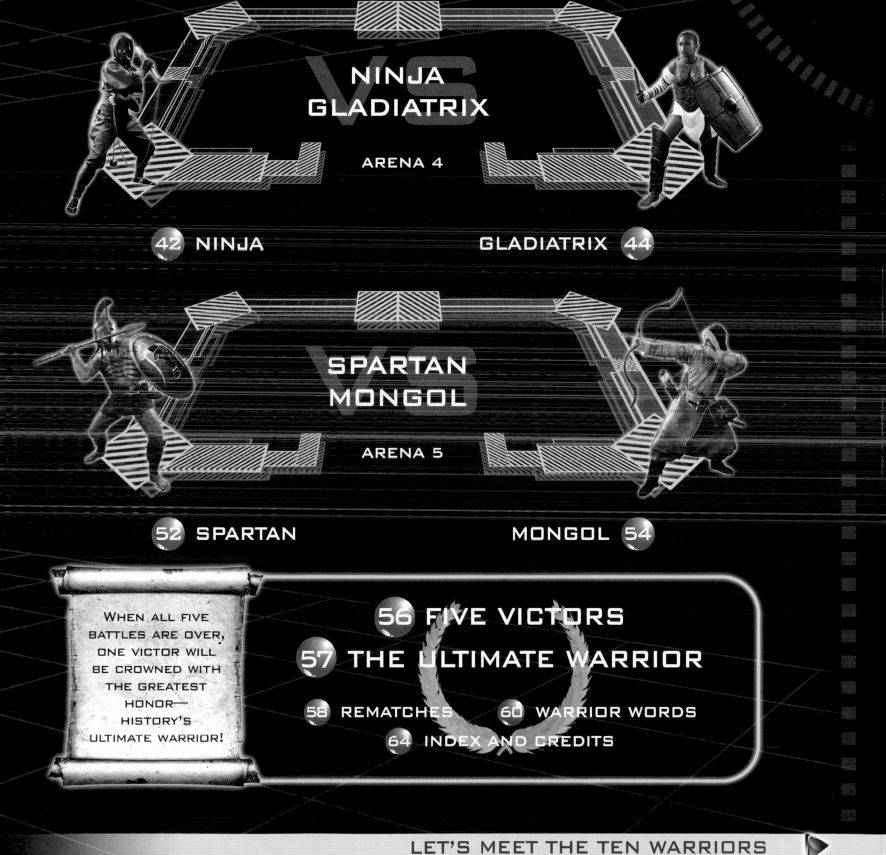

NINJA
GLADIATRIX

ARENA 4

SPARTAN
MONGOL

ARENA 5

WHEN ALL FIVE
BATTLES ARE OVER,
ONE VICTOR WILL
BE CROWNED WITH
THE GREATEST
HONOR—
HISTORY'S
ULTIMATE WARRIOR!

LET'S MEET THE TEN WARRIORS ▶

SPARTAN 480 B.C.
From the 700s to the 300s B.C., the ancient Greek city-state of Sparta was a military superpower. All of its citizens were soldiers—called hoplites—whose lives were dedicated to the art of war.

GLADIATRIX A.D. 100
The female gladiators of ancient Rome, like their male counterparts, were athletes rather than soldiers, fighting in one-to-one contests in the first and second century for public entertainment.

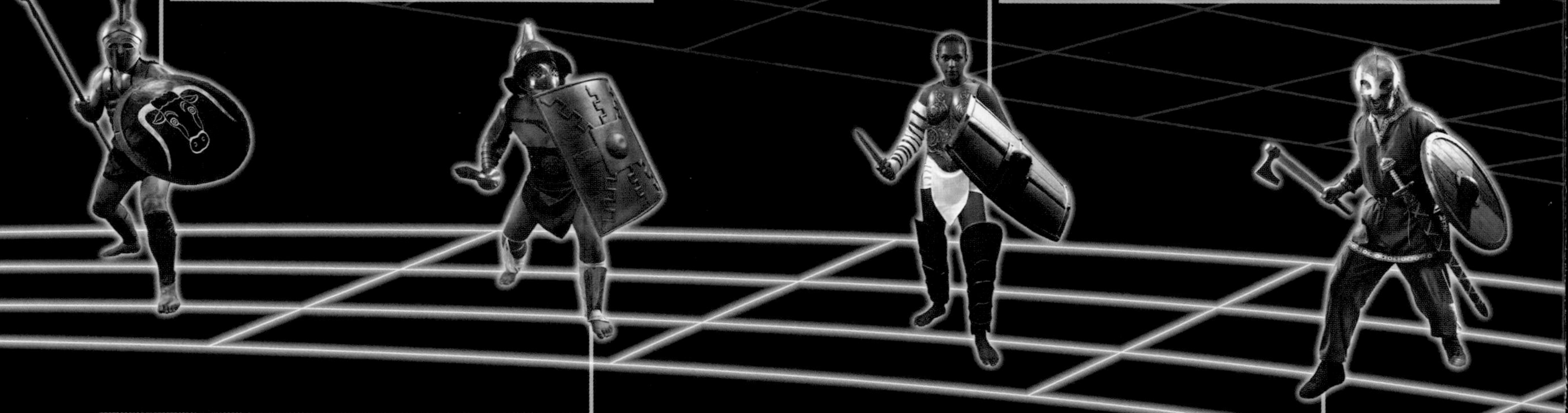

GLADIATOR 50 B.C.
In ancient Rome and its empire, contests involving gladiators—well-trained, well-armed athletes who fought in single combat—were hugely popular from the 300s B.C. to the A.D. 200s.

VIKING A.D. 840
From the late 700s to the 1000s, the Vikings, from Scandinavia, ransacked and conquered much of Europe. Skillful, fierce, and determined, Viking warriors were among the most feared fighters of their age.

LOCATION

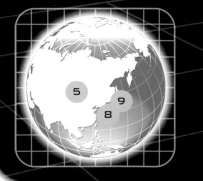

WARRIOR WORLD
HERE IS THE BATTLE-READY LINEUP: THE TEN FIGHTERS WHO WILL COMPETE TO BE HISTORY'S ULTIMATE WARRIOR. THEY COME FROM CENTURIES PAST AND FROM AROUND THE GLOBE. MOVE THROUGH THE BOOK AND INTO THE ARENAS AND PREPARE TO BE AMAZED BY DRAMATIC SCENES OF COMBAT. ALONG THE WAY, CONSULT EACH WARRIOR'S DATA PAGE FOR FACTS ABOUT THE SKILLS AND WEAPONS ON DISPLAY AND DISCOVER THE HISTORY AND CULTURE THAT SHAPED EACH COMBATANT.

5

MONGOL A.D. 1250
In the 1100s and 1200s, these warlike nomadic people from Central Asia amassed the largest empire in history. Mongol warriors were deadly archers—fast, ruthless, and cruel.

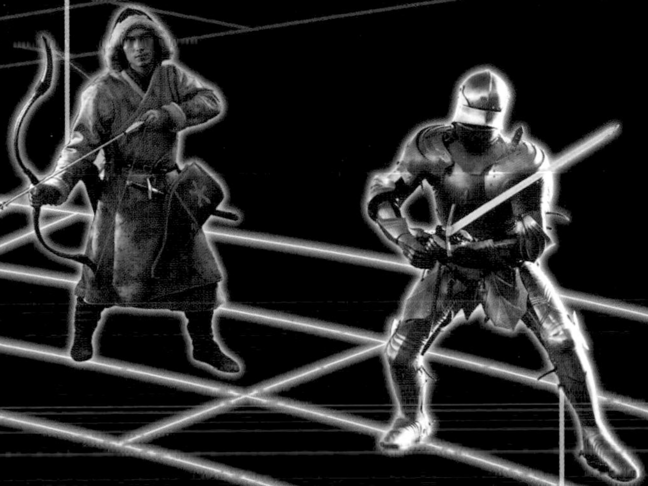

6

KNIGHT A.D. 1450
European knights fought in hundreds of bloody wars from the 800s to the 1500s. These noblemen soldiers had high-tech weapons and armor and spent their lives training for battle or waging war.

7

AZTEC A.D. 1500
The Aztec Empire in Mexico thrived from the 1100s until its fall in 1521. Aztec society was centered on warfare and the sacrifice of captured prisoners. All men were warriors.

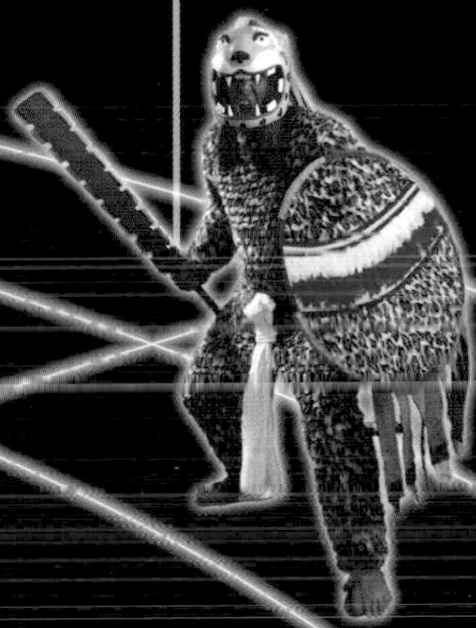

8

NINJA A.D. 1550
From the mid-1400s to the 1800s, the ninja were Japan's secret warriors. These martial arts experts were feared and despised by other warriors, but their skills as assassins were indispensable.

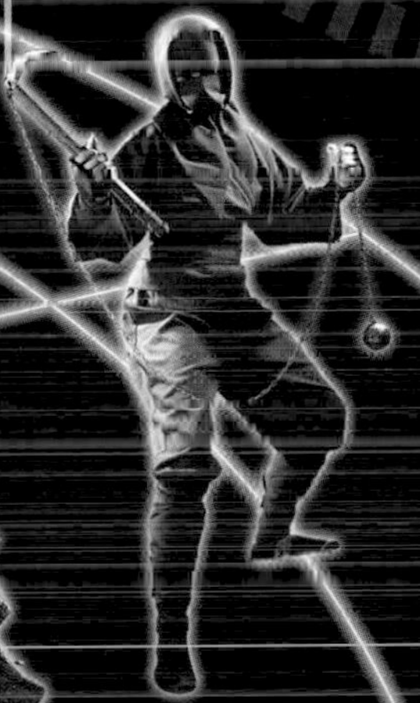

9

SAMURAI A.D. 1580
From the 700s to the 1800s, Japan was dominated by the samurai. These noble warrior knights had a strict code of honor and superb fighting methods. Rivalry between samurai clans was fierce.

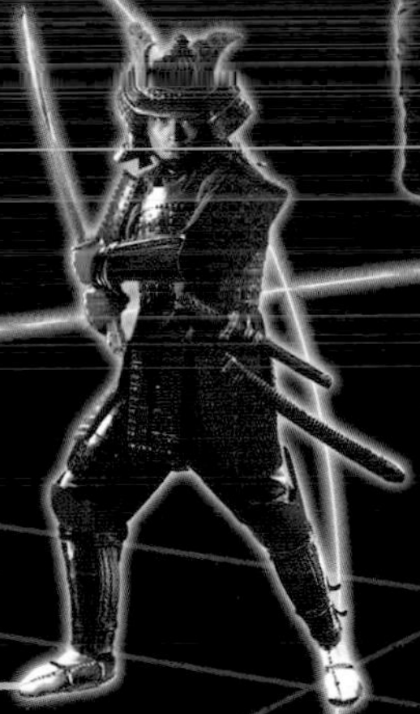

10

ZULU A.D. 1820
In the 1800s, the Zulu nation came to prominence in southern Africa. Zulu warriors had basic but deadly weapons, and they were aggressive and disciplined fighters, formidable in single combat.

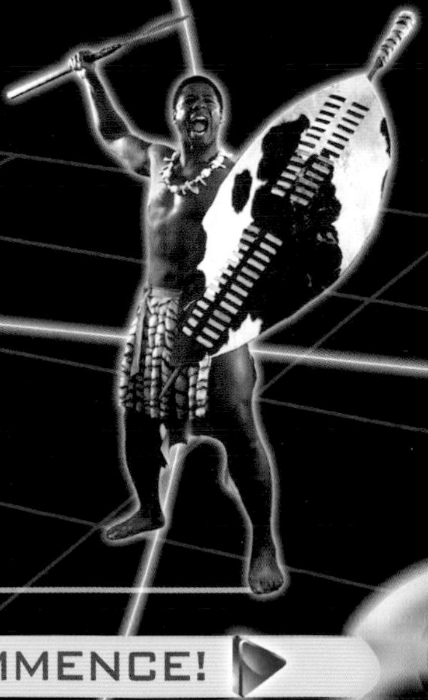

IT'S TIME FOR ACTION . . . LET THE BATTLES COMMENCE!

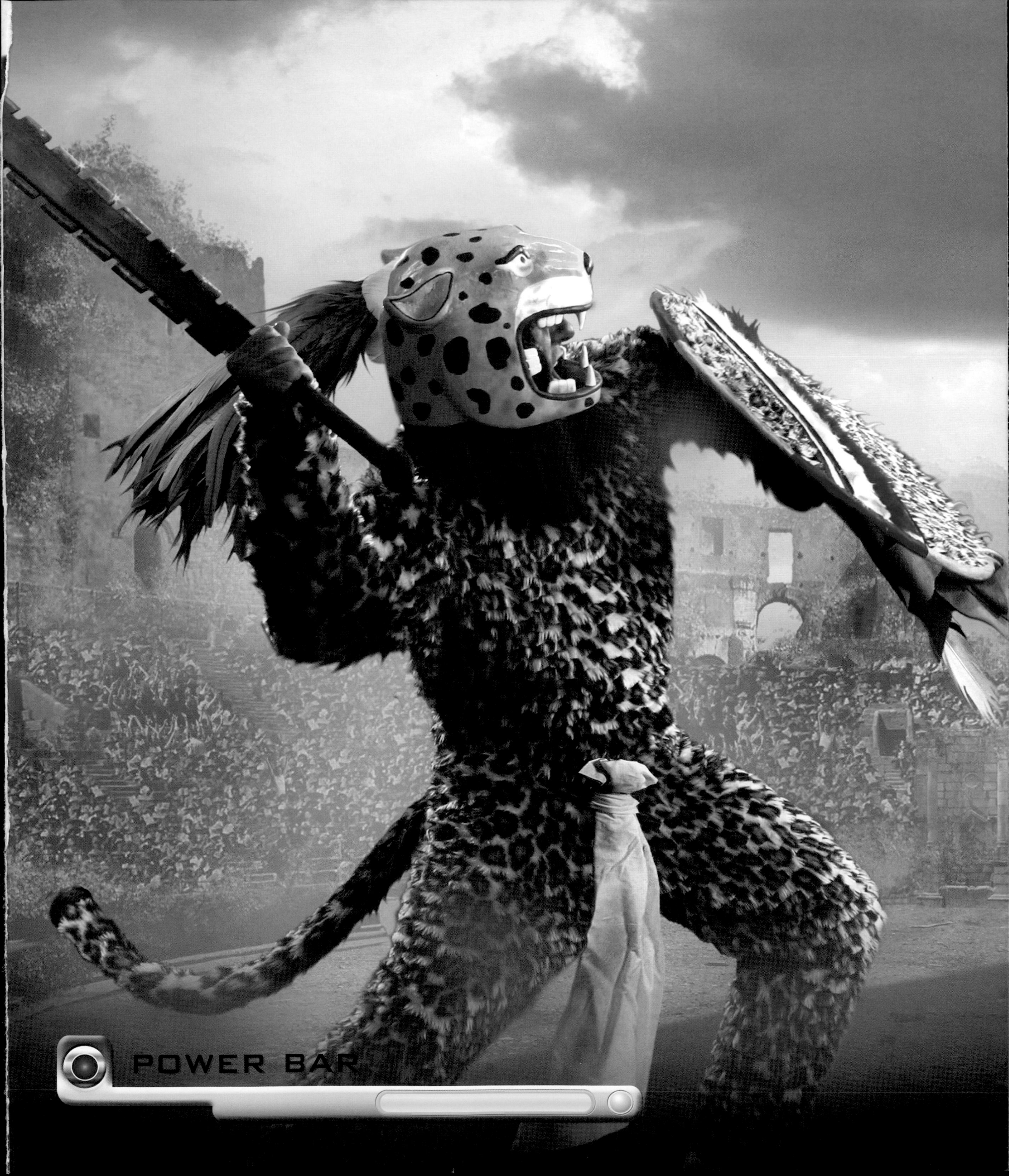
POWER BAR

JAGUAR

1. MACUAHUITL (SAW SWORD)

2. JAGUAR-HEAD HELMET

3. CHIMALLI (SHIELD)

4. TLAHUIZTLI (SUIT OF HONOR)—FEATHER-COVERED BODY SUIT

5. ICHCAHUIPILLI (QUILTED COTTON ARMOR, WORN UNDERNEATH THE TLAHUIZTLI)

A.D. 1550

AZTEC

DATA FILE

AZTEC WARRIORS TOOK THOUSANDS OF CAPTIVES AS THEY ADVANCED THROUGH MEXICO IN THE 1400S. IN BATTLE, A WARRIOR'S GOAL WAS TO MAIM AND CAPTURE HIS FOE. EACH CAPTURE BROUGHT HIM HONOR AND STATUS. THE JAGUARS WERE ONE OF SEVERAL ELITE WARRIOR SOCIETIES.

PICK A WEAPON

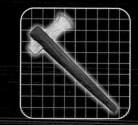

AX
This weapon is heavy, weighing over 8 lbs. (4kg). It may be basic, but it can still do real damage when swung at an enemy's head.

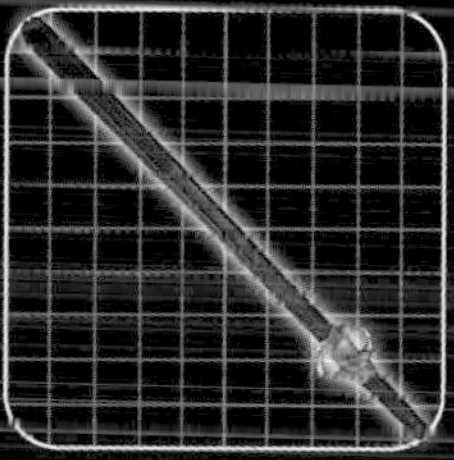

ATLATL
Use this throwing stick along with a dart or spear. It takes a lot of skill but will kill at a distance.

MACUAHUITL
This precision instrument is a 3-ft. (1-m)-long wooden sword inlaid with razor-sharp pieces of obsidian (natural glass). Use it to slice and slash—to maim, dismember, or even decapitate.

ADD STAMINA

FOOD

Keep in fighting form with the protein-rich Aztec staple diet of corn, beans, and squash—and an invigorating chili chocolate drink.

FIRST AID
Treat wounds with poultices, salves, and disinfectants made from aloes, cactus juice, and urine and prepared by healers.

ADVICE

Take heart knowing that at home your father is making daily offerings to the god of your birthday to ensure your safety in combat.

MAKE YOUR MOVE

CHARGE!
Run at your enemy at full speed to stun him with body impact.

ATTACK
Wave your macuahuitl fiercely, swinging as fast and furiously as you can.

PARRY
Defend with the shield while slashing at the enemy's arms and legs.

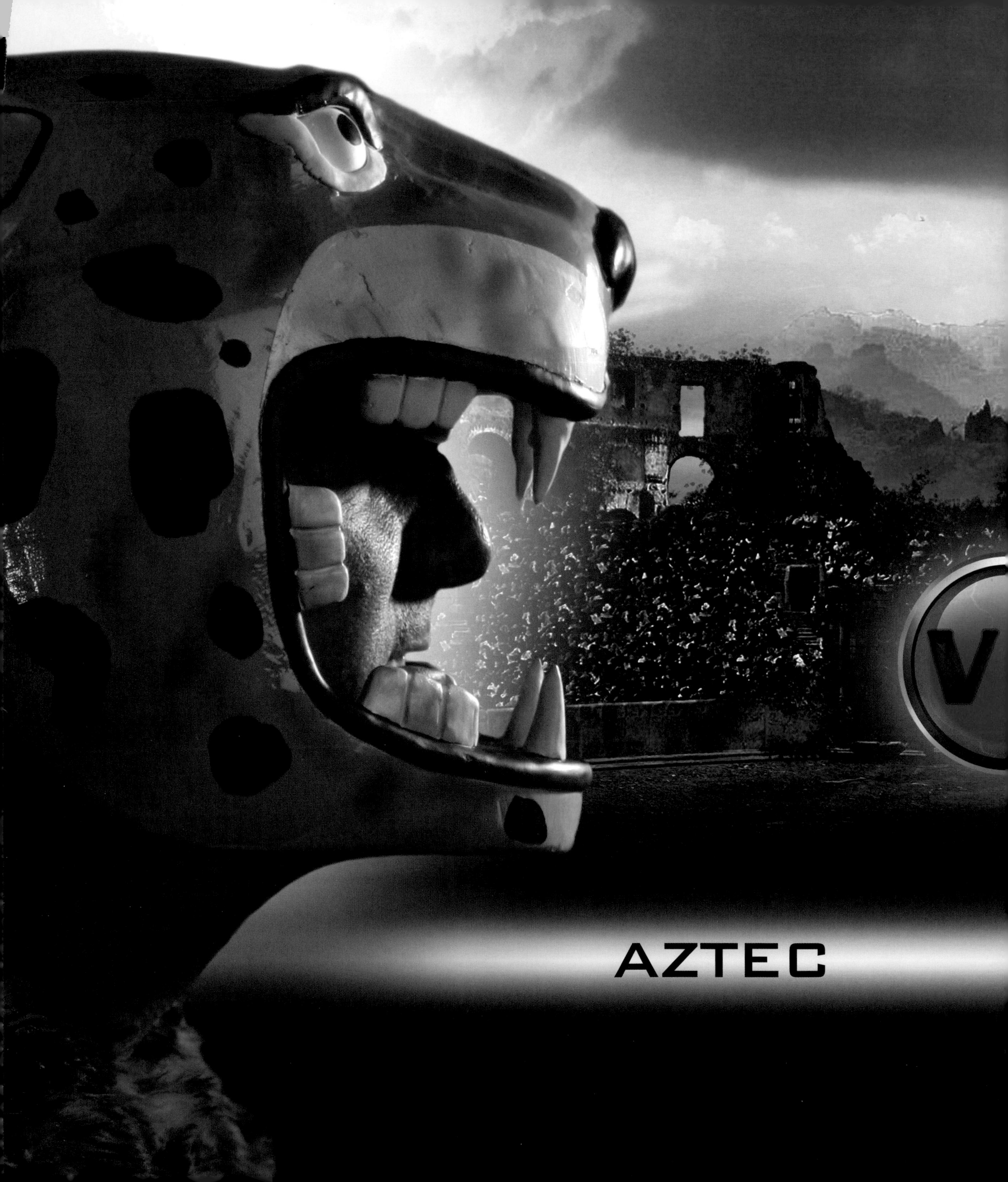
AZTEC

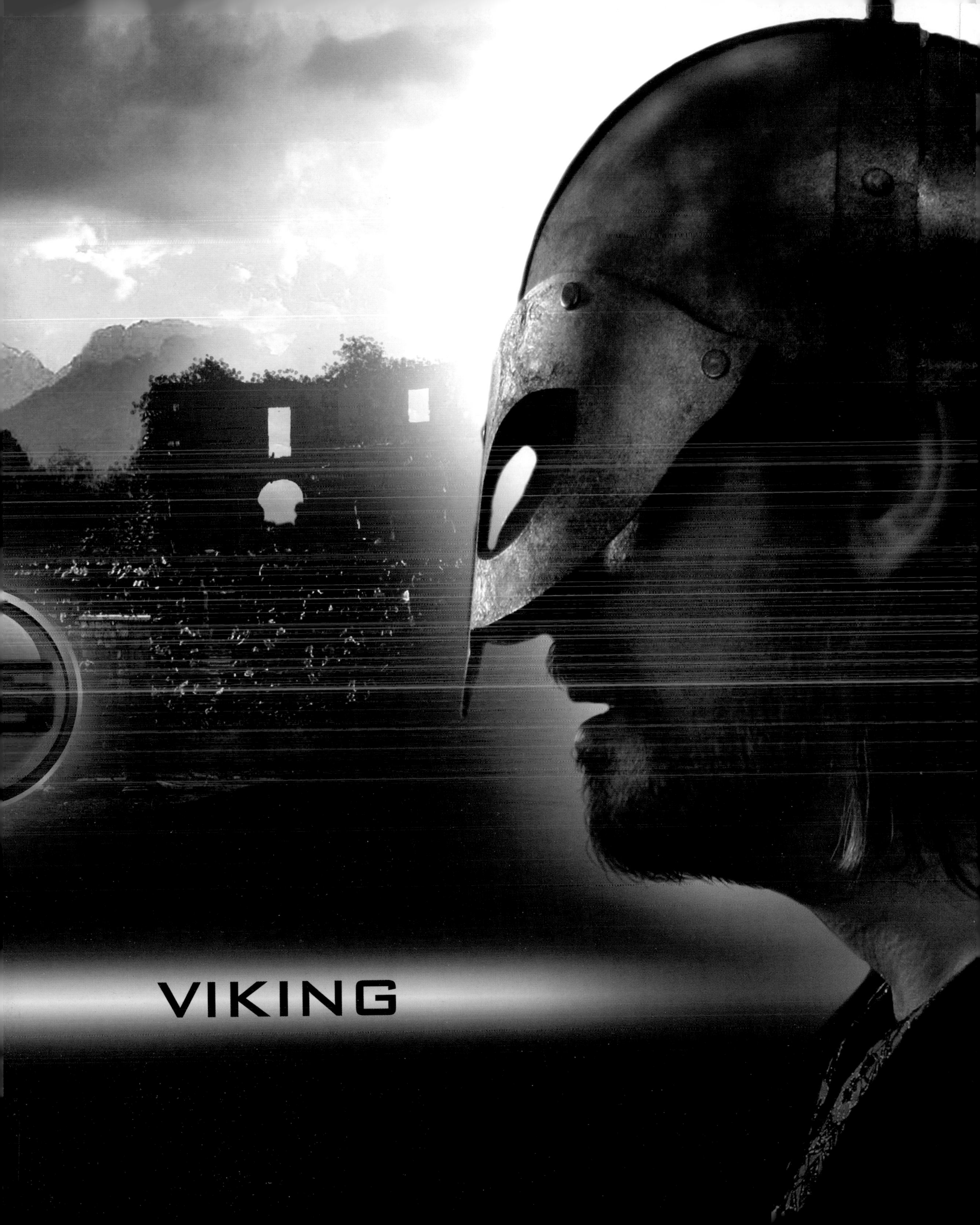

VIKING

VIKING

VS

DATA FILE

FROM THE LATE 700S TO THE 1000S, THE VIKINGS WENT FORTH FROM THEIR LANDS IN SCANDINAVIA TO CONQUER MUCH OF EUROPE. LITHSMEN WERE FREE WARRIORS SWORN TO SERVE THEIR LEADERS UNTIL DEATH. IN RETURN, THEY GOT FOOD, GOLD, AND LAND.

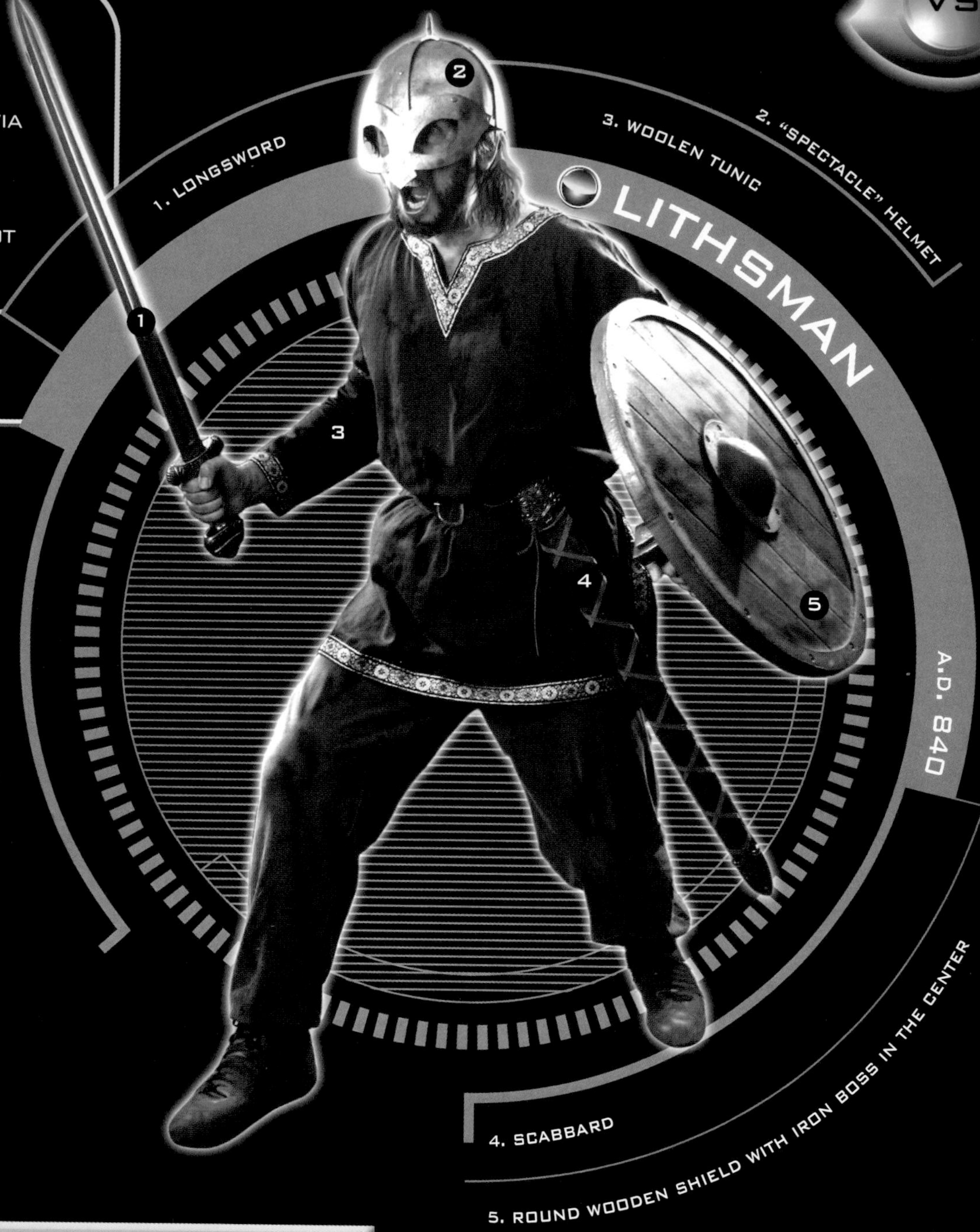

LITHSMAN
A.D. 840
1
2
3
4
5
1. LONGSWORD
2. "SPECTACLE" HELMET
3. WOOLEN TUNIC
4. SCABBARD
5. ROUND WOODEN SHIELD WITH IRON BOSS IN THE CENTER

PICK A WEAPON

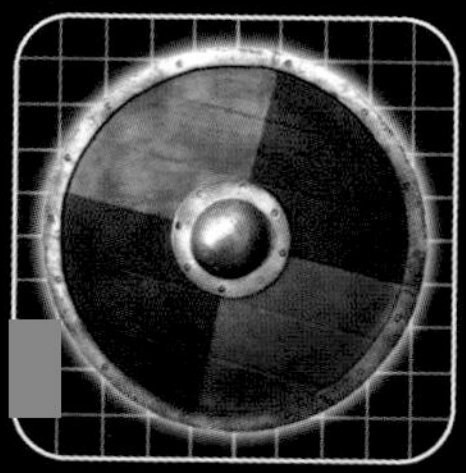

SHIELD
This war shield, with its heavy iron boss, can be smashed into an opponent's head. Many lined up together make a solid advancing wall.

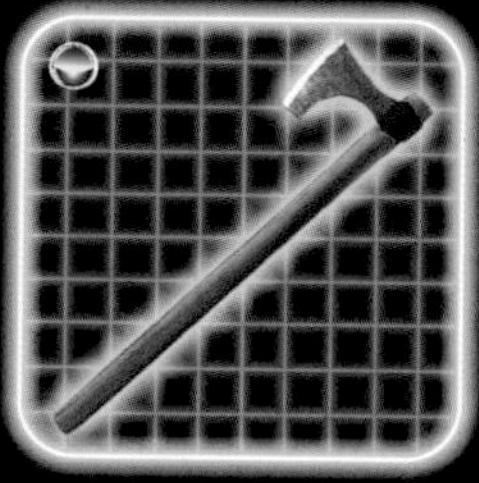

AX
This broad-bladed ax is wielded with one or both hands and is a powerful weapon to choose for a duel. It can deliver a skull-shattering blow to the enemy.

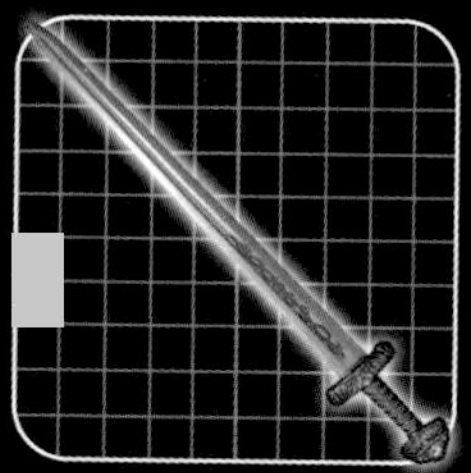

LONGSWORD
This 3-ft. (1-m)-long double-edged steel sword is the Viking warrior's most prized possession. Longswords are passed down from father to son.

MAKE YOUR MOVE

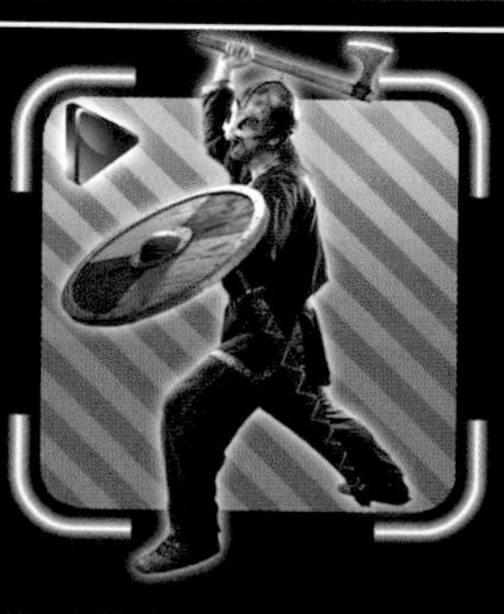

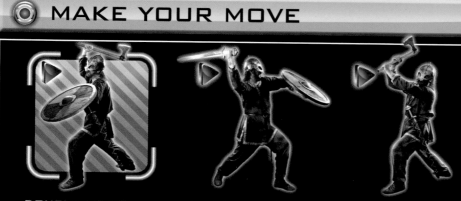

DOUBLE STRIKE
Close in with the shield to prevent being hit and strike hard with the ax.

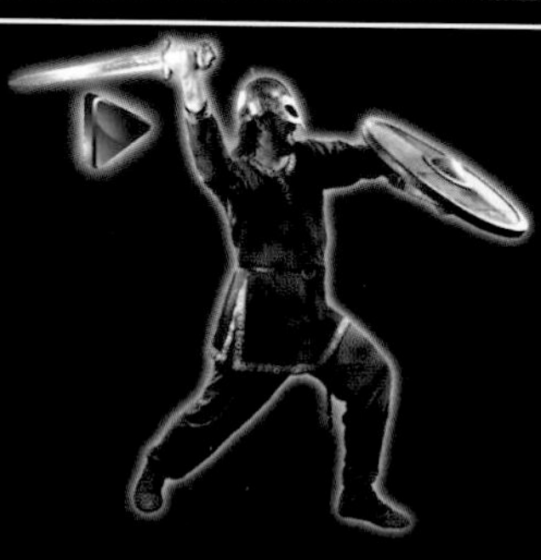

SHIELD STRIKE
Smash the shield into the head, chest, or weapon arm before slashing.

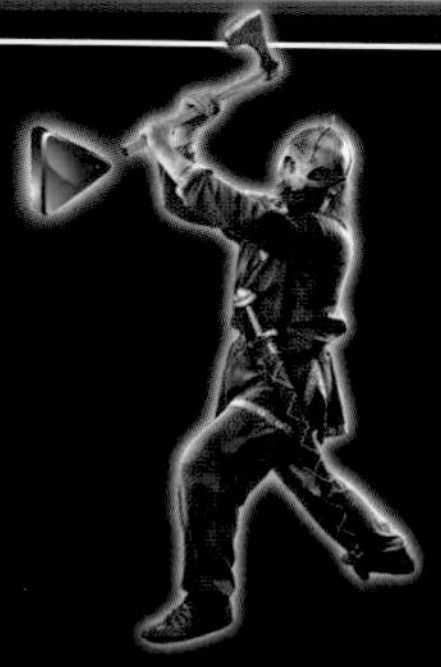

HIGH STRIKE
Whirl the ax around to confuse, then bring it down with great force.

ADD STAMINA

FOOD
Look forward to a victory meal of roast meat with a celebratory drink of beer or mead—better than your daily fare of porridge and cheese.

FIRST AID
When wounded, eat an onion-and-herb porridge. If the wound starts to smell like onions, WARNING!—you may die.

ADVICE
Take pride in your battle dress to intimidate the enemy. Keep hair and beard groomed, clean out ear wax, and wear fine clothes and jewelry.

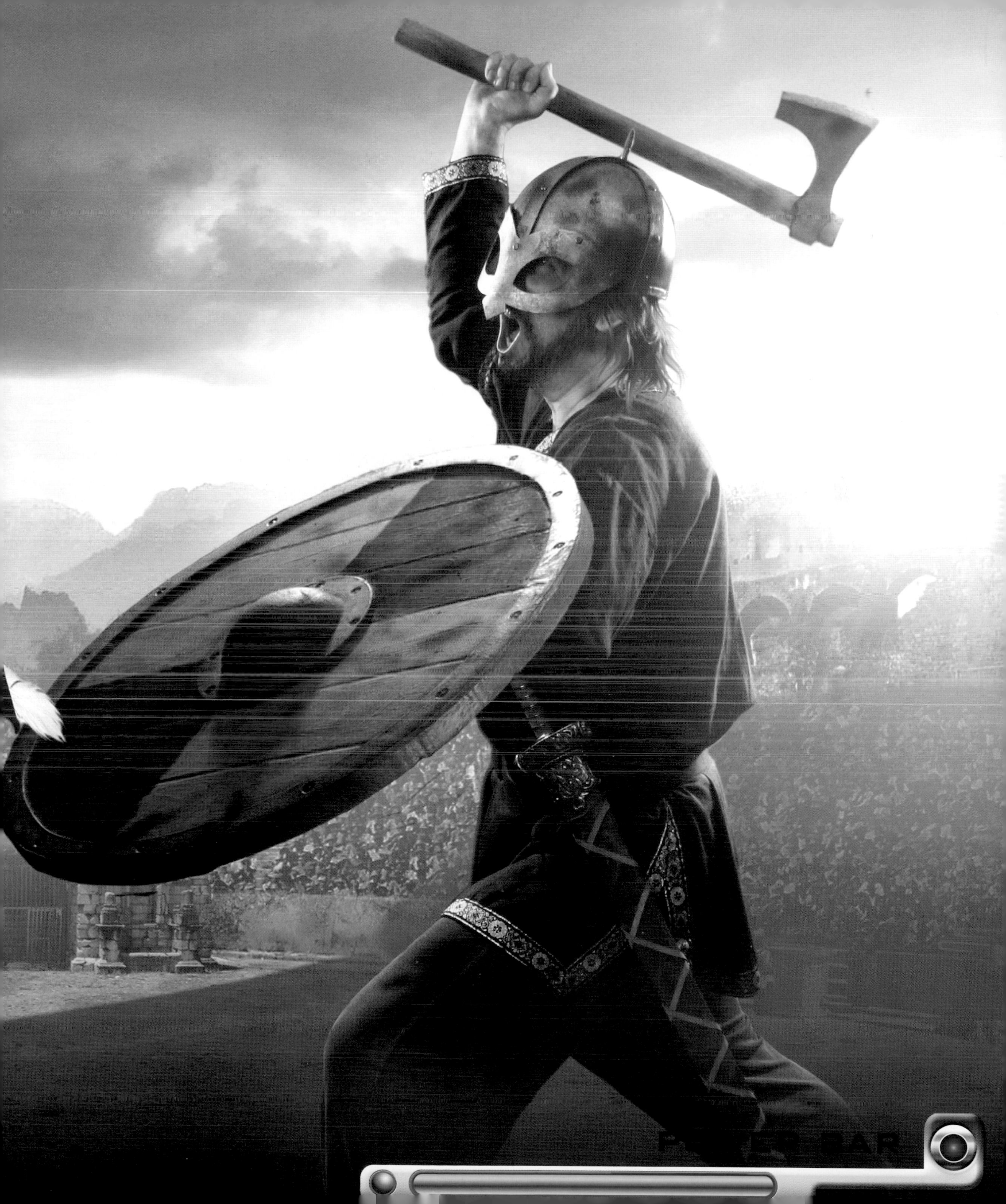

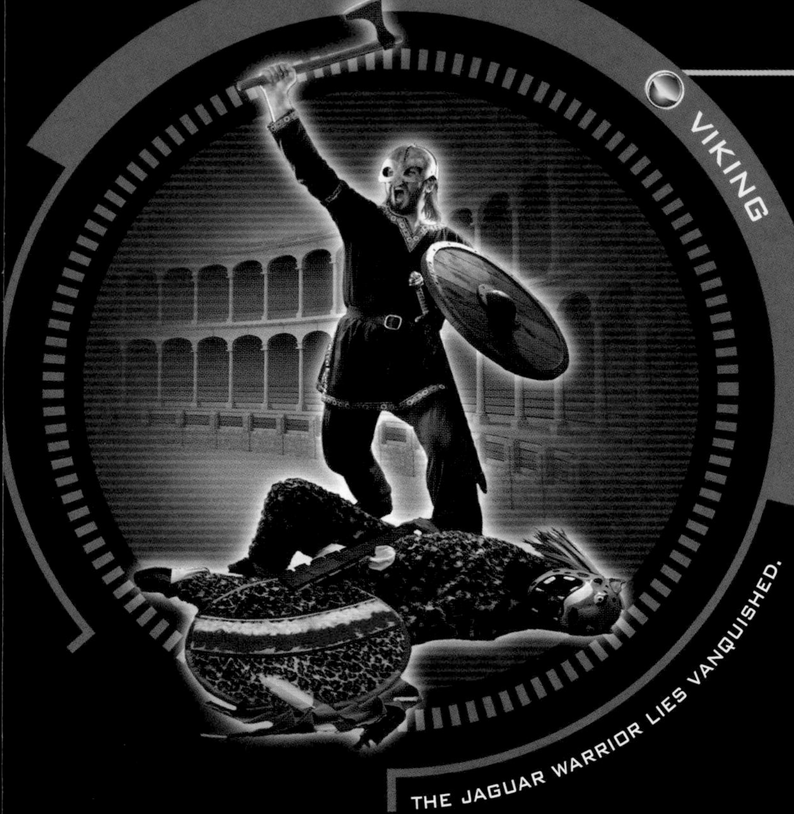

VIKING

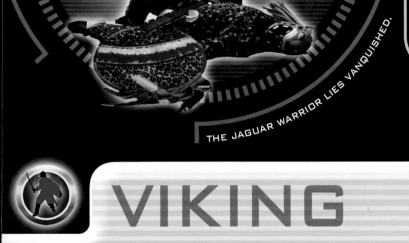

THE JAGUAR WARRIOR LIES VANQUISHED.

THE VIKING WINS

THE VIKING WINS WITH A BLOW OF HIS HEAVY BATTLE-AX. HE IS WELL TRAINED IN INDIVIDUAL COMBAT, HAS A LOT OF EXPERIENCE IN THIS KIND OF FIGHTING, AND IS KNOWN FOR HIS FEROCITY AND SKILL IN A DUEL. HE IS BIGGER AND STRONGER THAN THE AZTEC, AND HE WILL WIN HONOR FROM SLAYING THE ENEMY. THE AZTEC FIGHTS IN A VERY DIFFERENT WAY. HE HAS BEEN TRAINED TO CAPTURE PRISONERS FOR SACRIFICE RATHER THAN TO KILL THEM. HE SLASHES HAPHAZARDLY WITH HIS MACUAHUITL, BUT HE IS NO MATCH FOR THE VIKING.

VIKING

KNOWN AS NORTHMEN OR SEA WOLVES, THE VIKINGS FIRST SET SAIL FROM SCANDINAVIA ABOUT 1,200 YEARS AGO. FEARED WARRIORS, THEY STORMED ALONG THE COASTS AND RIVERS OF EUROPE IN SEARCH OF LAND AND PLUNDER.

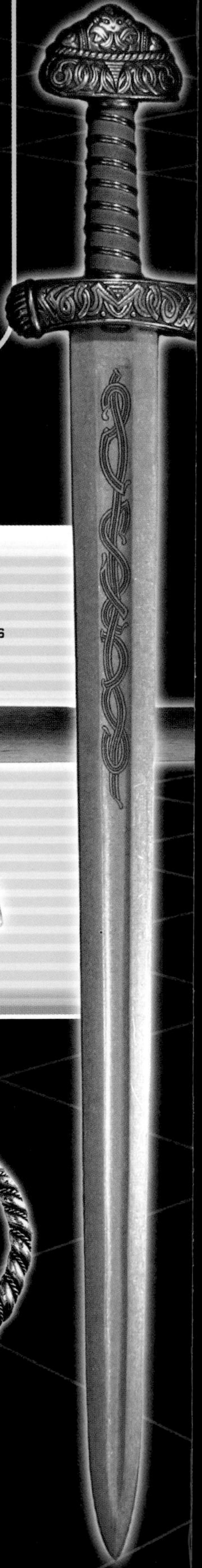

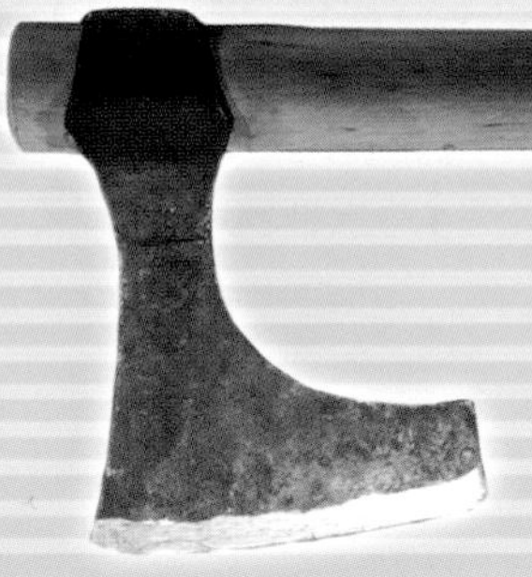

BATTLE-AX AND A NOBLE WARRIOR'S LONGSWORD

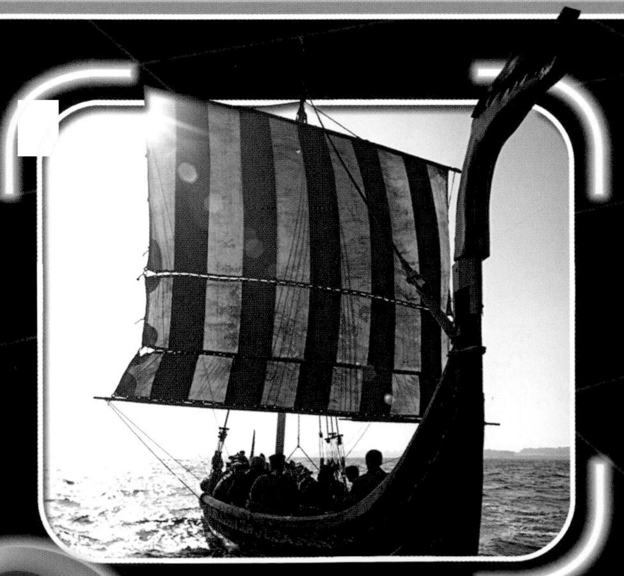

LONGSHIP RAIDERS

The sight of a Viking sail on the horizon struck terror into many hearts. Each longship was fast and sleek yet shallow enough to sail down a river or be dragged up a beach. Its prow was carved like a snarling dragon's head. Each longship carried 30 or more battle-scarred warriors, heavily armed and ready to fight. They burned down monasteries, churches, and towns, seizing gold, jewelry, cattle, or slaves.

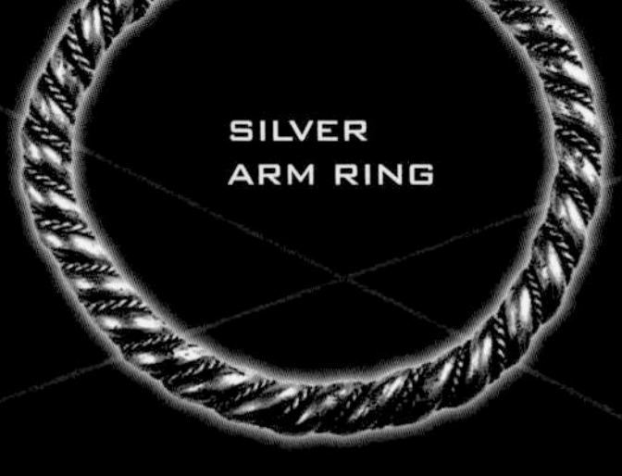

SILVER ARM RING

ERSERKER!

is chess piece shows a Viking biting
s shield in fury. He is a berserker.
erserkers were warriors from
particular cult who worked
emselves into a frenzied rage before
battle. They wore bearskin shirts,
ught without armor, and were said
t to feel pain. Today we still talk
out people "going berserk," or crazy.

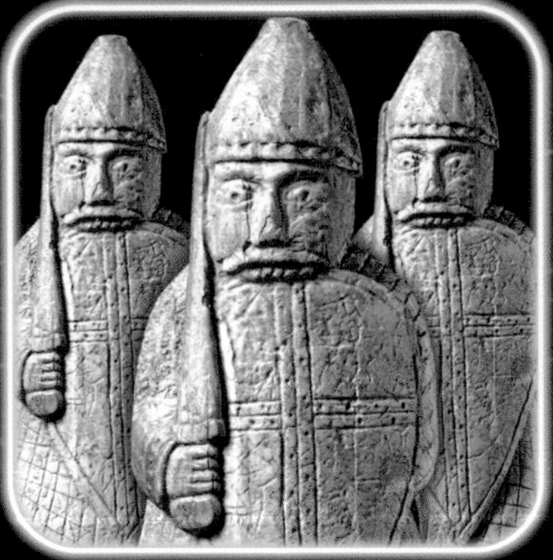

A BLAZE OF GLORY

A Viking longship is set on fire at a festival in Shetland, Scotland. Vikings fought in Ireland, the British Isles, France, and southern Europe. They served as bodyguards in Byzantium (now Istanbul) and traded in Russia and the Middle East. They settled in Iceland and Greenland, and they even reached North America.

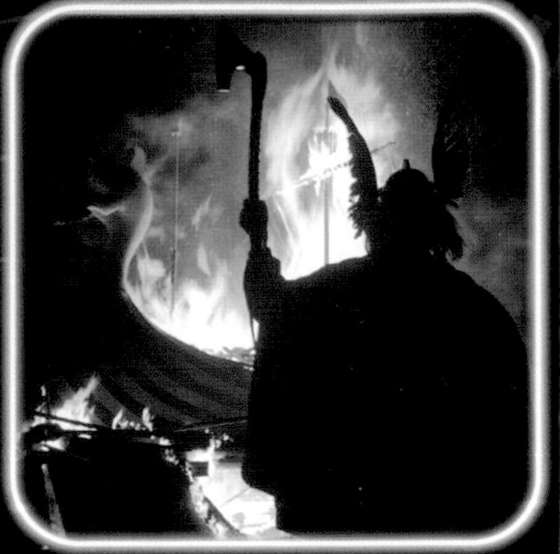

HEROES IN VALHALLA

INTO BATTLE

Vikings mostly fought in small bands but sometimes joined forces as an army. They were not highly organized, but they were strong, bloodthirsty, and well armed, with lethal swords and battle-axes, bows, and spears. They carried shields made of wood and iron. Most wore simple tunics and cloaks and helmets of metal or leather, but a jarl (rich chieftain) or hersir (noble warrior) might wear a fine shirt of mail and a metal helmet to protect the face.

WARLIKE GODS

The first Vikings worshiped gods who were believed to be just as violent as they were. Warriors who died bravely in battle were thought to go to Valhalla, the great hall of the gods. Odin, the father of the gods, rode through the sky on an eight-legged horse. He had two ravens that could fly around the world. Odin's raven emblem was a sight that brought fear to the Vikings' enemies. Although they were strong in battle, the Vikings usually overcame their enemies in fierce surprise attacks and secret raids.

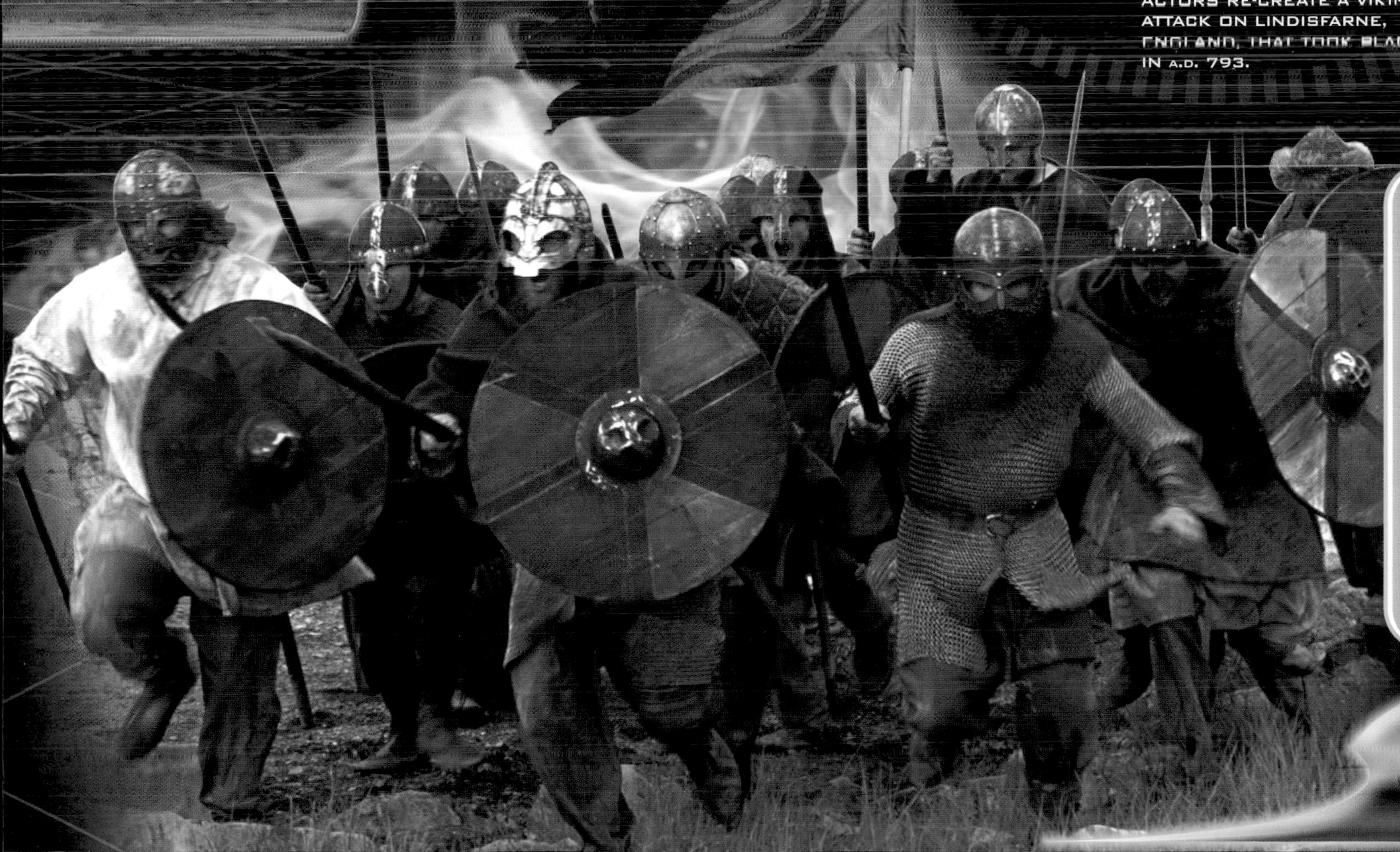

ACTORS RE-CREATE A VIKING ATTACK ON LINDISFARNE, ENGLAND, THAT TOOK PLACE IN A.D. 793.

ON THE LEFT IS A SOLDIER WHO HAS MADE FOUR CAPTURES. THE CENTER WARRIOR, WITH AN EAGLE MOTIF ON HIS SHIELD, HAS MADE FIVE. ON THE RIGHT IS A JAGUAR WARRIOR.

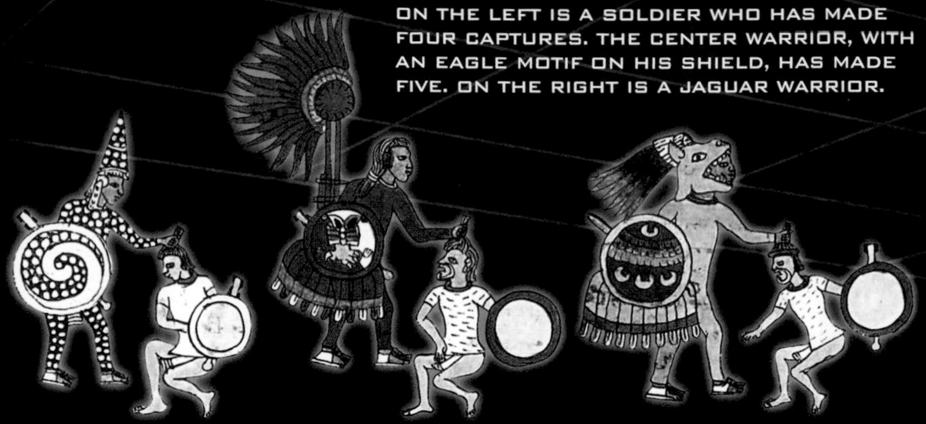

HONOR THROUGH CAPTURE

A WARRIOR GAINED PROMOTION WHEN HE CAPTURED AN ENEMY SINGLE-HANDEDLY AND BROUGHT THE PRISONER HOME FOR SACRIFICE. HE WAS GIVEN A SPECIAL FORM OF BATTLE DRESS TO MARK THIS ACHIEVEMENT. AFTER MAKING FIVE CAPTURES, A WARRIOR MIGHT JOIN ONE OF THE ELITE FIGHTING UNITS.

UNDER THREAT

STRANGE INVADERS

The Aztecs were the most powerful people in 15th-century Mexico. They defeated many enemies, but in 1519 the Spanish invaded. The pale-skinn strangers had horses, ships, guns, a swords. They did not fight by any of t Aztec rules of war. In 1521, the Aztec capital, Tenochtitlán, was besieged, and more than 240,000 warriors died in three months of bitter fighting. The Aztec Empire was crushed.

AZTEC

WHEN AN AZTEC BOY WAS BORN, HIS FIRST PRESENT WAS A BOW AND ARROW. HE WAS DESTINED FROM BIRTH TO BE A WARRIOR. A GRUESOME FATE AWAITED THOSE WHOM HE DEFEATED IN BATTLE . . .

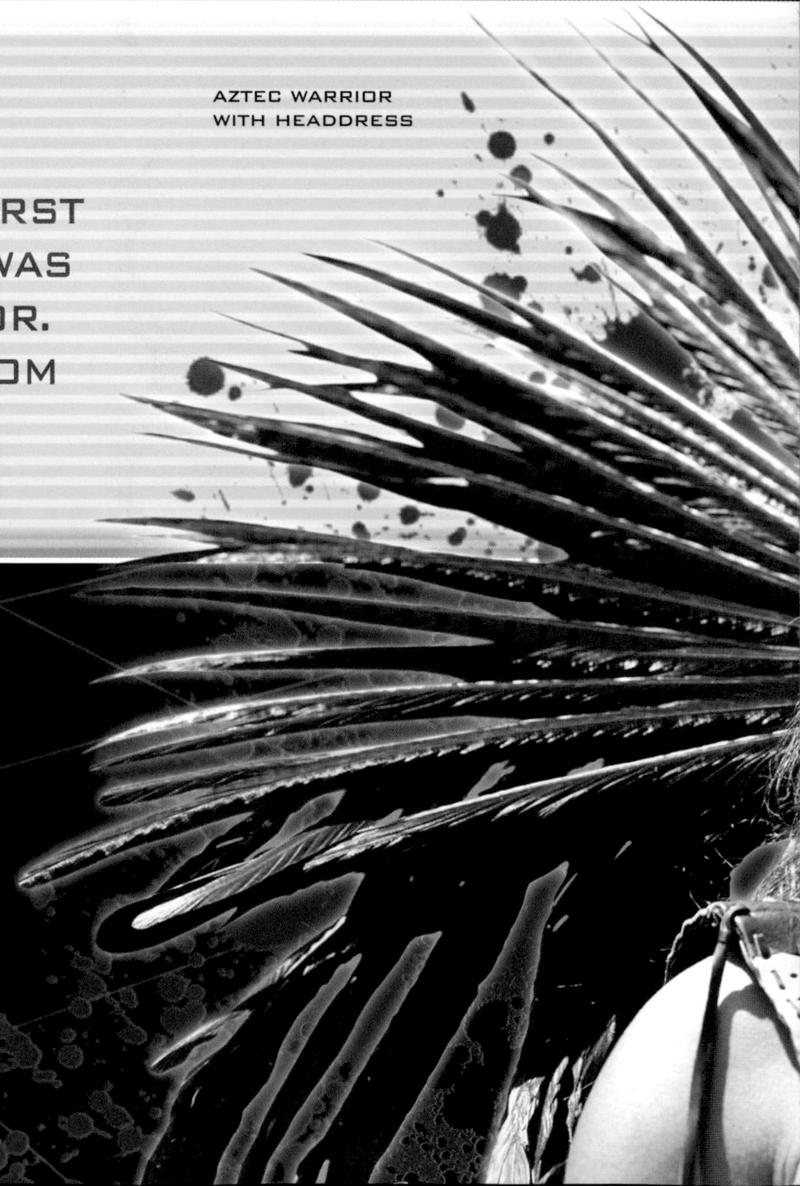

AZTEC WARRIOR WITH HEADDRESS

TRAINING FOR WAR

HOW TO BECOME A WARRIOR

In the Aztec Empire in the 1400s, all Aztec boys, whether nobles or commoners, started their warrior training at school. They learned how to obey orders, use weapons, and fight in battle. At the age of 18, they were sent to watch a kind of ritual battle with other tribes, known as a Flower War. When the next Flower War took place, they would participate and risk capture and sacrifice by the enemy. Once they had taken a prisoner themselves, they could become full Aztec warriors, fighting in real battles.

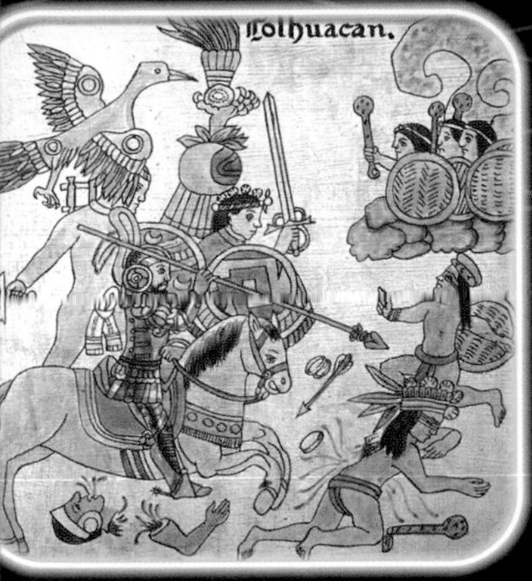
Colhuacan.

THE END OF AN AGE

Weapons like these were used at Aztec royal ceremonies. They included the atlatl, used to hurl pointed darts with great force, and decorative shields of gold and feathers. Aztec warriors fought in battle with bows and arrows, spears, slings, clubs, and the macuahuitl. They wore armor made of cotton padding. Unlike their enemies the Spanish conquistadors, they had no steel for swords or helmets.

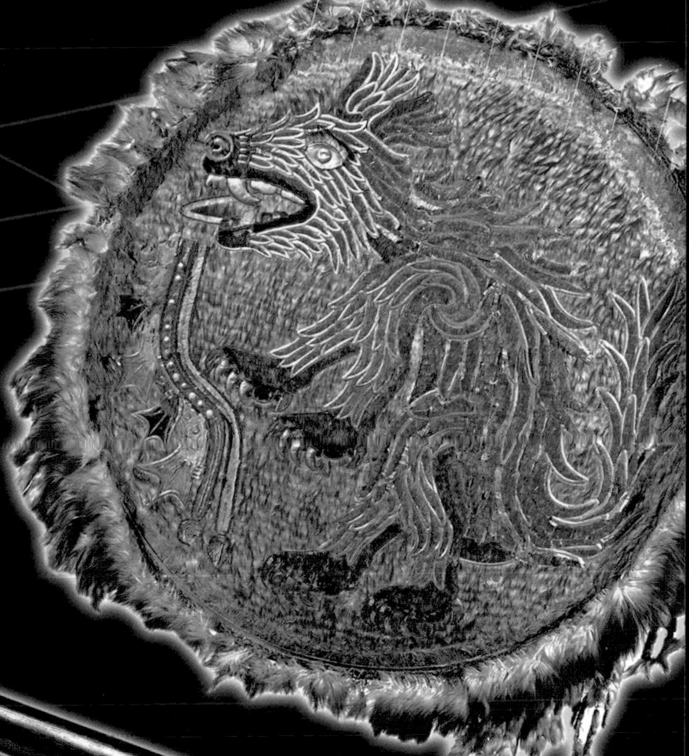

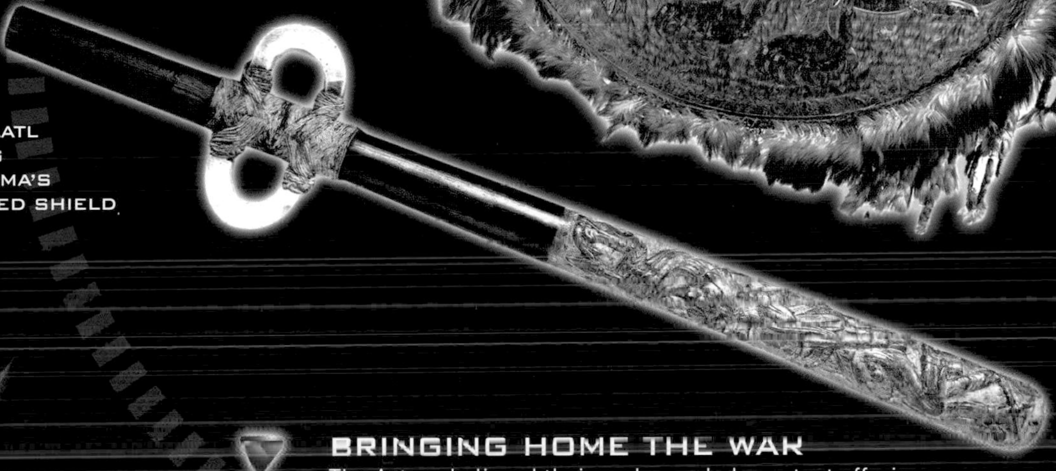

GOLD ATLATL AND KING MONTEZUMA'S DECORATED SHIELD

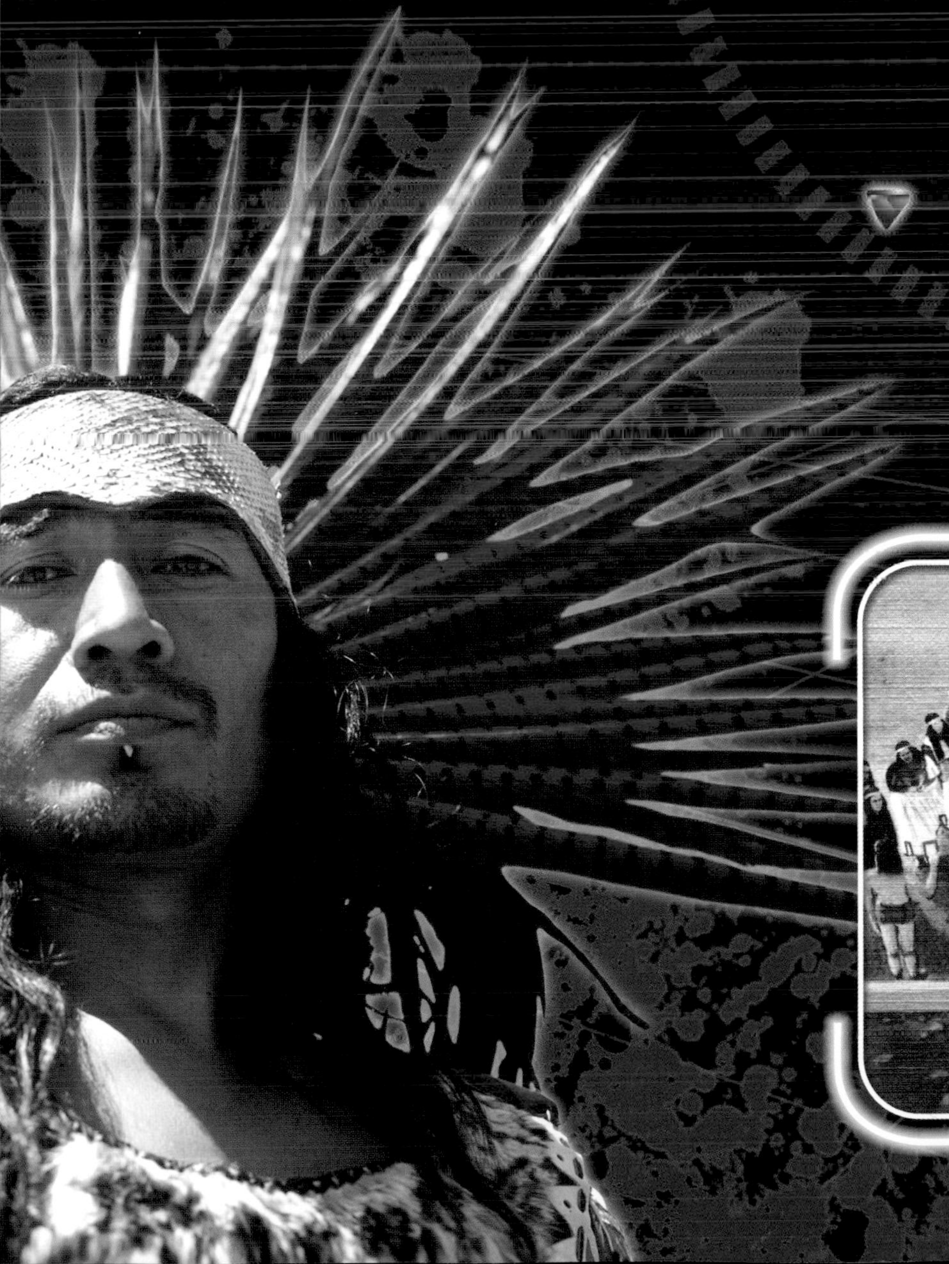

BRINGING HOME THE WAR

The Aztecs believed their gods needed constant offerings, including human lives. Warriors had to prove their worth by presenting prisoners, in the thousands, to be sacrificed to the gods. At the great temple in the center of Tenochtitlán, Aztec priests cut out prisoners' living hearts with a ceremonial knife. Blood poured down the steps. To the Aztecs, being chosen for sacrifice to the gods was not considered to be cruel or unjust but was a great honor. The scene below shows people acting out a sacrifice as part of a festival.

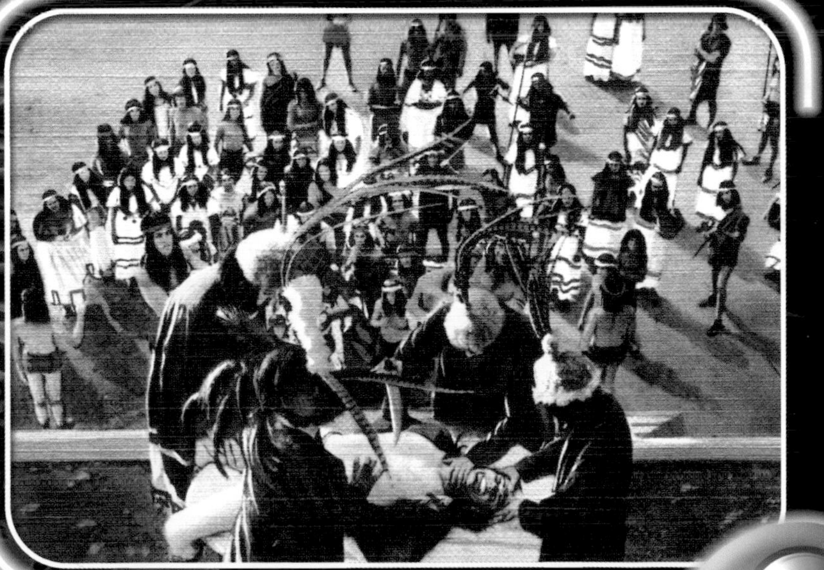

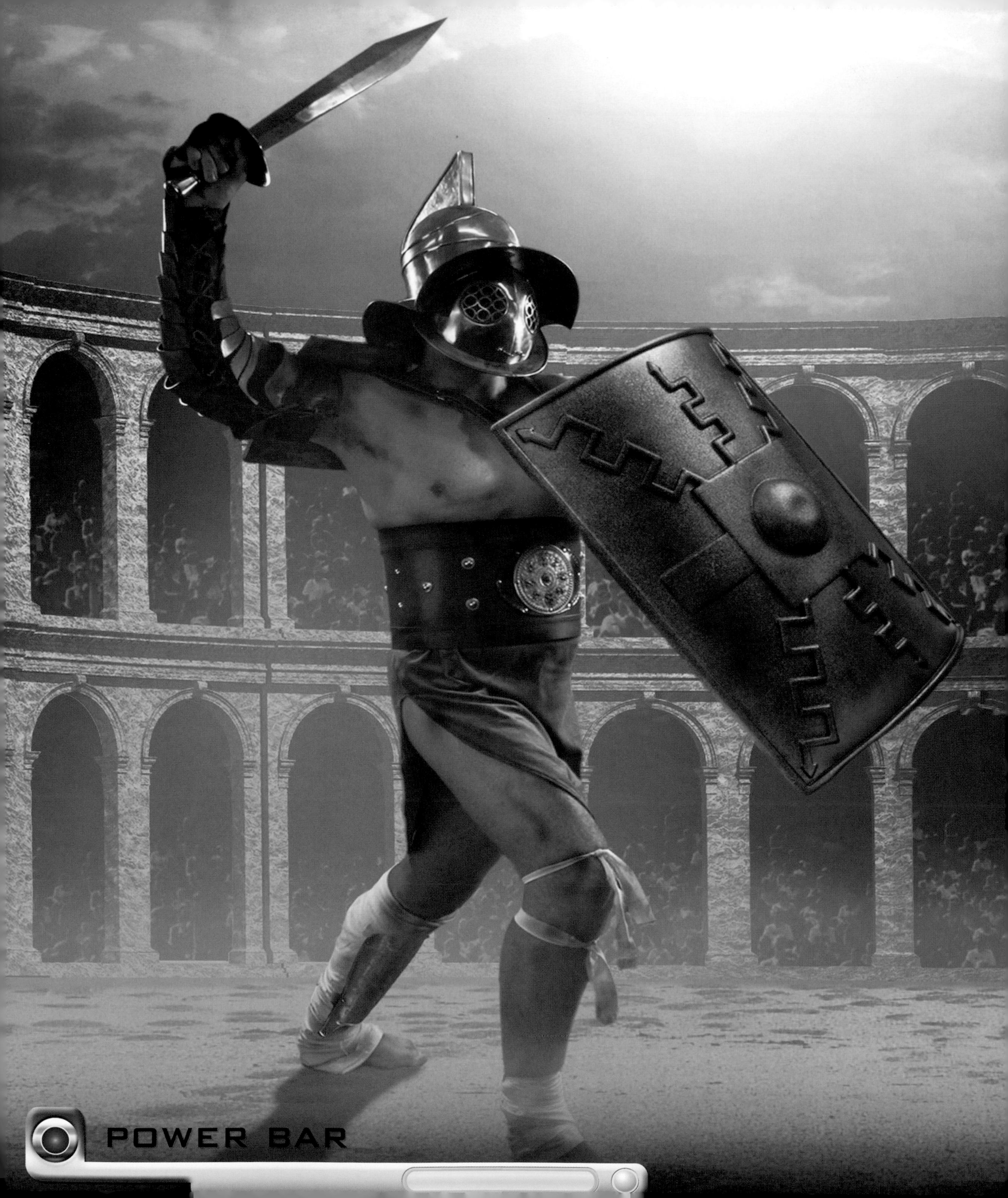
POWER BAR

VS

GLADIATOR

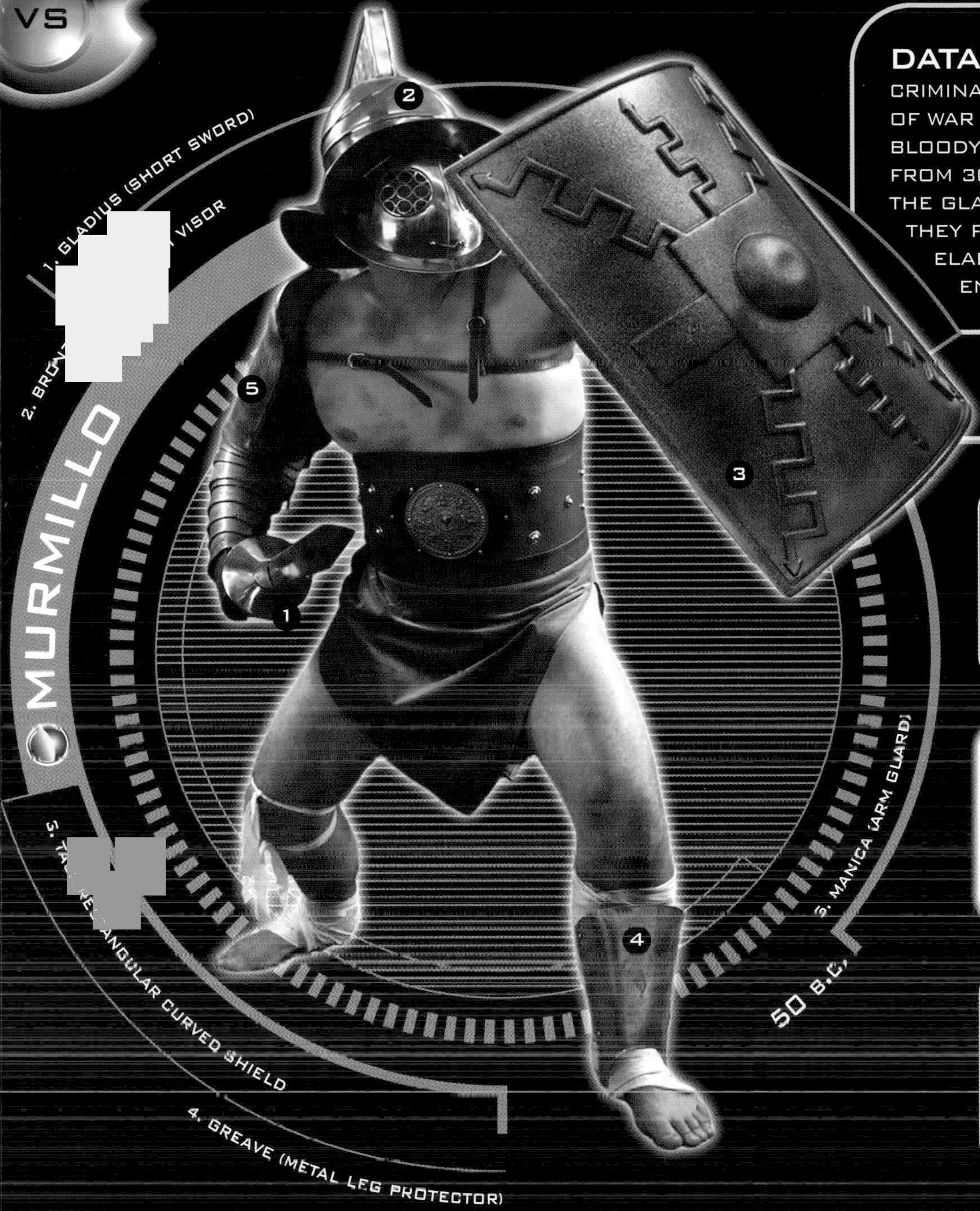

MURMILLO
1. GLADIUS (SHORT SWORD)
2. BRO
VISOR
3. TA
ANGULAR CURVED SHIELD
4. GREAVE (METAL LEG PROTECTOR)
5. MANICA (ARM GUARD)
50 B.C.

DATA FILE

CRIMINALS, SLAVES, AND PRISONERS OF WAR ALL LOST THEIR LIVES IN THE BLOODY ARENAS OF ANCIENT ROME FROM 300 B.C. TO A.D. 300. THESE WERE THE GLADIATORS. AGED ONLY 18–25, THEY FOUGHT AND EVEN DIED IN ELABORATE SHOWS STAGED TO ENTERTAIN THE ROMAN CROWDS.

PICK A WEAPON

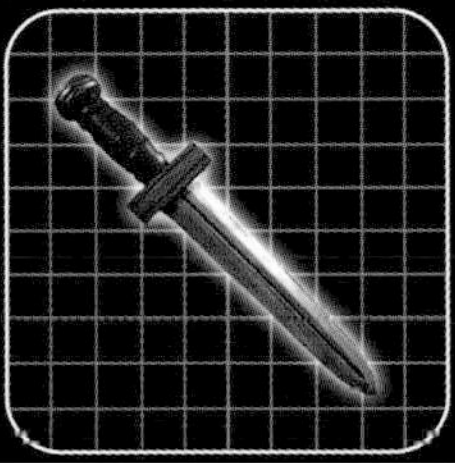

DAGGER
Although not as powerful a weapon as a sword, a steel dagger is a small, lightweight, and useful backup weapon.

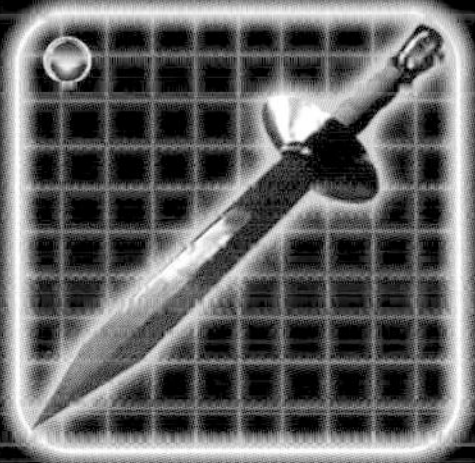

GLADIUS
The gladius, after which the gladiator takes his name, is a short double-edged sword. Light but deadly, it's perfect for hand-to-hand combat.

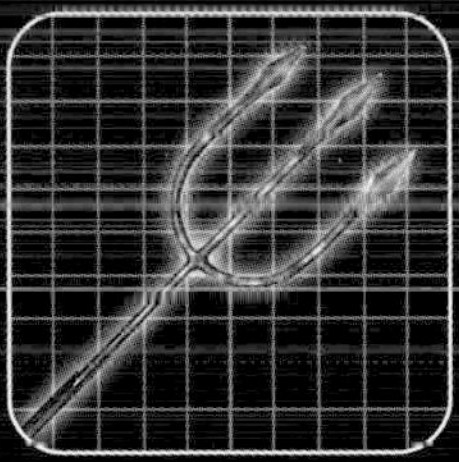

TRIDENT
WARNING! Tridents are for retiarii only! These gladiators fight with a net weighted by pieces of lead. They snare their victim under the net and then stab with the three-pronged trident.

ADD STAMINA

FOOD
Eat plenty of boiled beans, dried fruit, or barley for strength and to build up fat—it will give you some protection against sword blows.

FIRST AID
You can expect treatment from the best physicians and surgeons available—if you manage to get out of the arena alive!

ADVICE
For some last-minute tips on how to survive the fight, speak to the "doctor," an ex-gladiator who trains fighters at the gladiator school.

MAKE YOUR MOVE

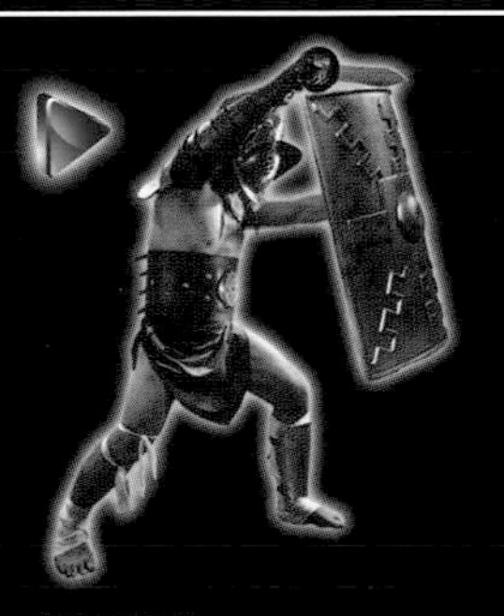

BLOCK
Thrust the shield forward to prevent the attacker from advancing on you.

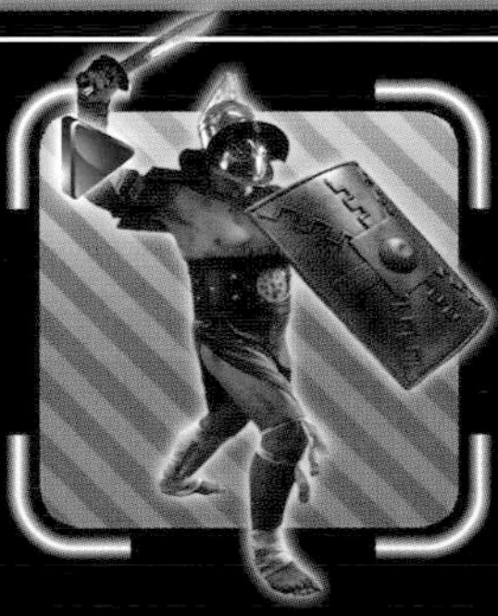

ATTACK
Charge, sword raised, but remember to shield your unarmored body!

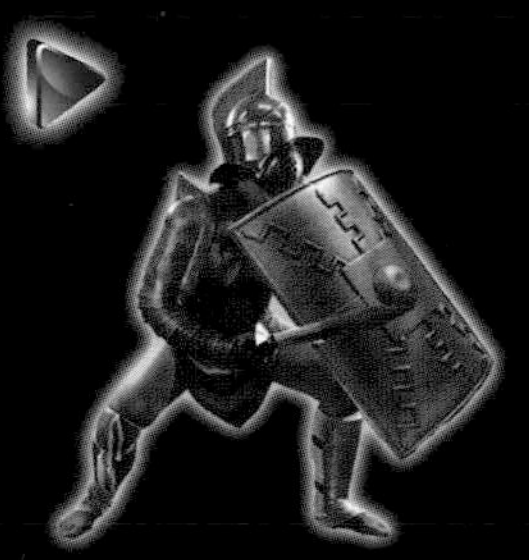

DEFEND
Crouch behind the shield to dodge and hide from the enemy's blows.

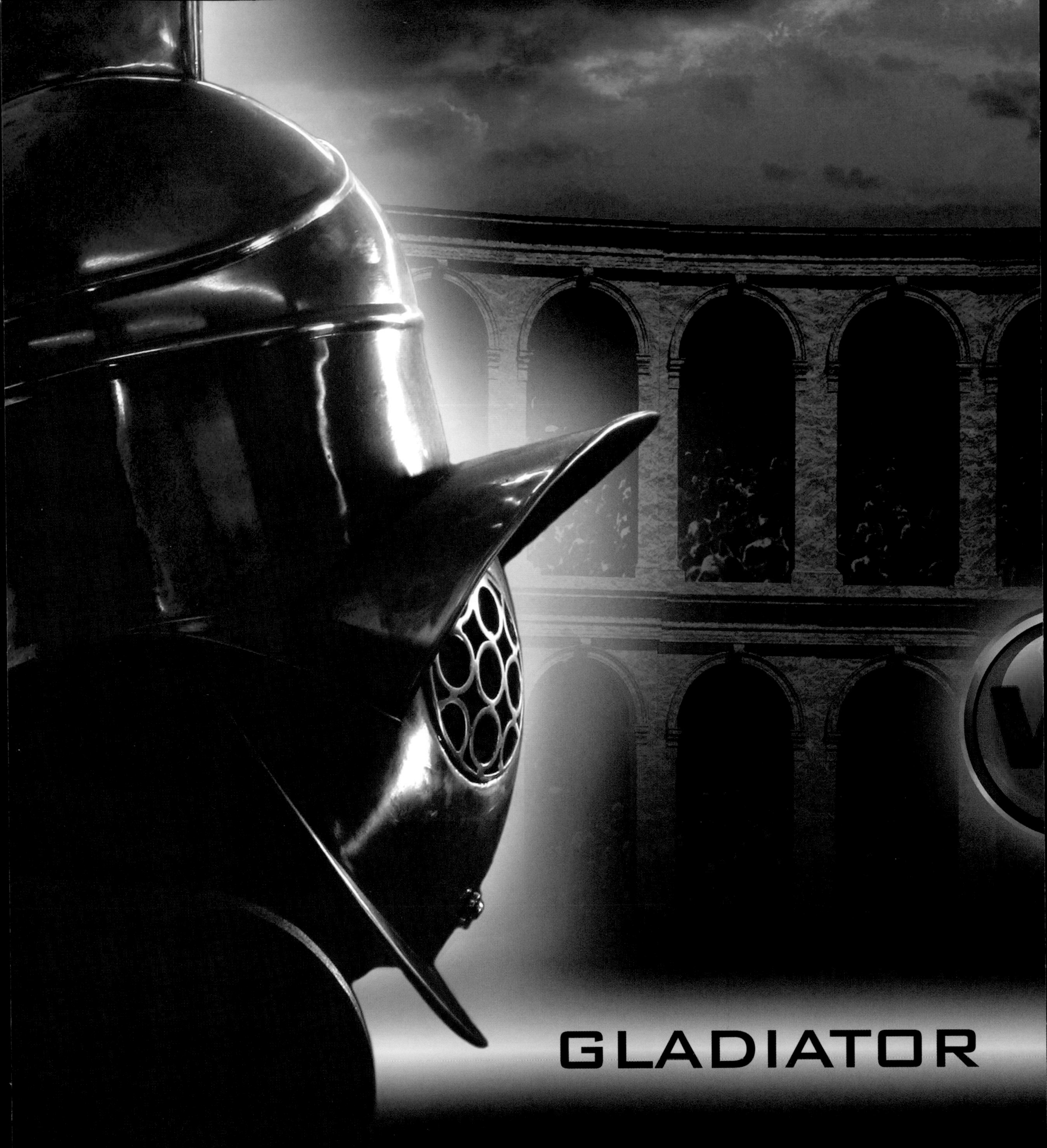

GLADIATOR

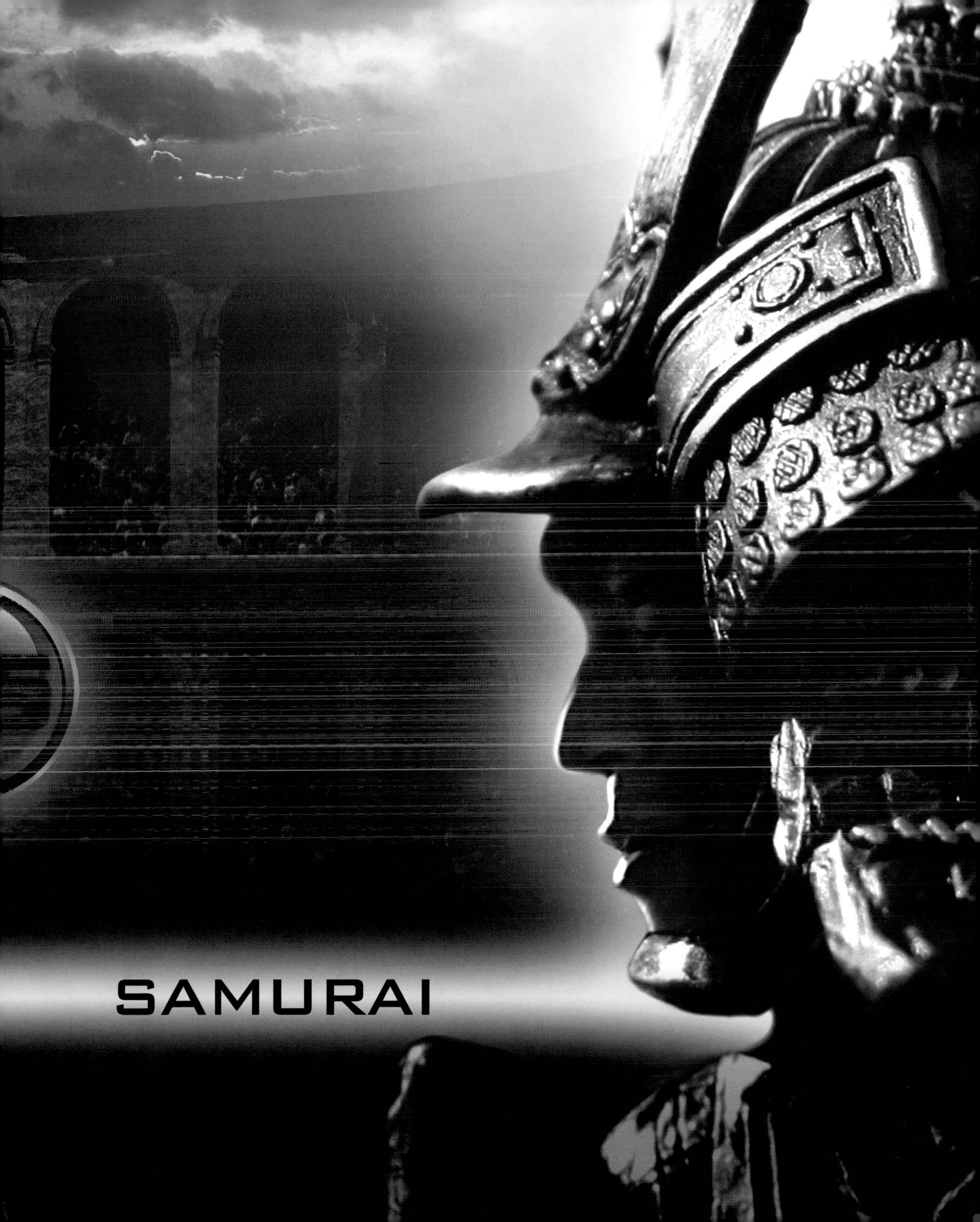
SAMURAI

SAMURAI

VS

DATA FILE

FROM THE 700S TO THE 1800S, NOBLE WARRIORS WAGED WAR AMONG THE TRIBAL CLANS OF JAPAN. THEY WERE THE SAMURAI, HIGHLY SKILLED IN HORSEMANSHIP, ARCHERY, AND DEADLY SWORDPLAY. THEY WERE FIERCE FIGHTERS WHO LIVED BY A WARRIOR CODE, THE BUSHIDO.

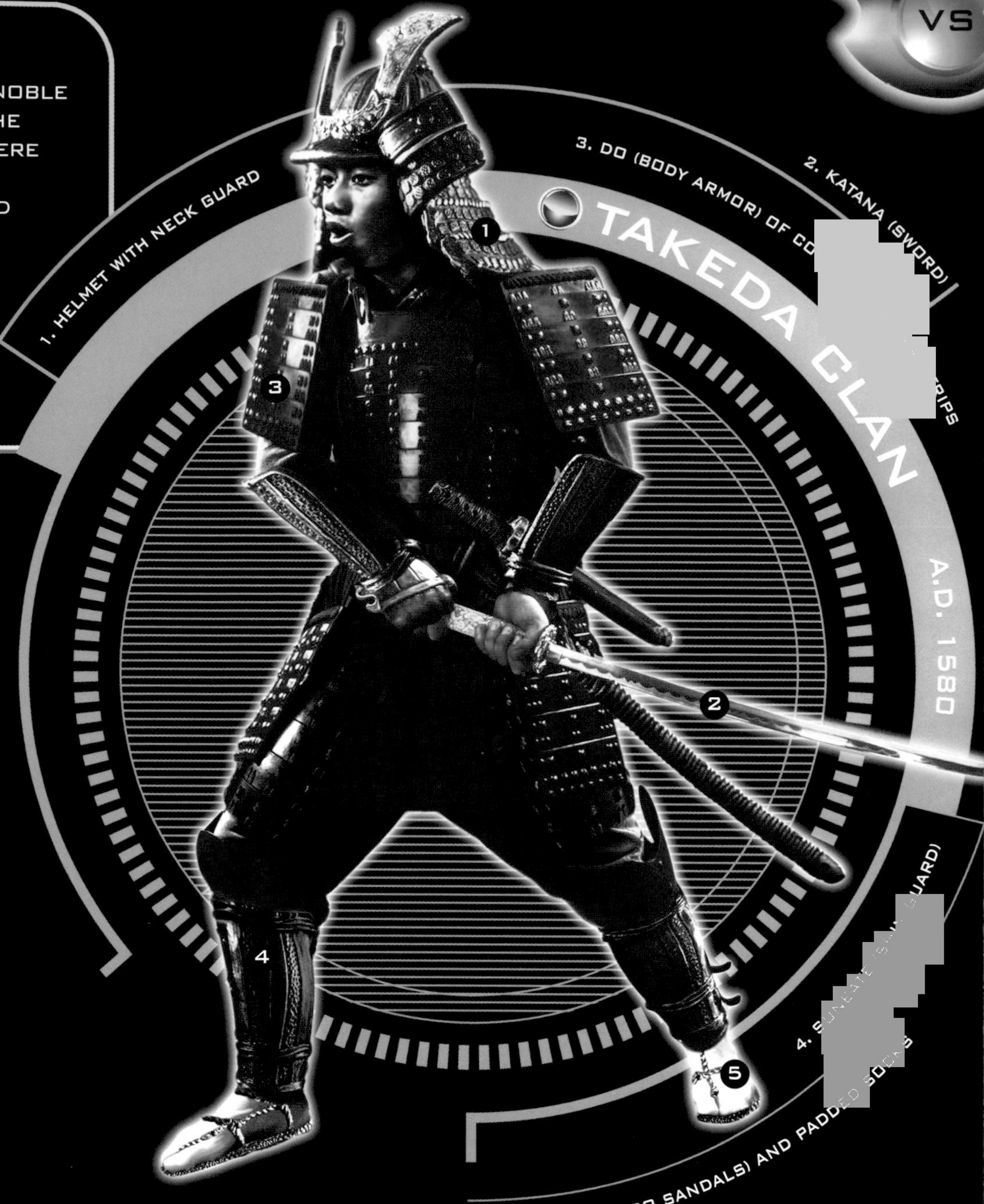

TAKEDA CLAN
A.D. 1580
1. HELMET WITH NECK GUARD
2. KATANA (SWORD)
3. DO (BODY ARMOR) OF CO [redacted] RIPS
4. [redacted] GUARD)
5. WARAJI (BAMBOO SANDALS) AND PADDED [redacted]

PICK A WEAPON

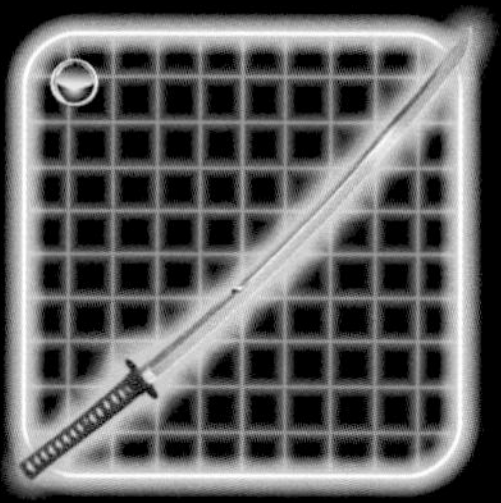

KATANA
The standard fighting sword is the katana. Long and curved, it has one razor-sharp cutting edge and a long handle for two hands to grip.

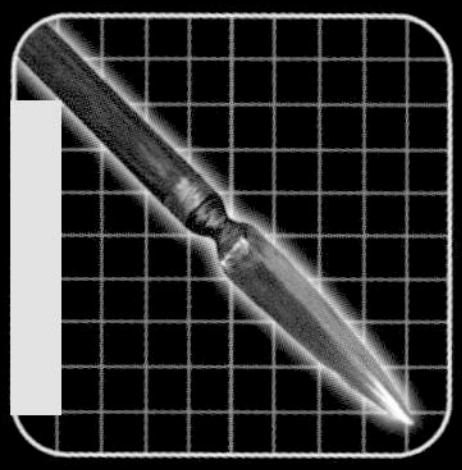

YARI
The yari (spear), which ranges from 3 to 20 ft. (1 to 6m) long, has a sharp steel blade. Samurai carry short, light yari on horseback and use them to stab their enemy.

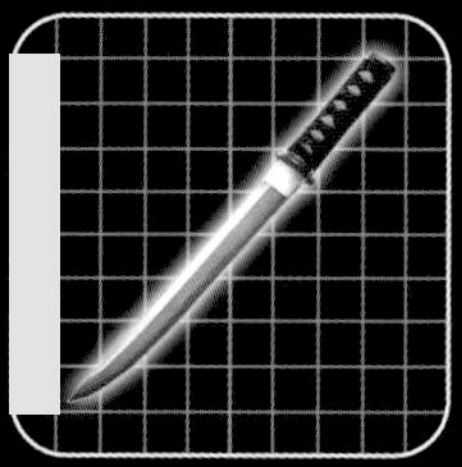

TANTO
This small double-edged dagger, tied to the belt or hidden inside the armor, is used for stabbing or slashing in close combat.

MAKE YOUR MOVE

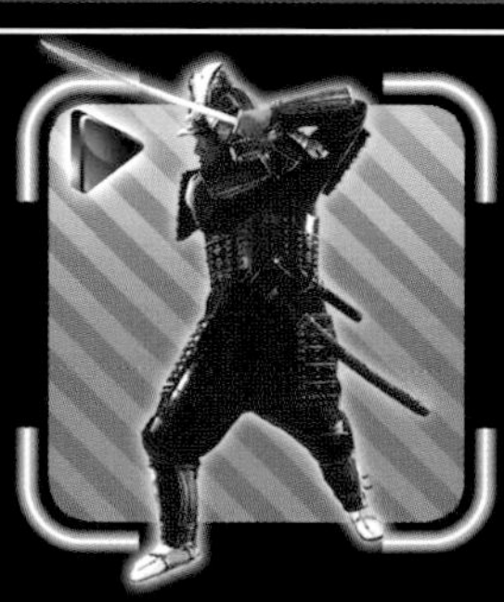

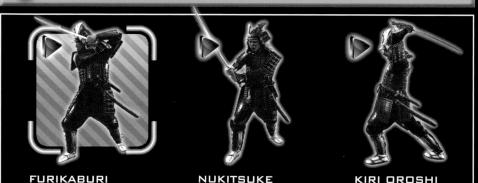

FURIKABURI
Raise the sword, keeping it horizontal as you do so, and prepare to attack.

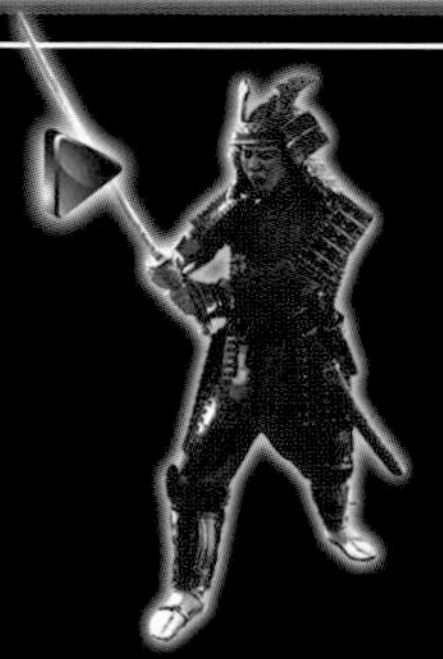

NUKITSUKE
Use the sword to block an attack—the samurai never carry shields.

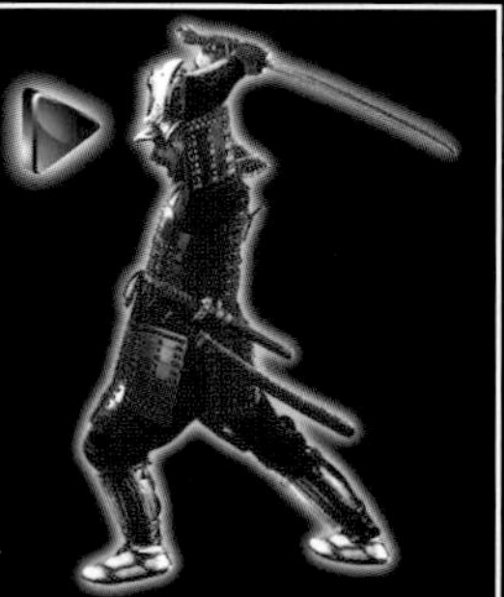

KIRI OROSHI
Finish an opponent with a fast, powerful downward cut.

ADD STAMINA

FOOD
Before battle, eat dried chestnuts—a sign of victory—with some strength-giving seaweed, shellfish, and a drink of sake (rice wine).

FIRST AID
Mash up some daffodil roots into a paste and apply this healing mixture to a sword wound.

ADVICE
Follow the Bushido warrior code that tells you, "To die when it is right to die; to strike when it is right to strike."

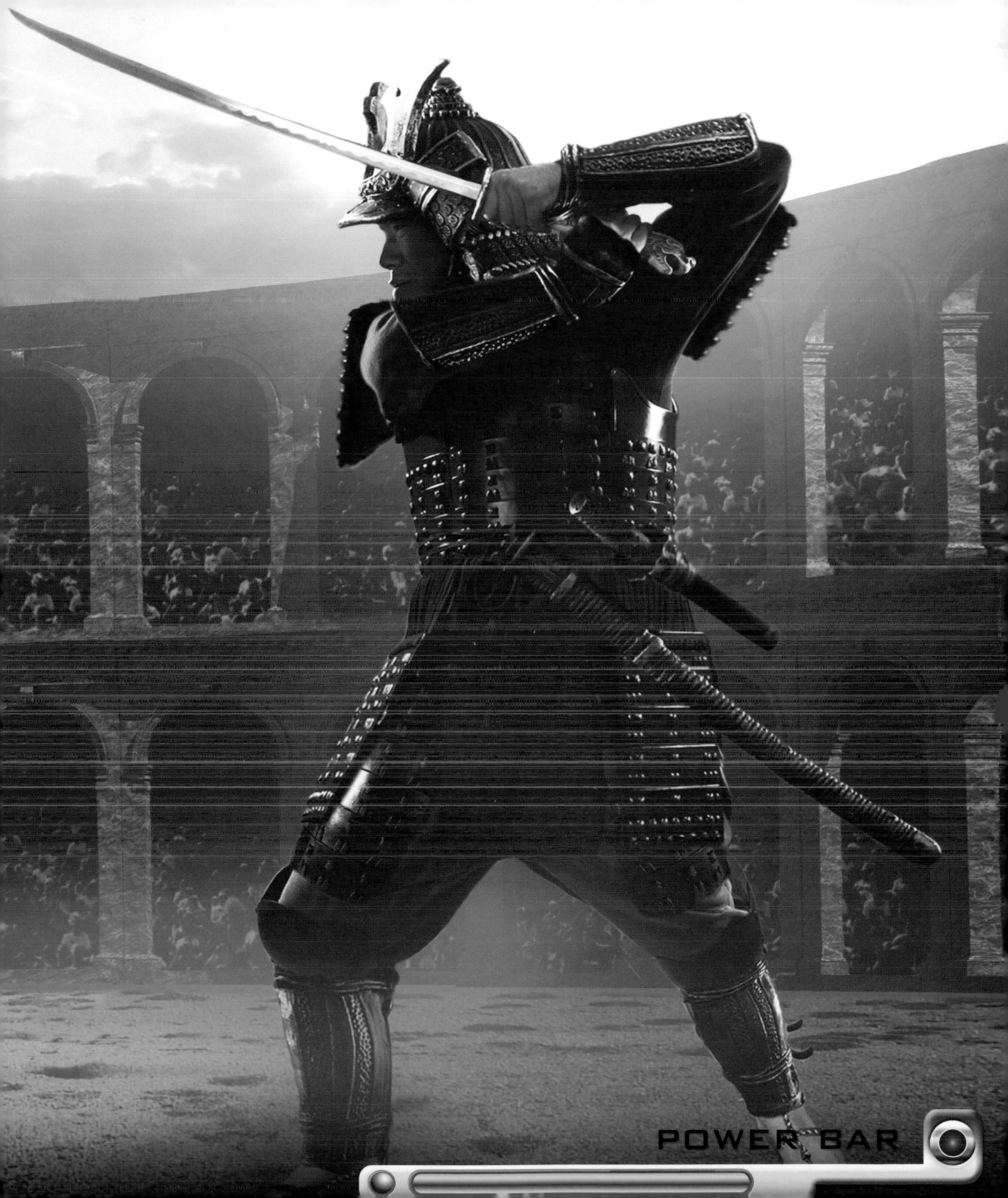
POWER BAR

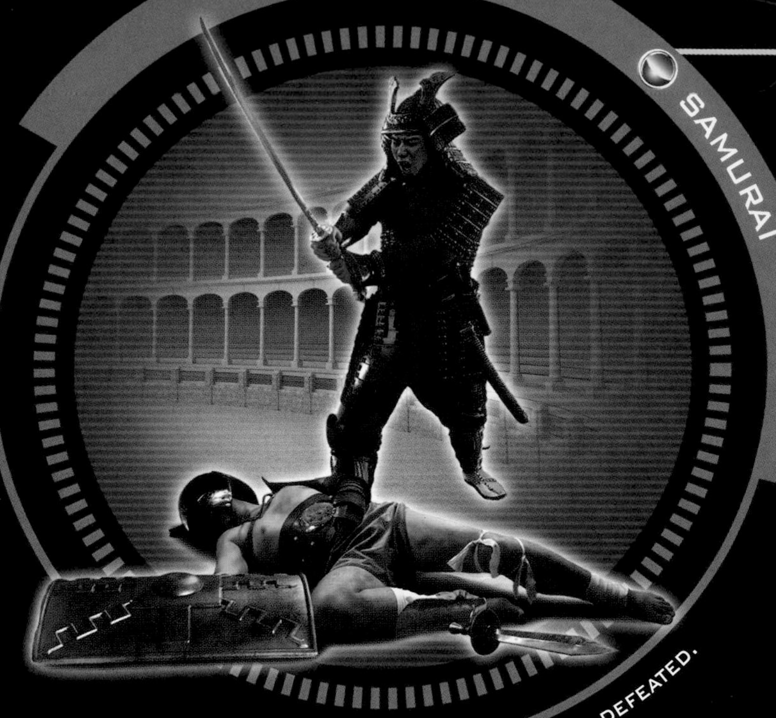
SAMURAI
THE GLADIATOR IS DEFEATED.

THE SAMURAI WINS

THE MURMILLO USUALLY FIGHTS HEAVILY ARMED GLADIATORS SUCH AS THE THRAEX OR HOPLOMACHUS, SO HE CAN CHALLENGE THE TAKEDA CLAN WARRIOR. BUT THE SAMURAI'S SUPERIOR BODY ARMOR ALLOWS HIM TO TAKE MORE RISKS, AND HE MAKES REPEATED CUTS WITH THE FINE BLADE OF HIS SWORD. THE GLADIATOR HAS BEEN TRAINED FOR A CROWD-PLEASING FIGHT, AND HIS SHOWY MOVES ARE EASY TO PREDICT. HE IS FORCED ONTO THE DEFENSIVE, AND THE SAMURAI SLASHES AT HIS UNARMORED TORSO AND LEGS. IT IS A CONVINCING SAMURAI VICTORY.

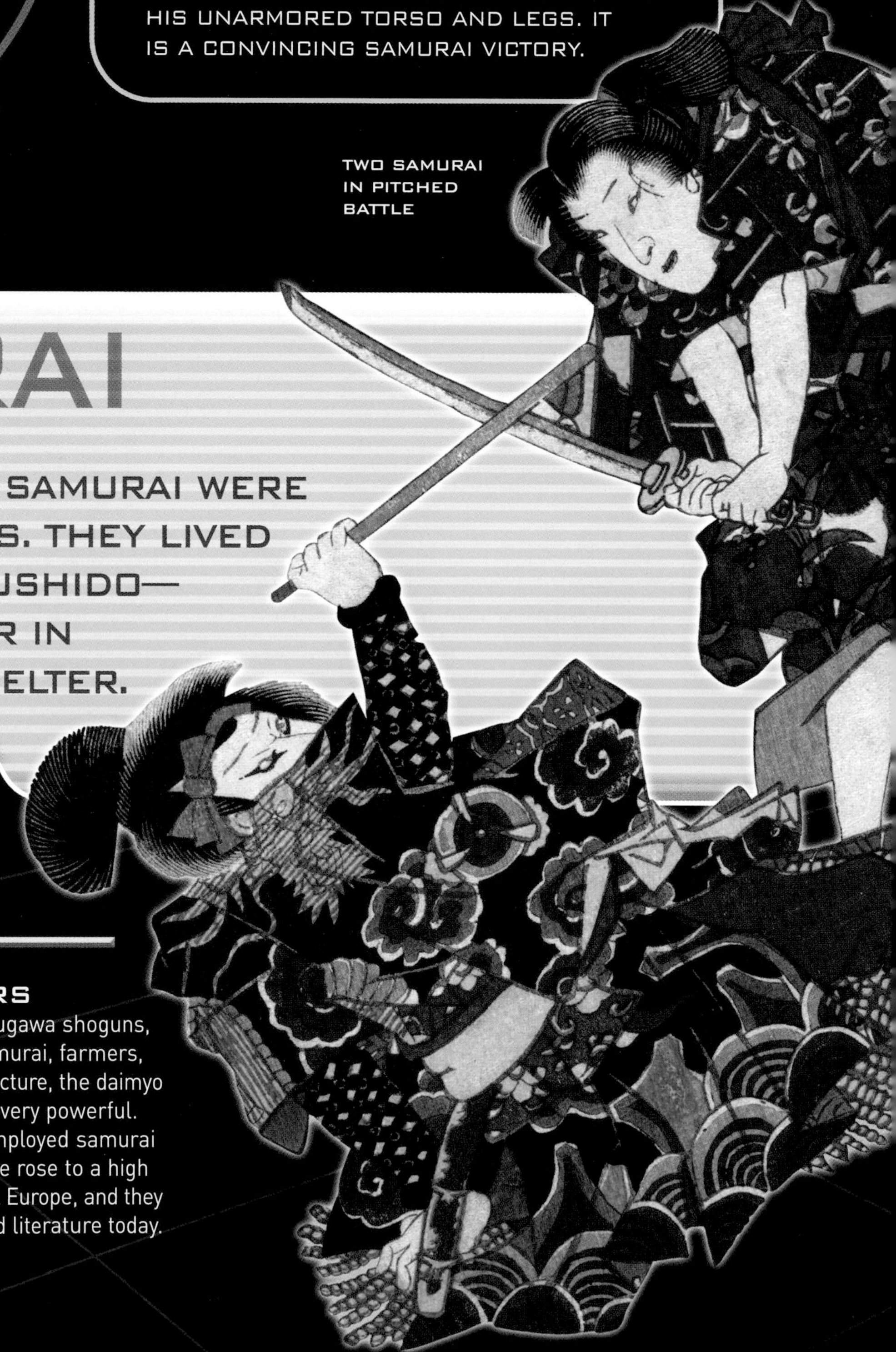
TWO SAMURAI IN PITCHED BATTLE

SAMURAI

IN MEDIEVAL JAPAN, ONLY THE SAMURAI WERE PERMITTED TO CARRY WEAPONS. THEY LIVED BY A WARRIOR'S CODE—THE BUSHIDO—AND SERVED A DAIMYO MASTER IN RETURN FOR PAYMENT AND SHELTER.

RISE OF THE SAMURAI

FROM SERVANTS TO WARRIORS

Between 1603 and 1868, under the rule of the Tokugawa shoguns, all Japanese people belonged to four classes—samurai, farmers, craftspeople, and merchants. Within this social structure, the daimyo lords (the top ranks of the samurai class) became very powerful. They had a responsibility to keep the peace and employed samurai warriors to help them do so. The samurai therefore rose to a high level in society, similar to that of knights in medieval Europe, and they are still depicted as heroes in Japanese movies and literature today.

Bushido: The Way of the Warrior

"Death shows greater nobility than capture or surrender."

"A samurai warrior must show no interest in material goods and wealth."

CASTLE KEEPS

The powerful Japanese daimyos built large castles. This enabled them to stamp their authority on the surrounding countryside, which they would dominate—and often terrorize—through the activities of their samurai warriors. By demonstrating their military power and increasing fear across the land, the samurai kept the peace.

RITUAL SUICIDE

Hara-kiri, or stomach cutting, was a way for Japanese warriors to die voluntarily. Originally it was performed only by the samurai on themselves as part of their Bushido heroic code. It allowed them to die with honor rather than fall into the hands of the enemy. It was also used as capital punishment if a warrior had brought shame upon himself.

THE AGE OF THE WARRING STATES

The Sengoku, or Warring States, period was a time of massive social change, political difficulty, and almost constant military conflict in Japan. It lasted from the middle of the 1400s to the beginning of the 1600s. During this period, many samurai lost their lives fighting for their daimyo masters.

CONFLICT

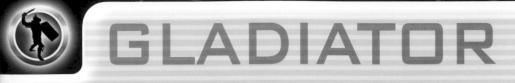

GLADIATOR

HOW COULD THE SCUM OF THE EARTH WIN FAME AND FORTUNE IN ANCIENT ROME? BY PROVING THEIR BRAVERY IN THE ARENA AS GLADIATORS. THERE WAS JUST ONE PROBLEM—HOW TO SURVIVE . . .

Oath of the Gladiator

"I will put up with being burned, bound, beaten, or killed by cold steel."

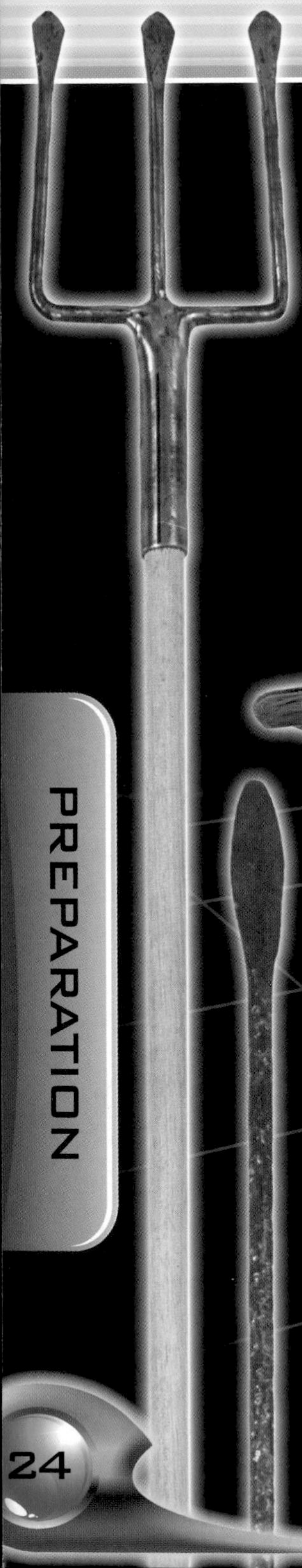

TRIDENT, USED BY A RETIARIUS

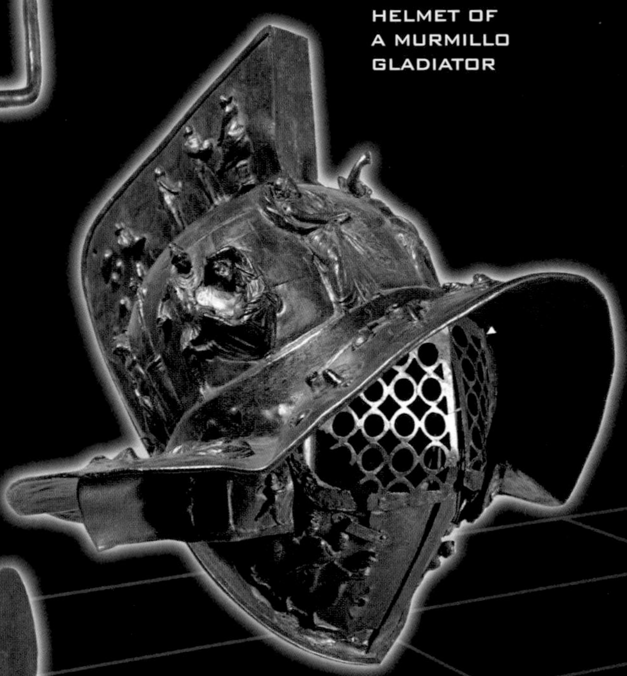

HELMET OF A MURMILLO GLADIATOR

WHO BECAME A GLADIATOR?

Gladiators were usually the lowest of the low. They might be slaves, criminals, or prisoners of war. A few free Romans sometimes chose to fight as gladiators, too. Gladiators who managed to stay alive and please the crowd became hugely popular, like celebrity athletes today. They could win big prizes and even be presented with their freedom, symbolized by a wooden sword. Once freed, they might become a trainer in a ludus.

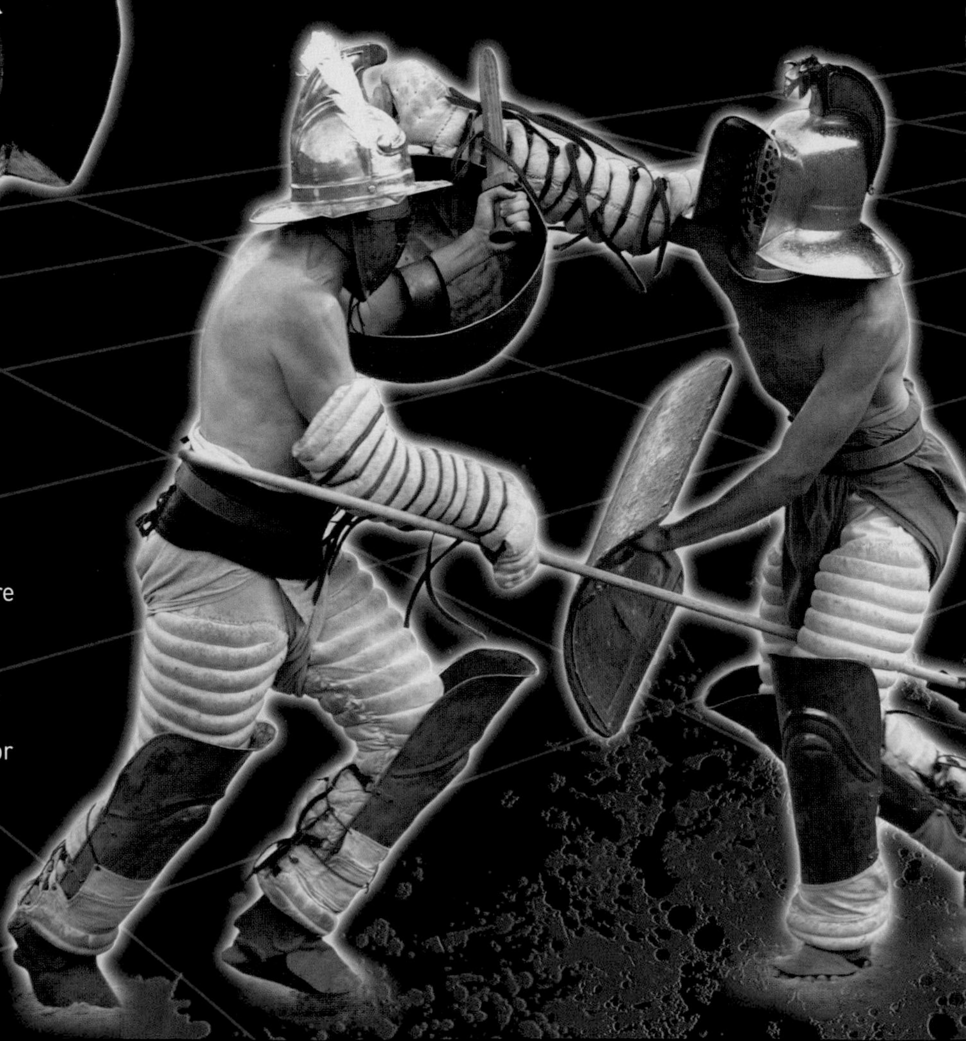

LIFE IN THE LUDUS

A gladiator school was called a ludus. It was often next to the amphitheater where the fights took place. There were barracks where the gladiators slept, rested, and ate special meals to build up their strength. In the exercise area, the gladiators would be worked hard under the watchful eye of the owner, or lanista. They were taught how to stab and slash with a short sword, how to use a shield, a net, and a spear, how to put on a show, and how to die heroically.

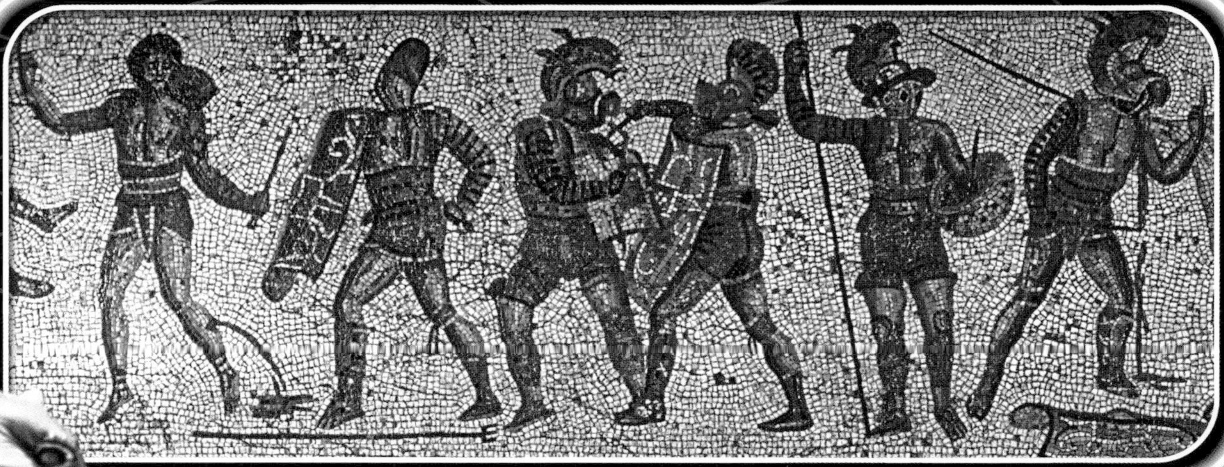

IS GLADIATOR
UM A MOVIE
LEASED IN
OO IS
REALISTIC BUT
RY DRAMATIC!

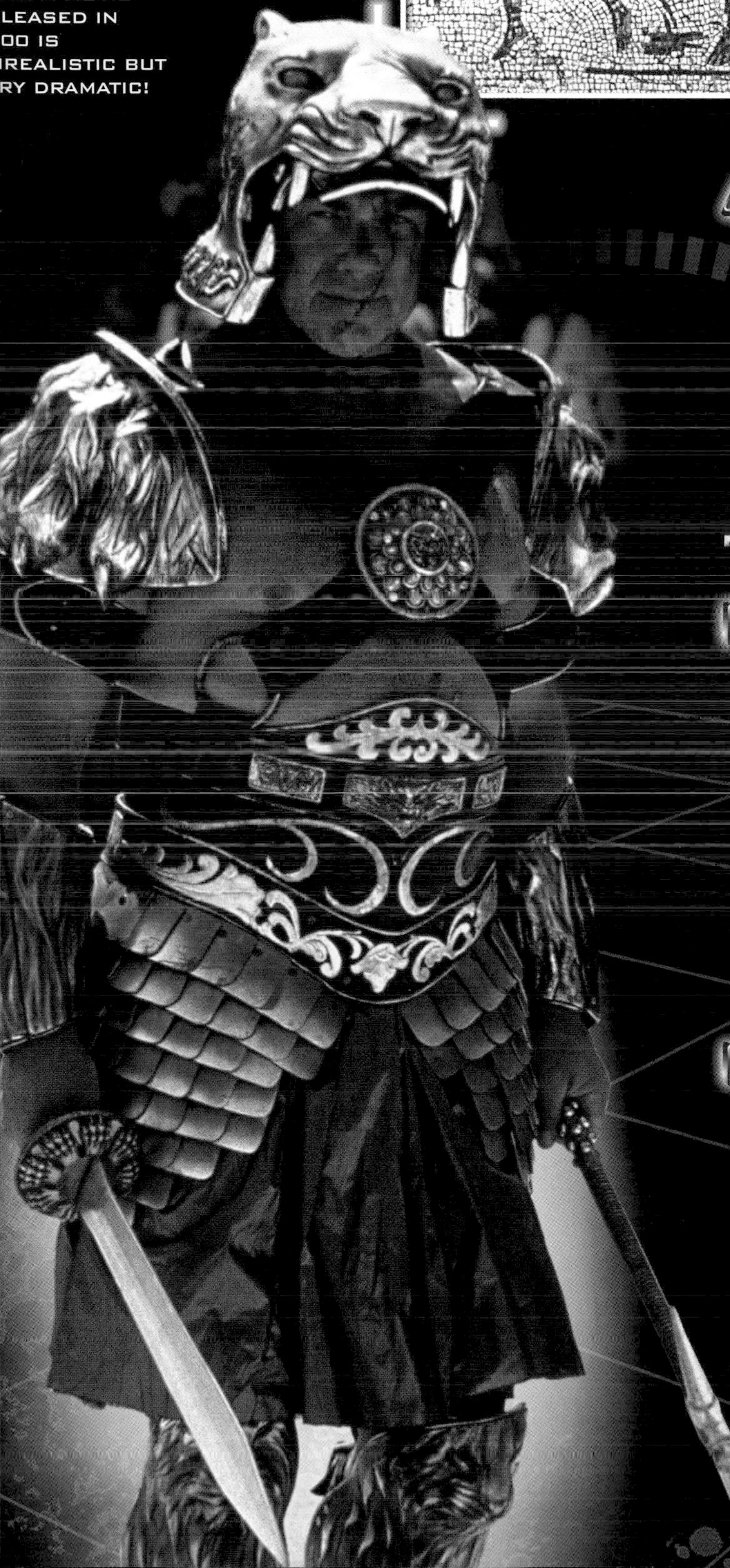

GLADIATOR TYPES

Several distinct types of gladiators entered the arena. This mosaic shows (from left to right): a retiarius, secutor, thraex, murmillo, hoplomachus, and another murmillo. Each had his own type of weapons and armor and his own way of fighting. The secutor, or "follower," carried a shield and sword. He would fight against the retiarius, or "net man," armed with a trident. The murmillo wore an ornate helmet, while the thraex (Thracian) fought with a small round shield and dagger. The fighters clashed and the crowd bellowed.

DEATH OR GLORY

THE CRUEL ARENA

Amphitheaters were built in hundreds of towns across the Roman Empire. On a day when gladiator shows were held, these stadiums would fill with spectators eager to watch the action. Gladiators would fight in pairs. The most spectacular and cruelest gladiator fights were held in the Colosseum in Rome. It could seat 50,000 spectators.

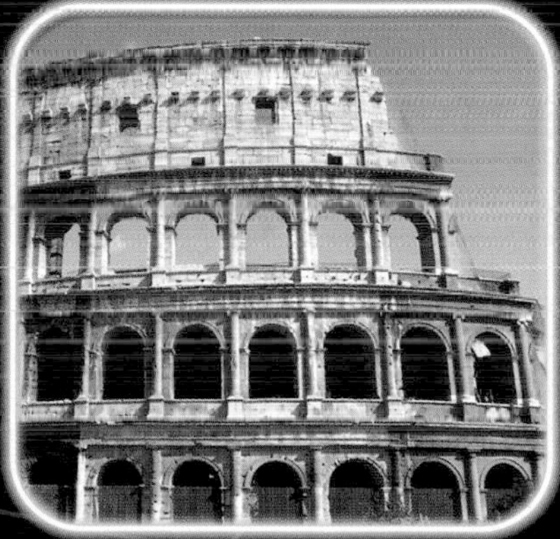

GLADIATOR REBEL

Spartacus (c. 109–71 B.C.) made his name by leaving the arena for the battlefield. He had been a soldier and a slave before being sold into a ludus. He and his fellow gladiators joined forces and fought their way to freedom. Soon they headed an army of perhaps 140,000 runaway slaves and outlaws. Eventually they were defeated by the Roman army.

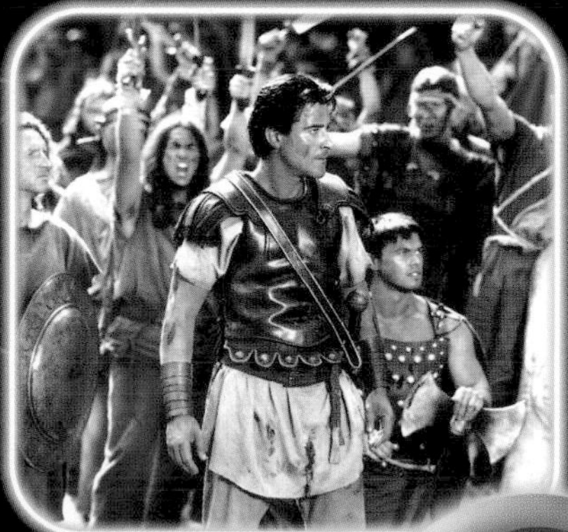

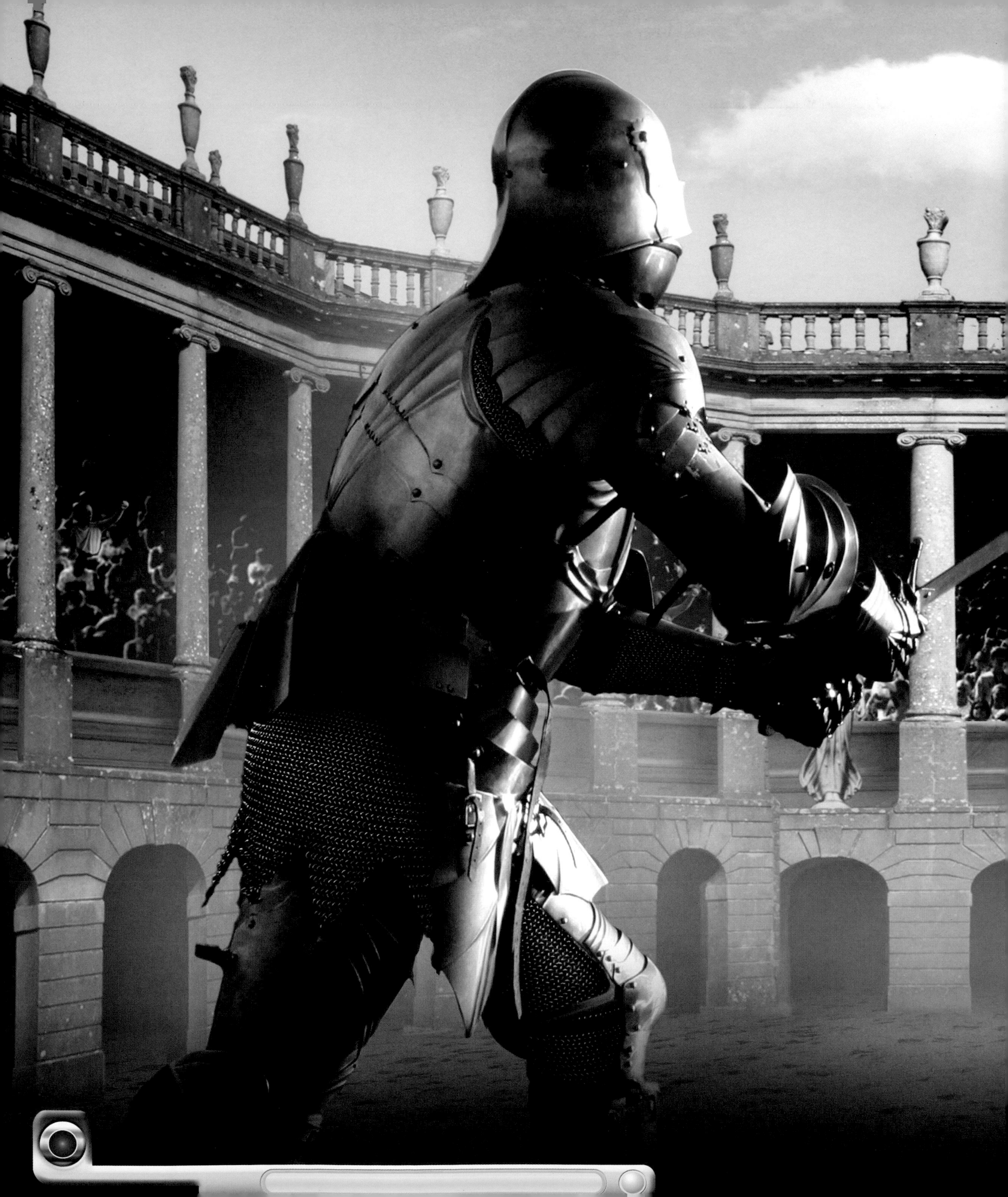

VS

KNIGHT

EARL

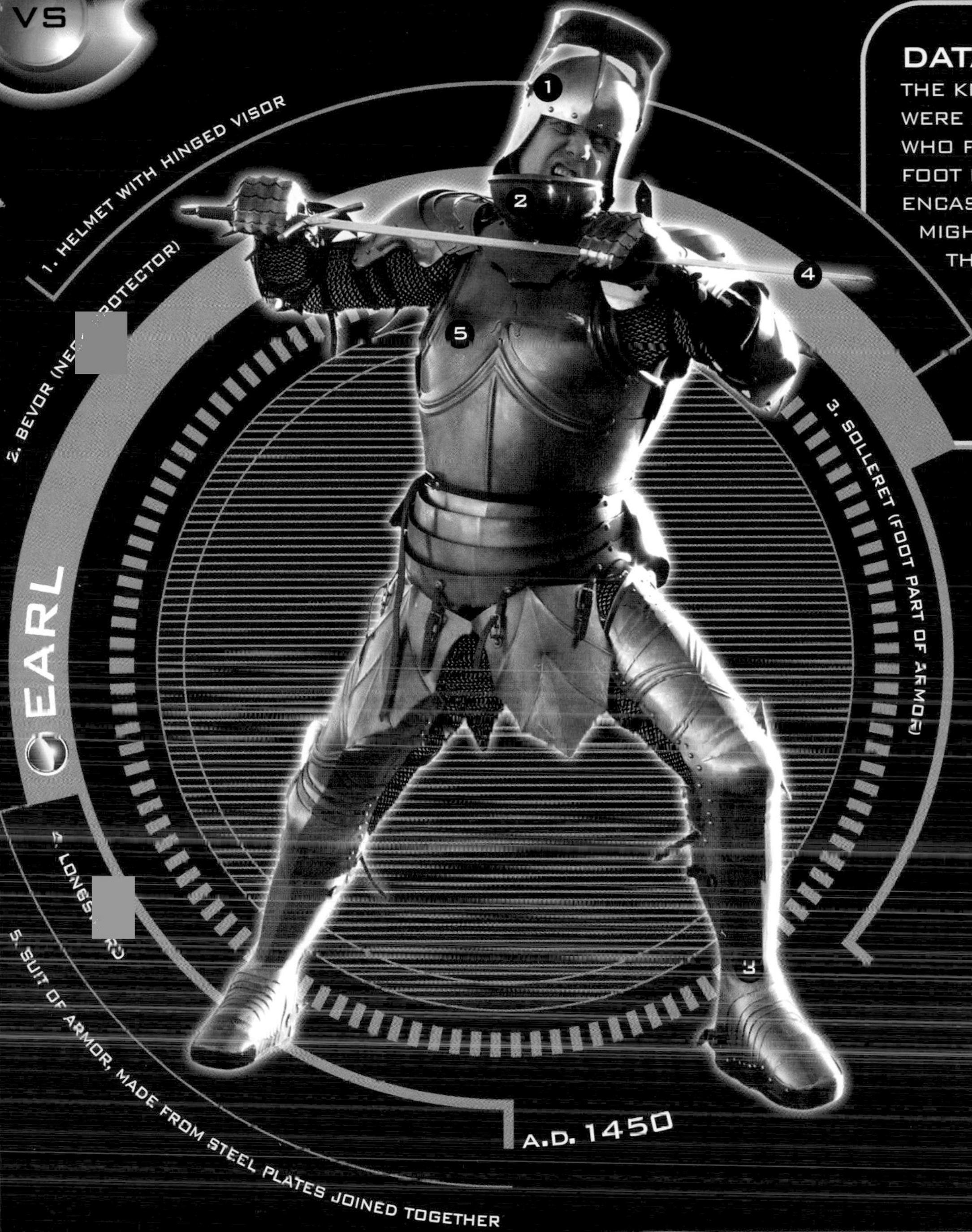
1. HELMET WITH HINGED VISOR
2. BEVOR (NE[redacted]OTECTOR)
3. SOLLERET (FOOT PART OF ARMOR)
4. LONGS[redacted]RD
5. SUIT OF ARMOR, MADE FROM STEEL PLATES JOINED TOGETHER
1
2
3
4
5
A.D. 1450

DATA FILE

THE KNIGHTS OF MEDIEVAL EUROPE WERE A POWERFUL WARRIOR CLASS WHO FOUGHT ON HORSEBACK AND ON FOOT FROM THE 800S TO THE MID-1500S. ENCASED IN ARMOR AND ARMED WITH MIGHTY SWORDS, THEY DEDICATED THEIR LIVES TO SEEKING VICTORY AND GLORY IN BATTLE.

PICK A WEAPON

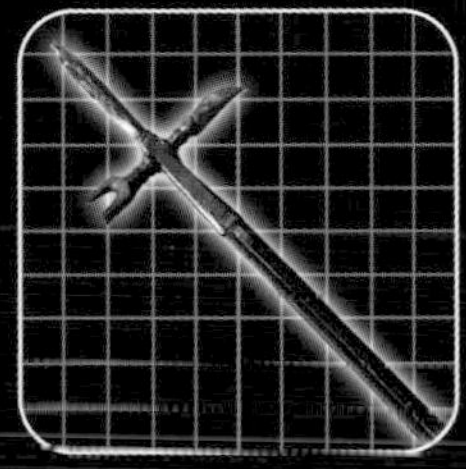

POLEAX
This war hammer is an essential weapon. Strike with the front or back of the "hammer" head or launch a deadly thrust with the spike on top.

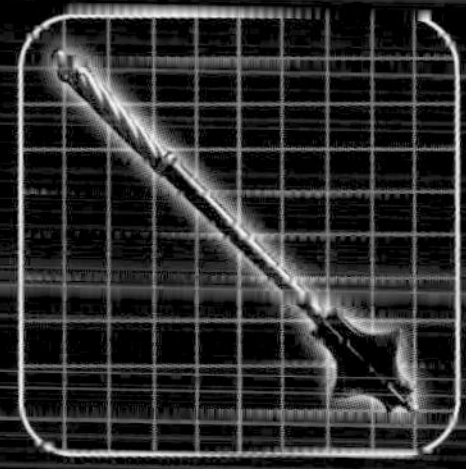

LIGHT MACE
This spiked club can be wielded from horseback or in foot combat and is designed to smash through armor and cause serious injury.

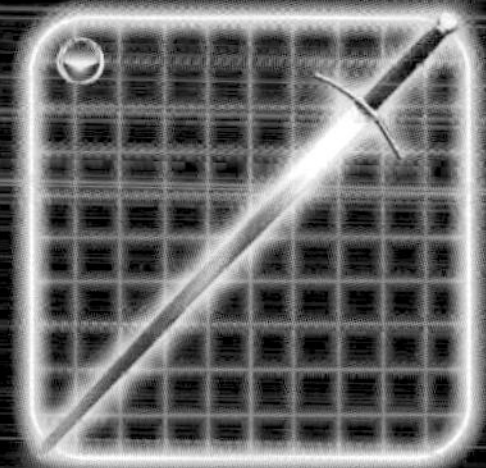

LONGSWORD
This superb weapon has a double-edged steel blade that is straight and flexible. Use it to slash or stab—it can even pierce metal armor.

ADD STAMINA

FIRST AID
Clean wounds with vinegar. Apply a potion of garlic to reduce the risk of infection or a balm made from yarrow, an herb, to stem bleeding.

ADVICE 1
Take heart from the thought that your stamina is excellent—you've trained to wear your heavy armor for many hours at a time.

ADVICE 2
Always follow the chivalric code of honor. Be fierce, brave, and merciless in battle but courteous and well mannered to others.

MAKE YOUR MOVE

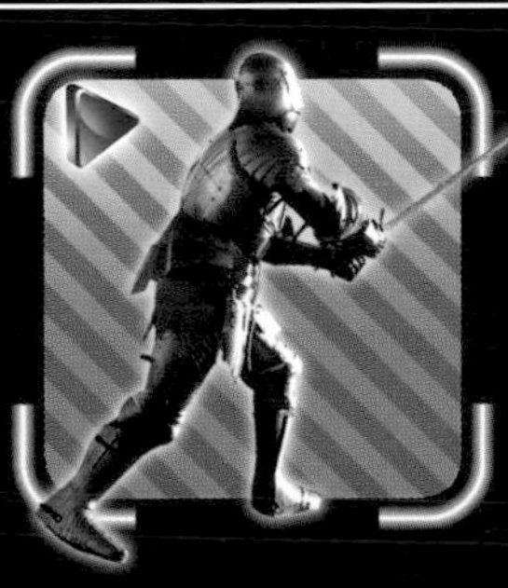

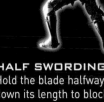

FRONTAL WARD
This forward position allows you to thrust, cut, or deflect from any angle.

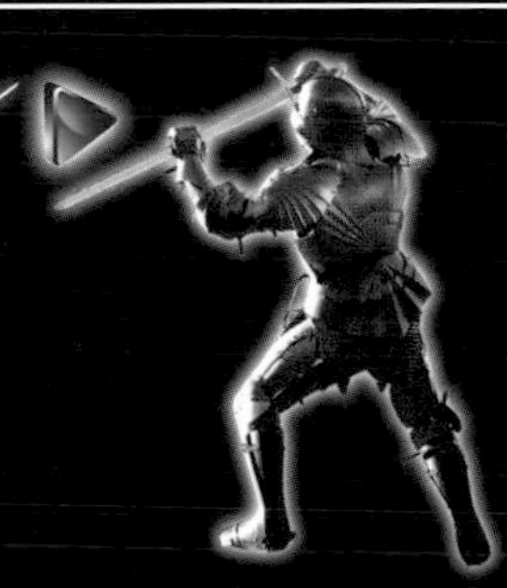

HALF SWORDING
Hold the blade halfway down its length to block or close in, hit, and stab.

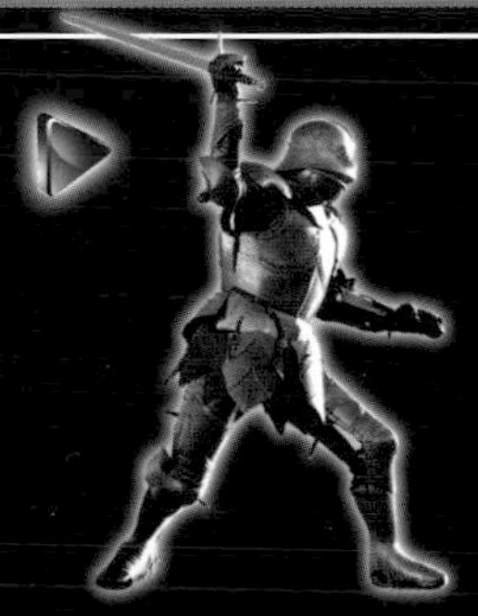

HIGH WARD
Make devastating blows in any direction, even from beneath your foe.

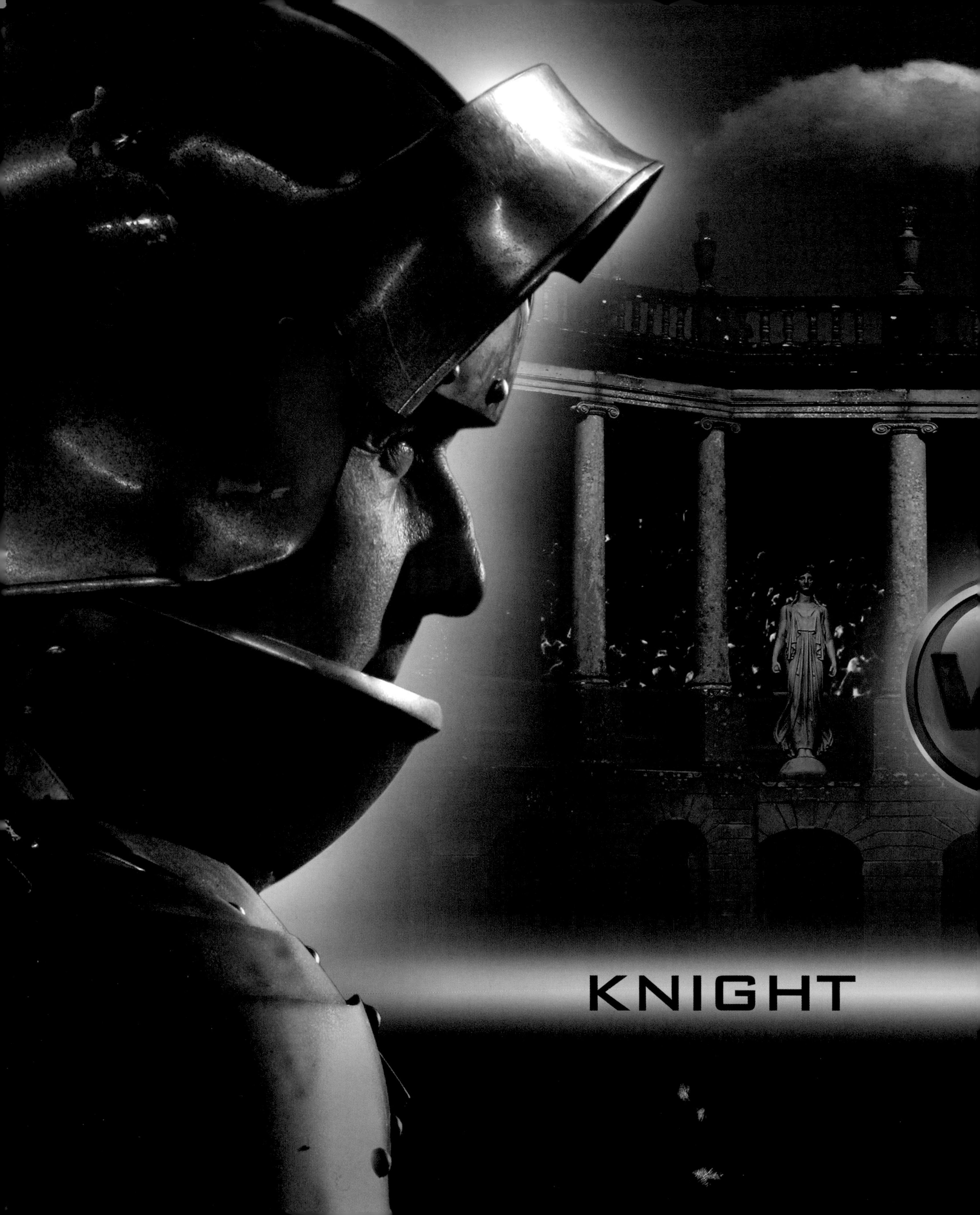
KNIGHT

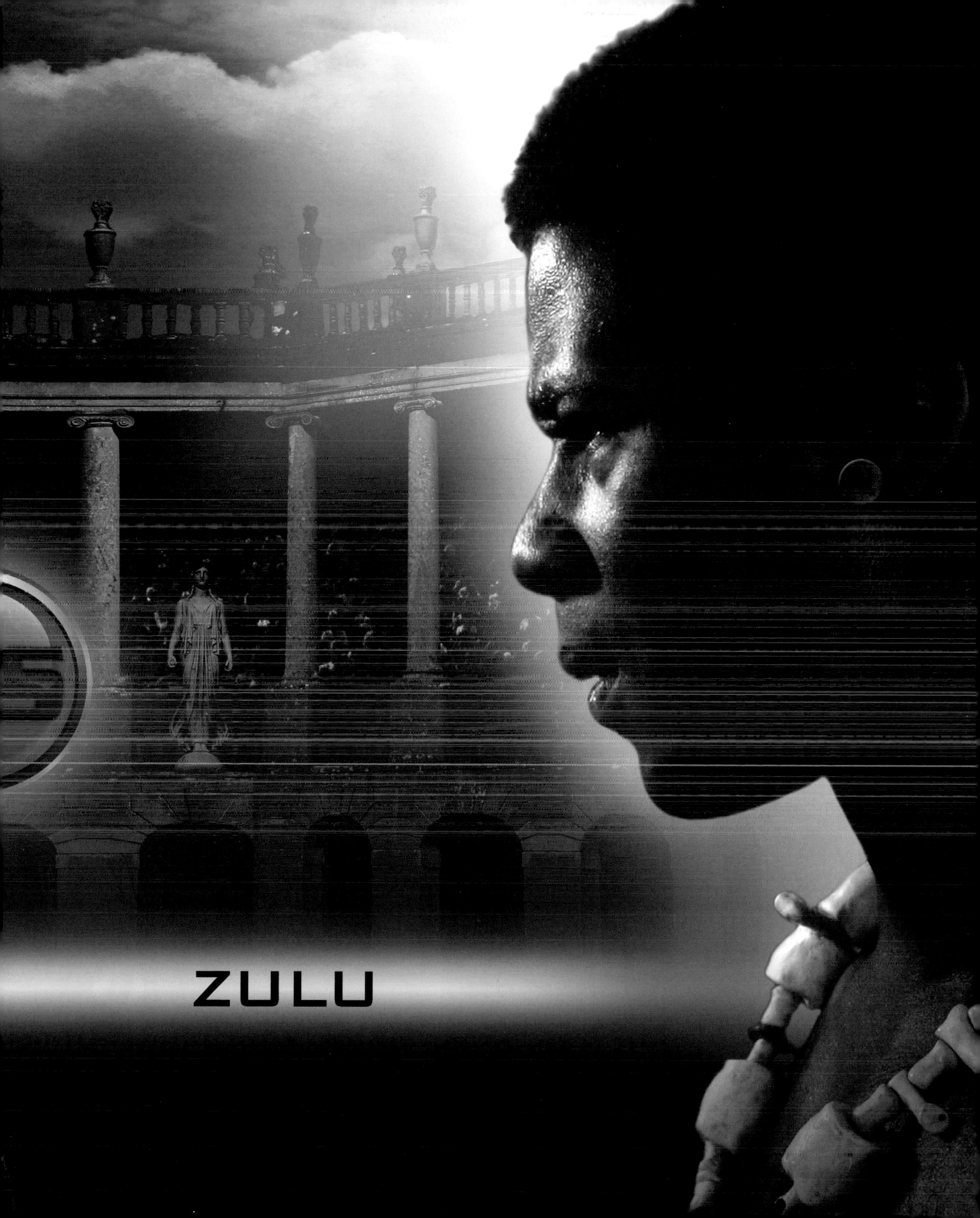
ZULU

VS

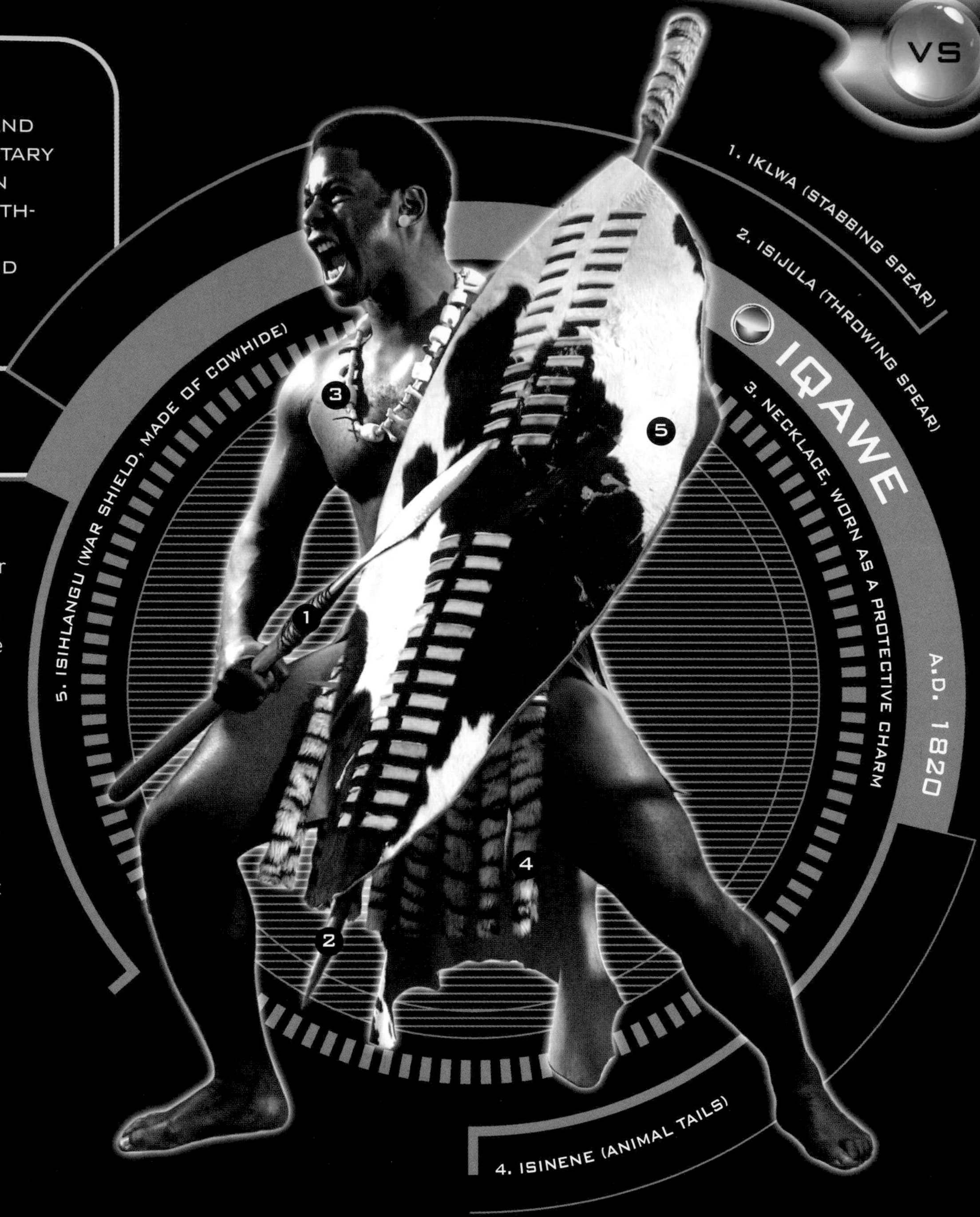

IQAWE
A.D. 1820
1. IKLWA (STABBING SPEAR)
2. ISIJULA (THROWING SPEAR)
3. NECKLACE, WORN AS A PROTECTIVE CHARM
4. ISINENE (ANIMAL TAILS)
5. ISIHLANGU (WAR SHIELD, MADE OF COWHIDE)
1
2
3
4
5

DATA FILE

ARMED WITH DEADLY WEAPONS AND BOASTING A SOPHISTICATED MILITARY ORGANIZATION, THE ZULU NATION WAS A FORMIDABLE FORCE IN 19TH-CENTURY SOUTHERN AFRICA. AN IQAWE WAS A GREAT WARRIOR AND RENOWNED HERO FROM AMONG THE ZULU FIGHTERS.

PICK A WEAPON

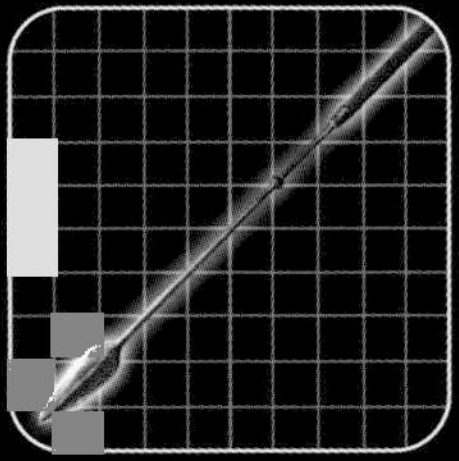

ISIJULA
Use this throwing spear with great accuracy and speed to wound an enemy's torso or pierce a shield from almost 100 ft. (30m) away.

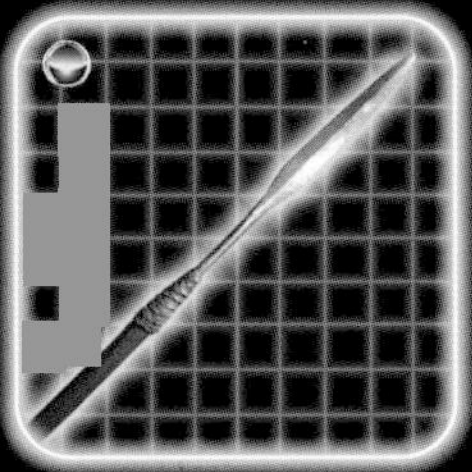

IKLWA
This heavy-bladed war weapon is named after the sucking sound it makes when pulled out of the enemy's flesh. Aim at the stomach.

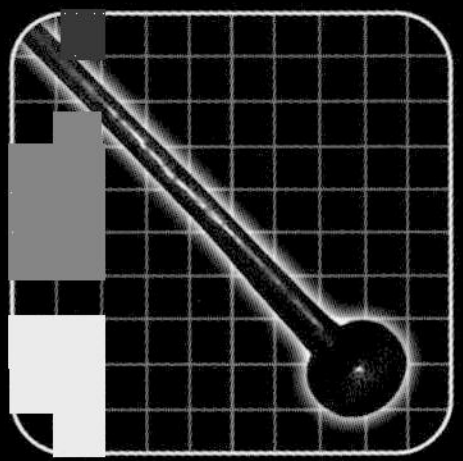

IWISA
This club is beautifully crafted from a single piece of wood, but its purpose is not pretty—you can use it to beat an enemy's brains out.

MAKE YOUR MOVE

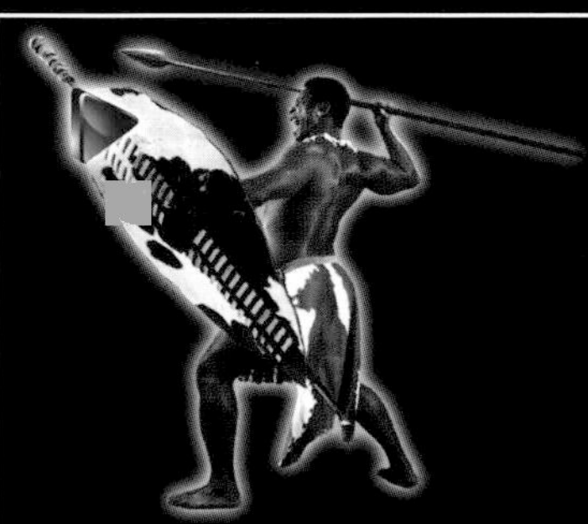

DISTRACT
Move the shield and spear back and forth to distract and confuse your enemy.

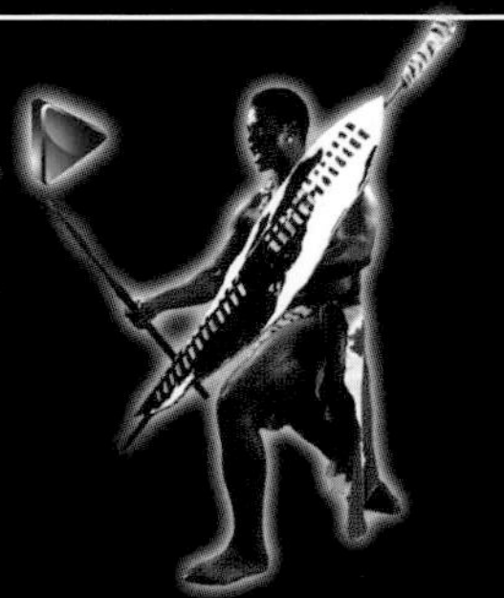

QUICK THROW
When your enemy is off guard, quickly grab and throw the isijula at him.

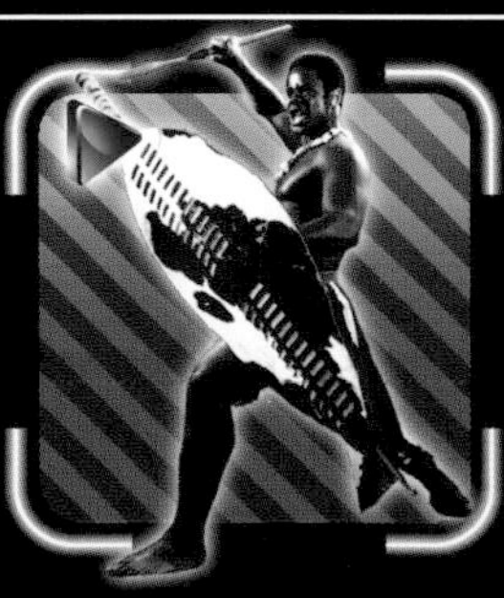

THRUST
Deliver a powerful underarm thrust to the torso with the iklwa.

ADD STAMINA

FOOD
Eat up your beef rations—you'll have more of this nutritious food when serving in the army than at any time in civilian life.

FIRST AID
Bind wounds with grass until you can see the inyanga (healer), who will wash and stitch your wounds and give you powerful medicines.

ADVICE
Ensure the protection of ancestral spirits by taking part in rituals, staged by an inyanga, before battle.

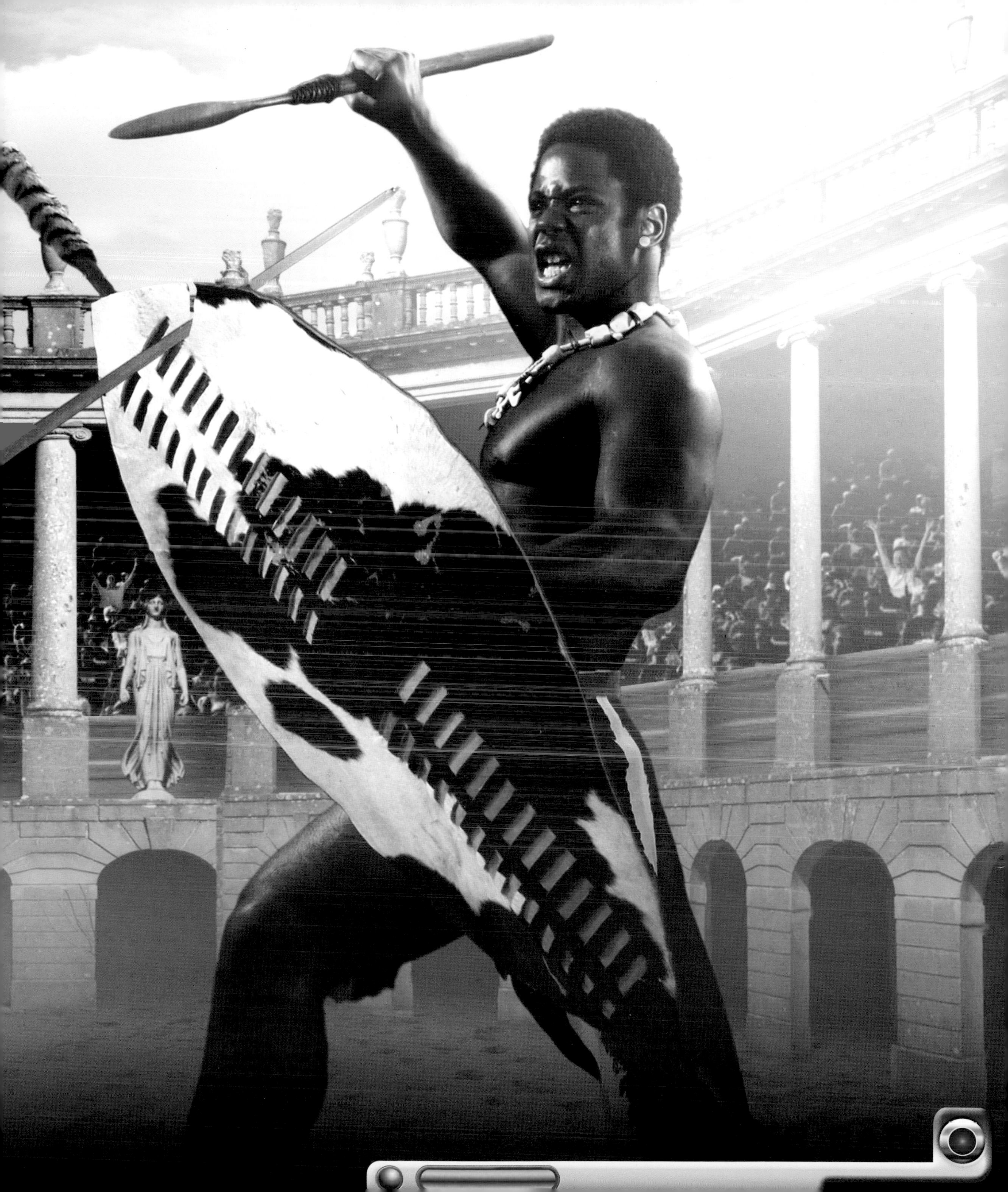

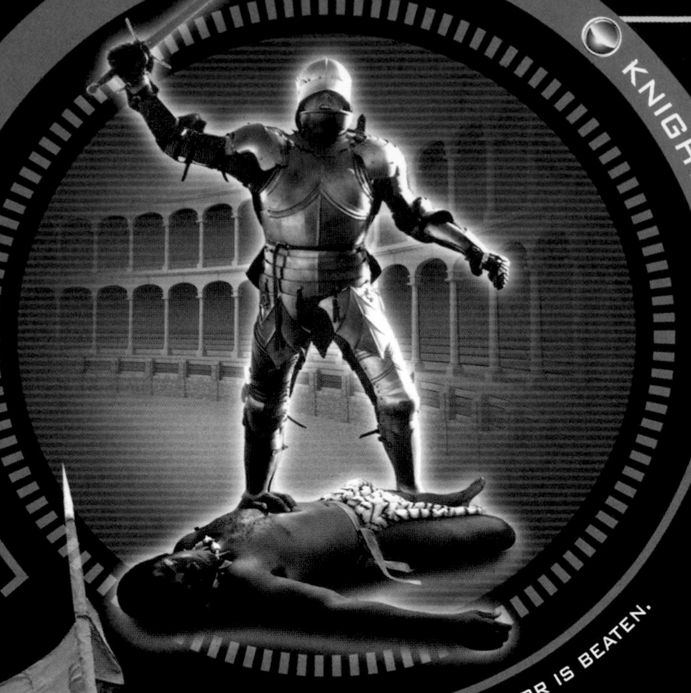
KNIGHT
THE ZULU WARRIOR IS BEATEN.

THE KNIGHT WINS

THE ZULU WEARS NEITHER ARMOR NOR A HELMET. HE LACKS A DEVASTATING WEAPON SUCH AS A METAL SWORD OR MACE. A ZULU WARRIOR IS DISCIPLINED AND USES CLEVER TACTICS IN BATTLE BUT IS LESS SUITED TO A SINGLE-COMBAT CHALLENGE. THE HEAVILY ARMORED KNIGHT IS A PROFESSIONAL FIGHTER WHO HAS PRACTICED SWORDSMANSHIP EVERY DAY FROM A YOUNG AGE. HE HAS BEEN TRAINED TO USE A RANGE OF WEAPONS AND TO MEET A VARIETY OF FIGHTING STYLES IN WHATEVER OPPONENT HE HAS TO FACE.

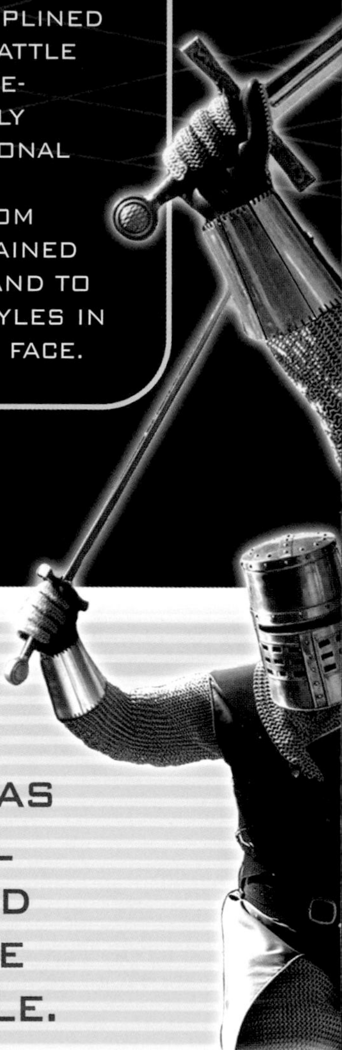

KNIGHT

THE HISTORY OF MEDIEVAL EUROPE WAS MADE BY ARMORED HORSEMEN, LOYAL TO THEIR LORD AND GREEDY FOR LAND AND POWER. A KNIGHT'S LIFE WAS ONE OF PERMANENT READINESS FOR BATTLE.

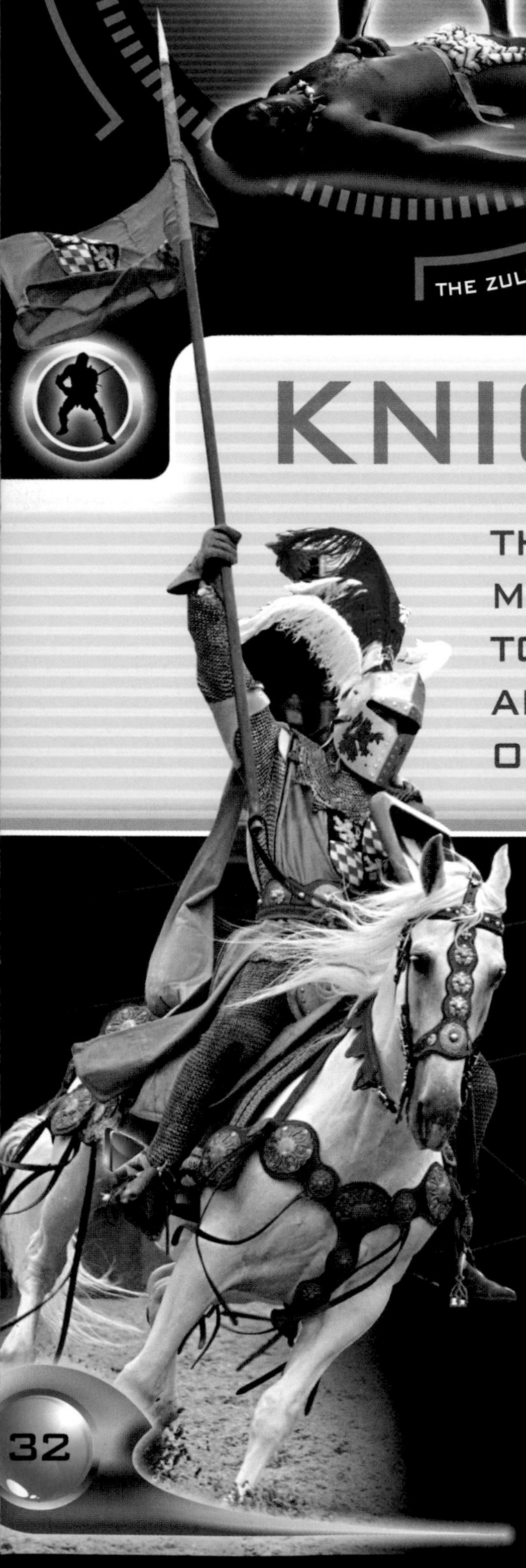

WAR CHARGE!

In the turmoil of battle, a knight and his powerful warhorse would act together. Mounted knights, charging through enemy lines, were vital in battle. From around A.D. 800 to 1500, European knights fought countless bloody wars, including the Crusades (a series of invasions of lands in the Middle East) and wars between nations, such as the Hundred Years' War between France and England.

From the code of chivalry:

- Fear God
- Serve your Lord
- Respect women
- Protect the weak
- Honor your fellow knights
- Live by honor and fight for glory

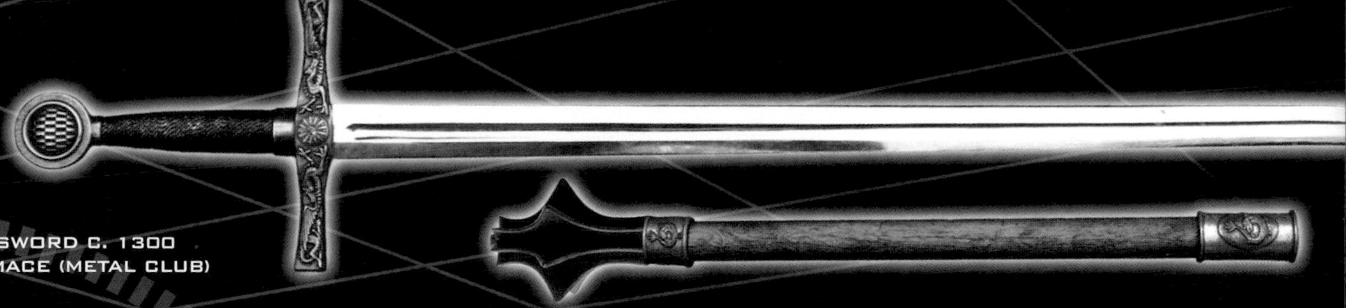

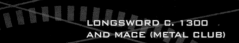

LONGSWORD C. 1300
AND MACE (METAL CLUB)

MEN OF STEEL

These knights wear coats and leggings of mail, made up of interlinking rings of iron. Their helmets, or "great helms," are like buckets, covering the whole head. During the 1300s, knights began to protect some parts of the body with solid metal plates. The emblems on the shield and cloth tunic, or surcoat, are called coats of arms. They identify each knight in the heat of battle.

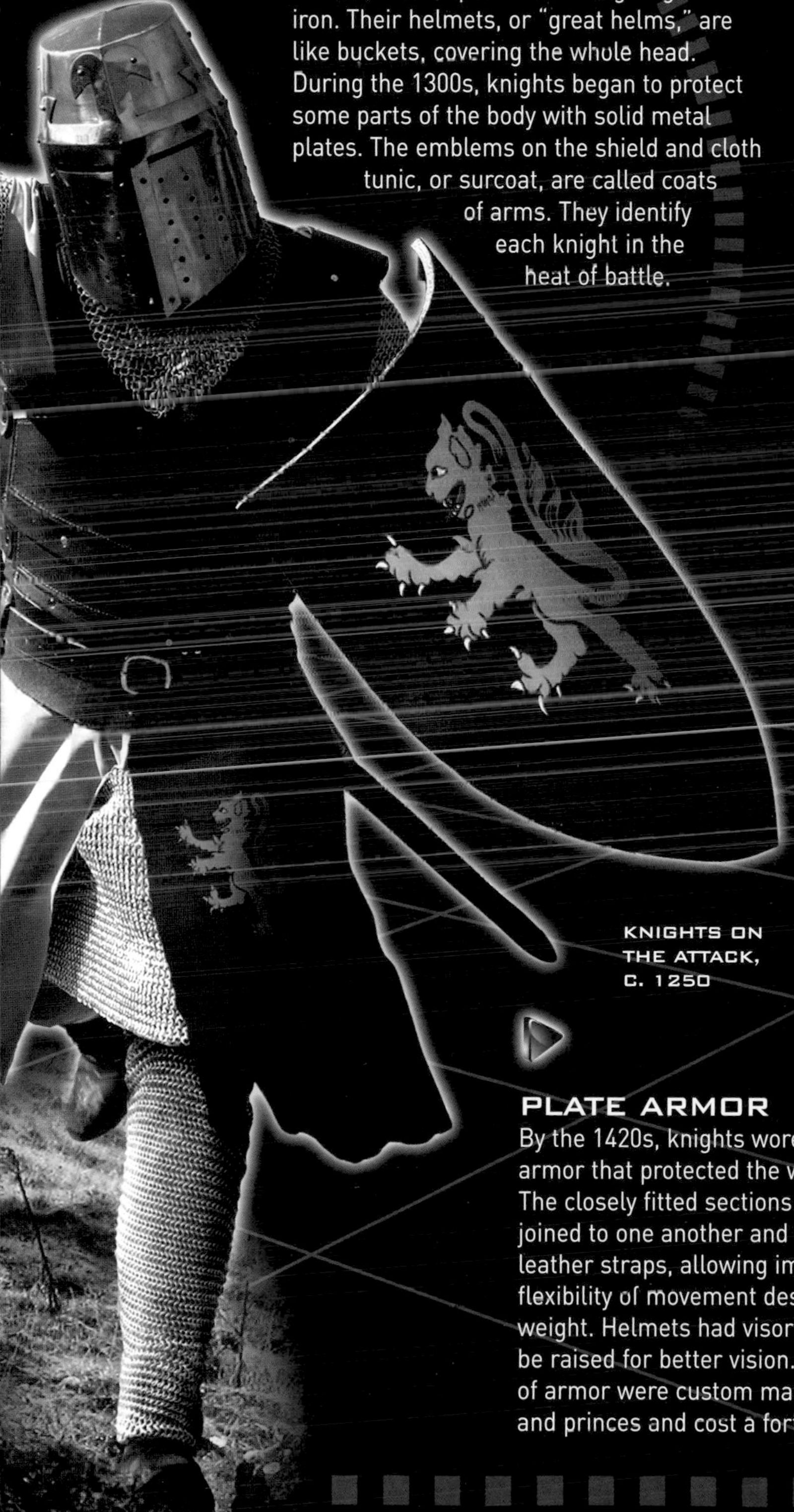

KNIGHTS ON THE ATTACK, C. 1250

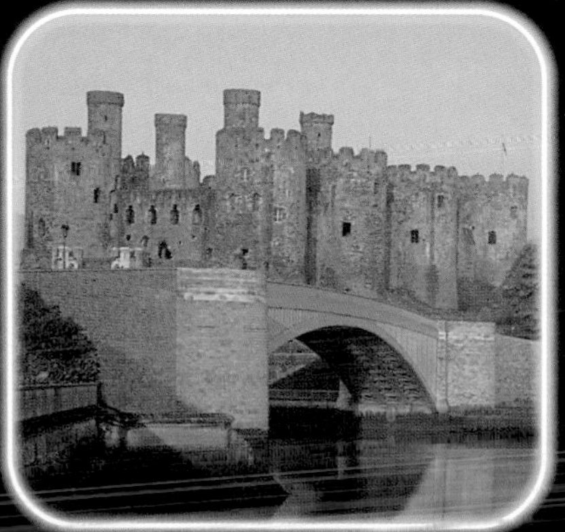

HUGE WALLS

Kings, lords, and knights lived in great castles with high stone walls. Their goal was to control the surrounding region. Enemies would attack the castle by surrounding it and cutting off supplies—a siege. This castle was built in Conwy, Wales, in the 1280s, after the English king Edward I (reigned 1272–1307) invaded Wales.

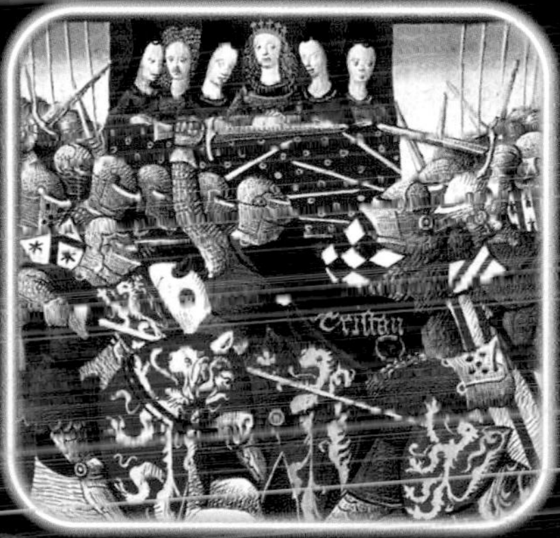

THE TOURNAMENT

Tournaments were mock battles in which knights would practice their fighting skills in combat with one another. They were also festivals of chivalry. The knights showed off to the ladies and wore fancy armor and plumed helmets. Stories and poems were written about the heroic deeds of knights in battle and at tournaments.

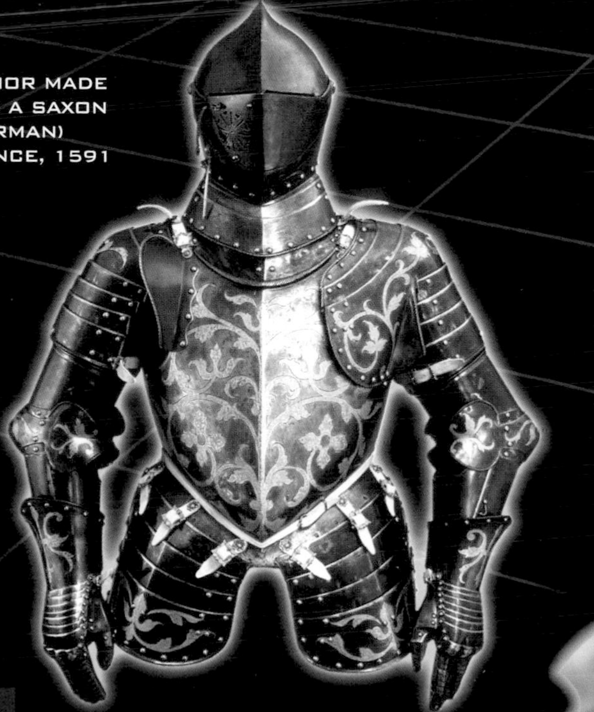

ARMOR MADE FOR A SAXON (GERMAN) PRINCE, 1591

PLATE ARMOR

By the 1420s, knights wore suits of plate armor that protected the whole body. The closely fitted sections of steel were joined to one another and the body by leather straps, allowing impressive flexibility of movement despite the heavy weight. Helmets had visors, which could be raised for better vision. The best suits of armor were custom made for kings and princes and cost a fortune.

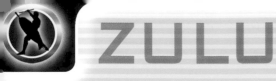

ZULU

DURING THE 1800S, FEW SOUTHERN AFRICAN WARRIORS COULD WITHSTAND THE ONSLAUGHT OF THE ZULU ARMIES. ONCE A PEACEFUL FARMING PEOPLE, THE ZULU EMERGED AS A POWERFUL FORCE—ORGANIZED AND EXTREMELY AGGRESSIVE.

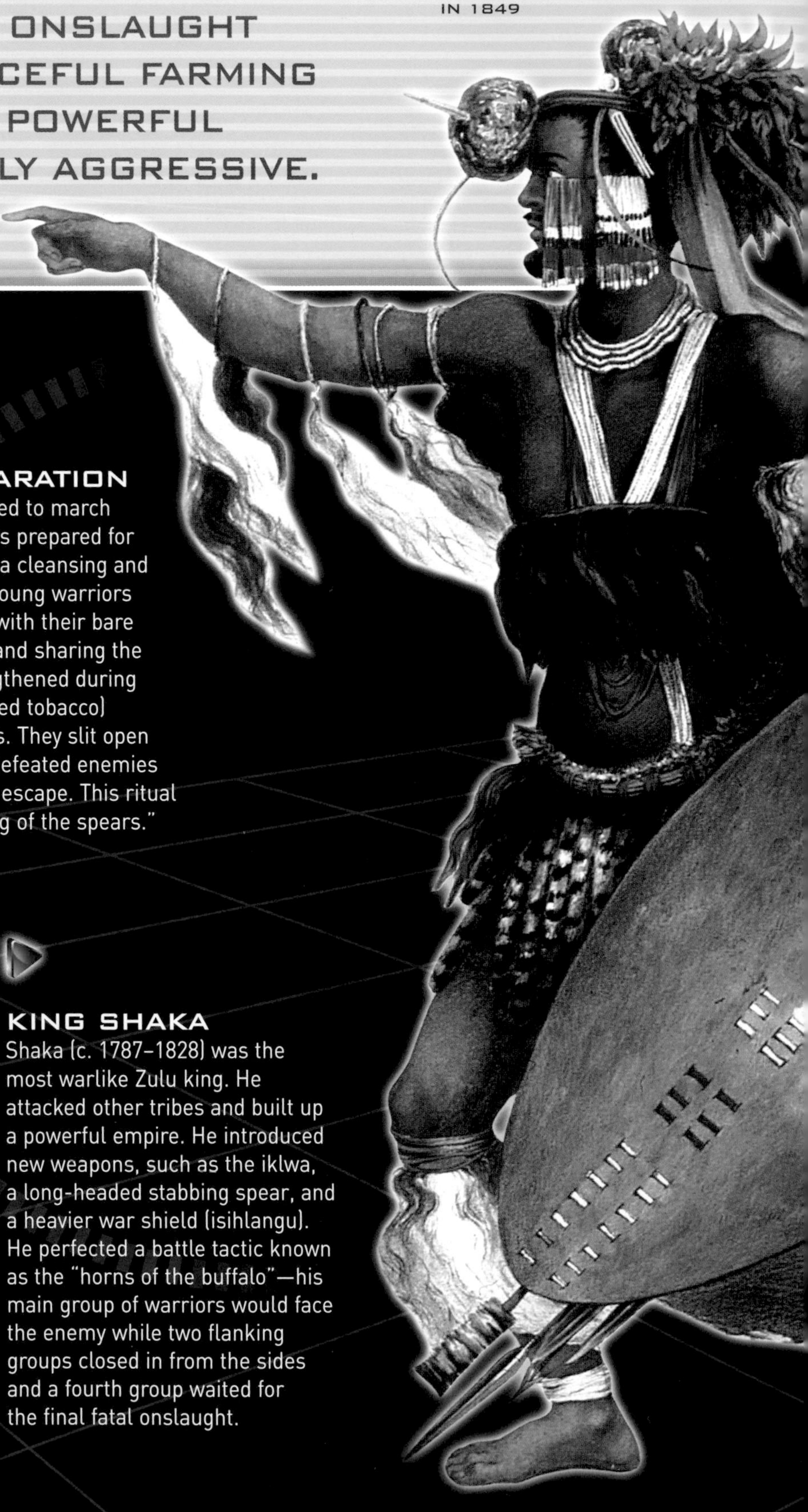

UTIMUNI, A NEPHEW OF KING SHAKA, IN 1849

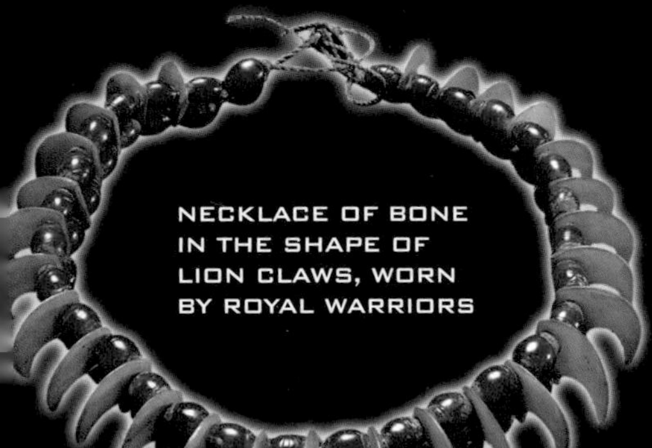

NECKLACE OF BONE IN THE SHAPE OF LION CLAWS, WORN BY ROYAL WARRIORS

BATTLE PREPARATION

Zulu armies were trained to march at great speed. Warriors prepared for battle by taking part in a cleansing and strengthening ritual—young warriors would kill a black bull with their bare hands before roasting and sharing the meat. They were strengthened during battle by snuff (powdered tobacco) containing potent herbs. They slit open the stomachs of their defeated enemies to allow their spirits to escape. This ritual was called the "washing of the spears."

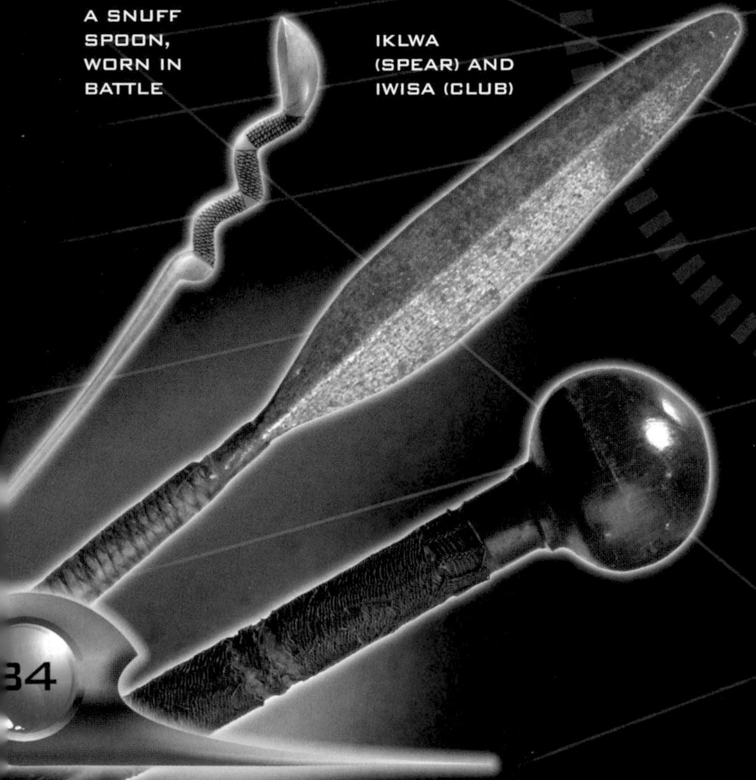

A SNUFF SPOON, WORN IN BATTLE

IKLWA (SPEAR) AND IWISA (CLUB)

KING SHAKA

Shaka (c. 1787–1828) was the most warlike Zulu king. He attacked other tribes and built up a powerful empire. He introduced new weapons, such as the iklwa, a long-headed stabbing spear, and a heavier war shield (isihlangu). He perfected a battle tactic known as the "horns of the buffalo"—his main group of warriors would face the enemy while two flanking groups closed in from the sides and a fourth group waited for the final fatal onslaught.

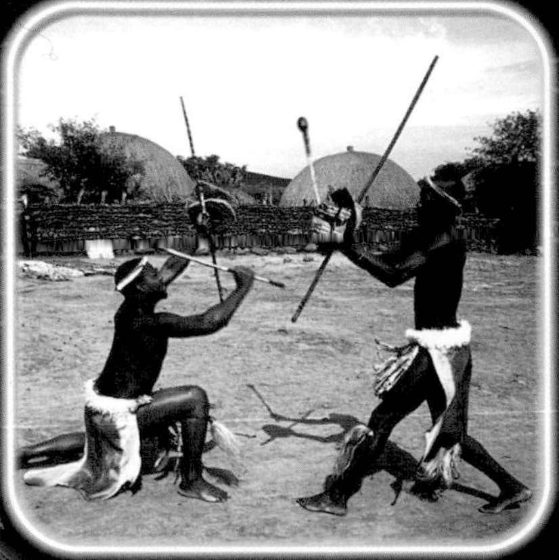

TOUGH AND READY

A Zulu fighting group was called an impi. Boys were trained for combat when still young, and warriors learned to endure pain by stamping—barefoot—on thorns. From the age of 20, men enlisted in a regiment (iButho) of 1,000 warriors. They were not permanent soldiers but would be called up in the event of war. Shaka could call upon around 20,000 trained fighters.

"They were giving vent to no loud war cries but to a low musical murmuring noise, which gave the impression of a gigantic swarm of bees getting nearer and nearer."

A Zulu army approaches, from an eyewitness account of the battle of Isandlwana (1879)

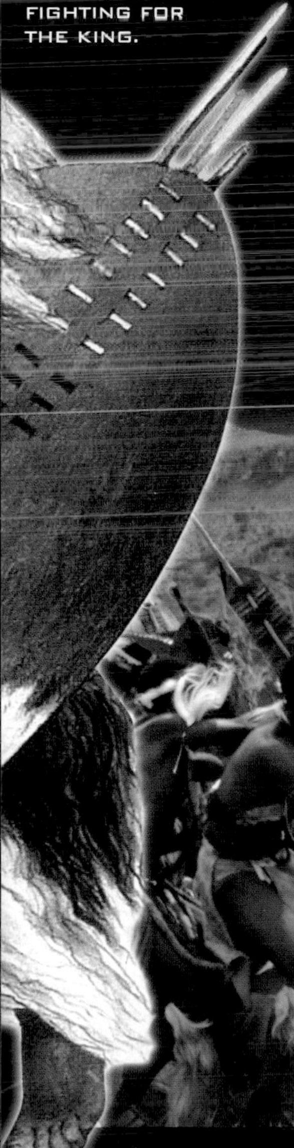

THE WAR SHIELD WAS ISSUED TO A SOLDIER FIGHTING FOR THE KING.

ZULU WARS

In the 1860s and 1870s, the Zulu clashed with European invaders, such as Afrikaner settlers and British soldiers, who had modern firearms. In 1879, King Cetshwayo, a nephew of Shaka, went to war. His warriors defeated a British army at Isandlwana. Some Zulu had by then acquired firearms, but their success was due more to surprise, tactics, and numbers. The shocked British defeated the Zulu at Ulundi later that year.

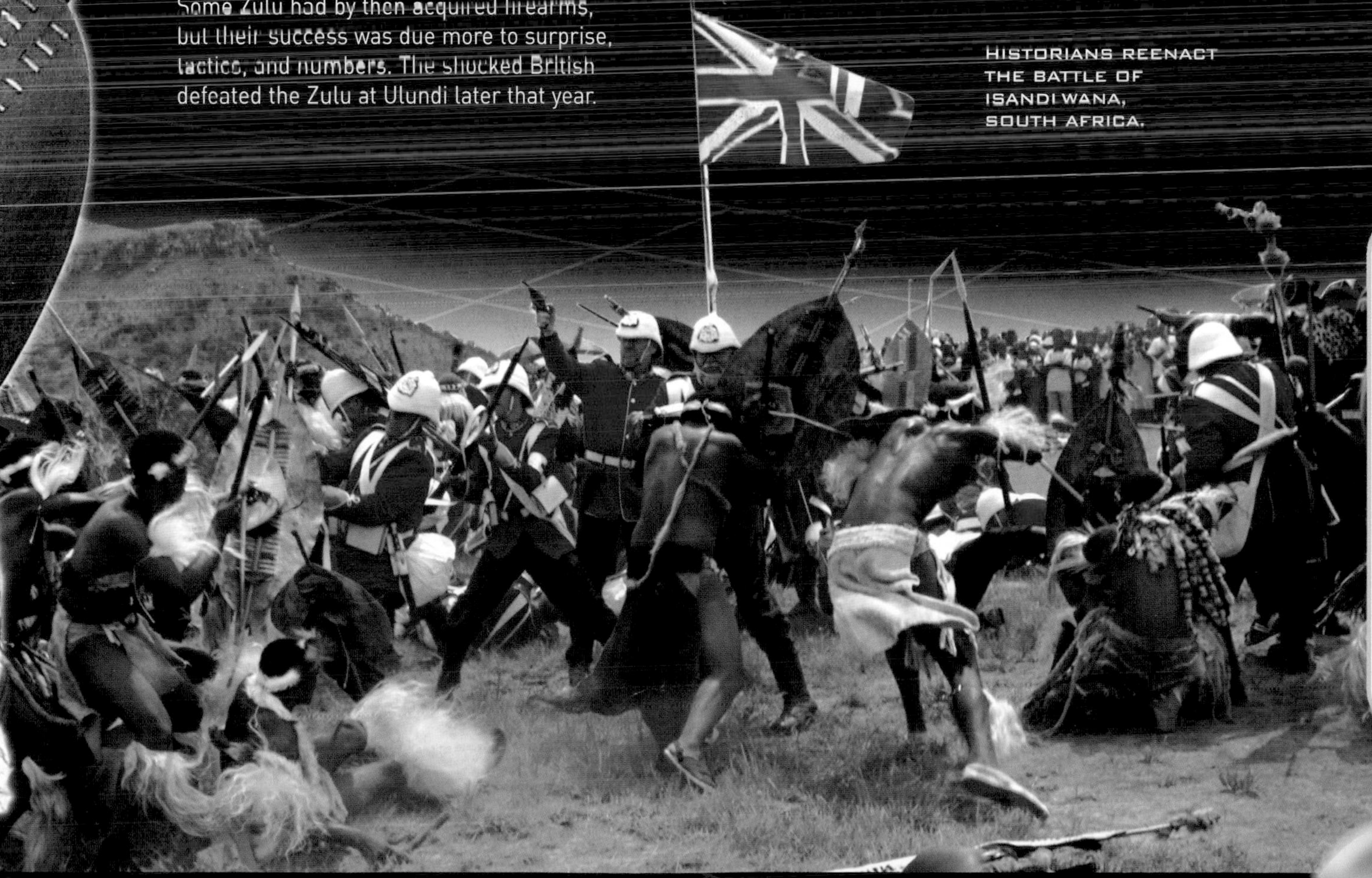

HISTORIANS REENACT THE BATTLE OF ISANDLWANA, SOUTH AFRICA.

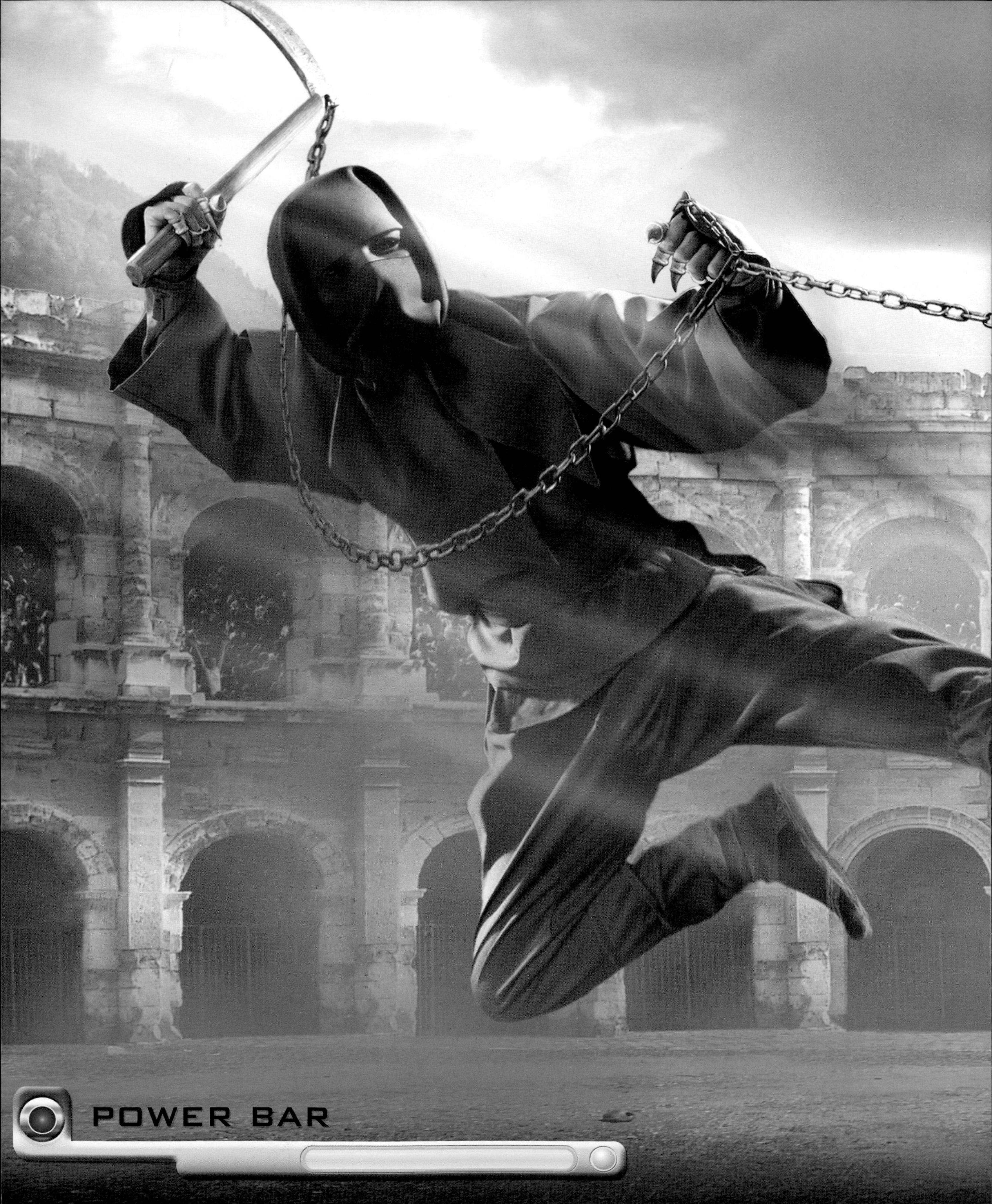
POWER BAR

VS

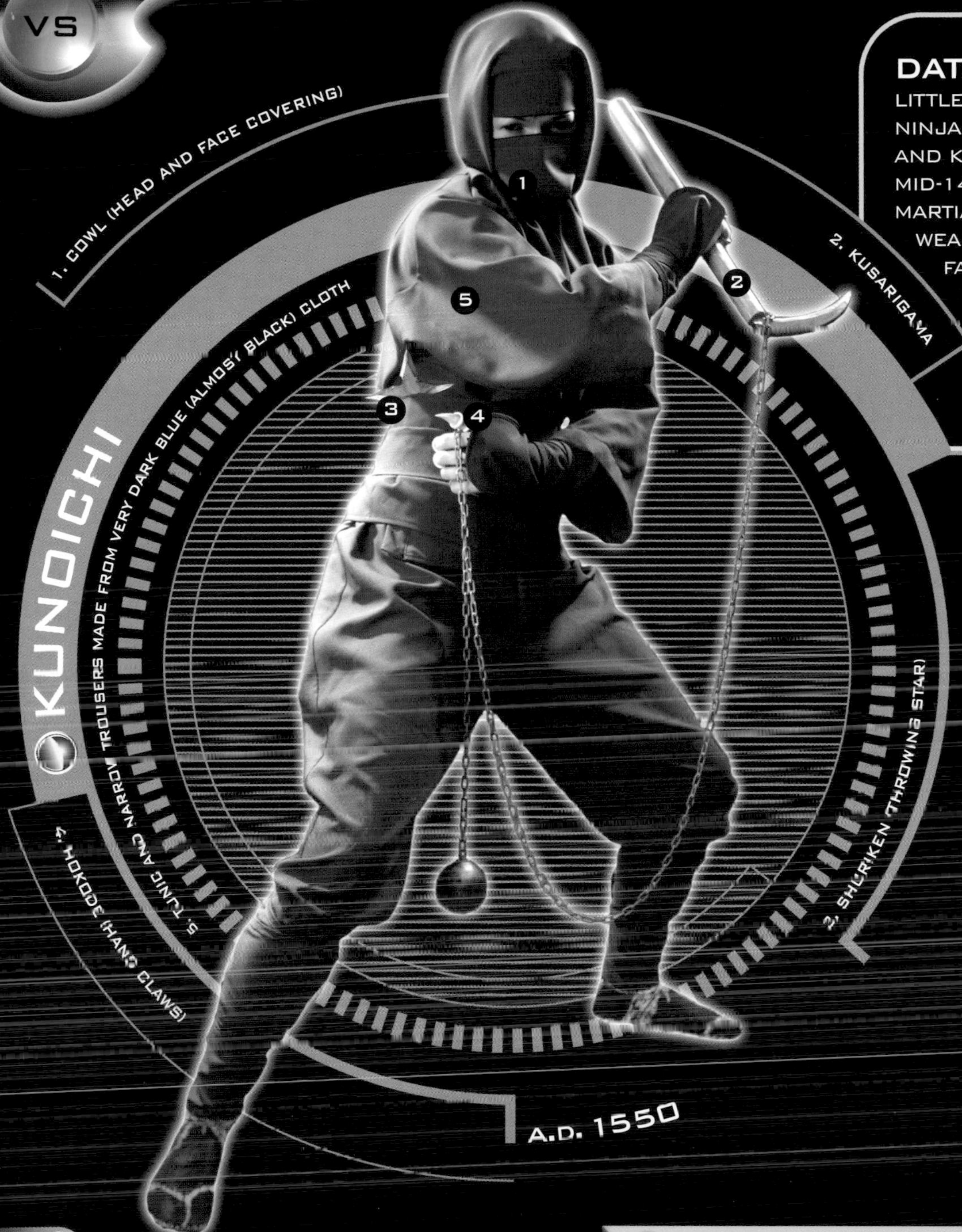

KUNOICHI
1. COWL (HEAD AND FACE COVERING)
2. KUSARIGAMA
3. SHURIKEN (THROWING STAR)
4. HOKODE (HAND CLAWS)
5. TUNIC AND NARROW TROUSERS MADE FROM VERY DARK BLUE (ALMOST BLACK) CLOTH
1
2
3
4
5
A.D. 1550

DATA FILE

LITTLE IS KNOWN FOR CERTAIN ABOUT THE NINJA, SECRET ASSASSINS WHO FOUGHT AND KILLED IN JAPAN FROM ABOUT THE MID-1400S TO THE 1800S. SKILLED IN MARTIAL ARTS, WITH MANY OF THEIR WEAPONS ADAPTED FROM EVERYDAY FARM AND HOUSEHOLD TOOLS, THEY WERE UNPREDICTABLE ENEMIES.

PICK A WEAPON

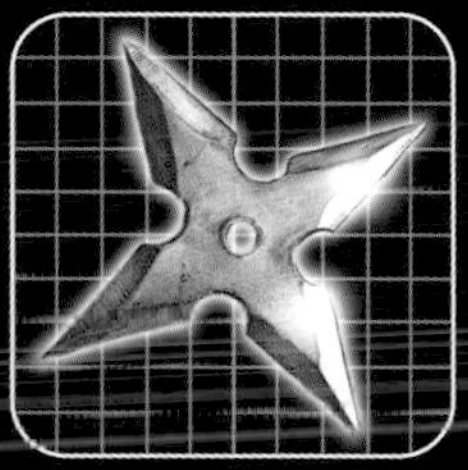

SHURIKEN
These throwing stars, hidden in a pocket, are small but deadly. Thrown with spin and speed, they can give your enemy a fatal cut.

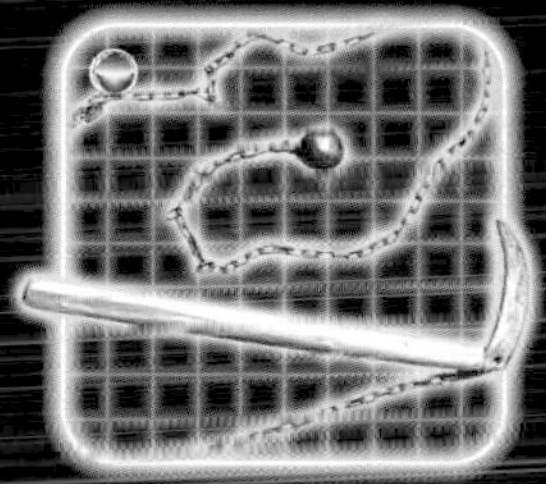

KUSARIGAMA
This is made up of a chain, sickle, and heavy ball. Entangle your opponent by hurling the ball at her and then strike with the sickle blade.

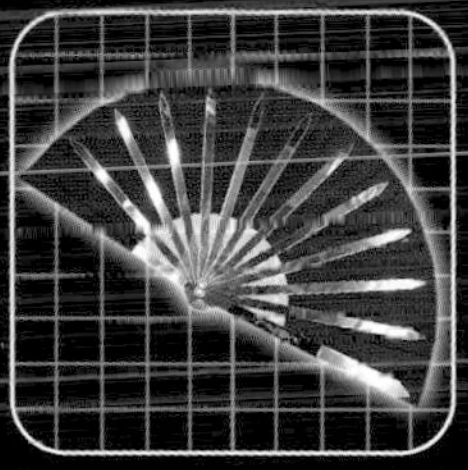

TESSEN
This feminine-looking object looks like a normal fan, but its concealed iron blades make it a menacing defensive weapon.

ADD STAMINA

FOOD
Carry a "hunger ball" made from carrots, different kinds of flour, licorice root, and yams preserved in sake (rice wine).

ADVICE 1
Dodge your opponent's sword blows by leaping over the blade and high in the air—so high that she might think you can fly!

ADVICE 2
Seishin teki kyoyo, or spiritual discipline, is the first skill of the ninja. Control yourself and you can control the enemy.

MAKE YOUR MOVE

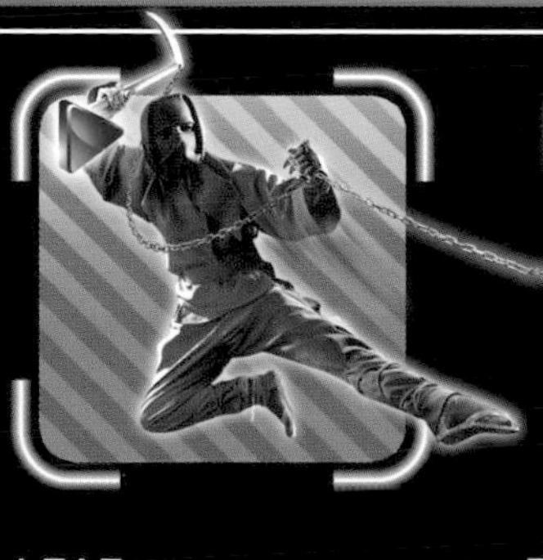

LEAP
Jump high in the air to give more force as you strike with the sickle.

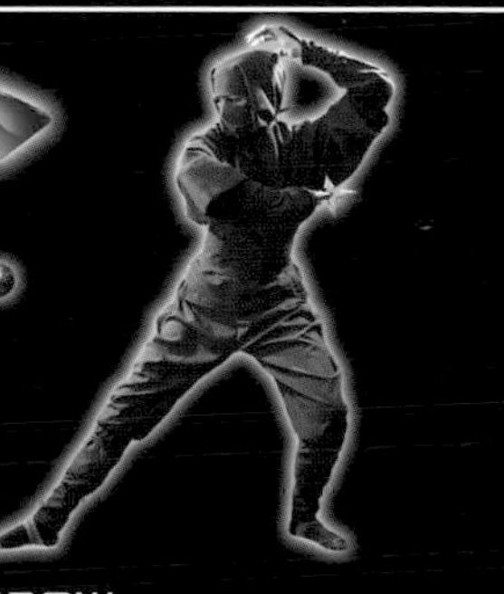

THROW
Fire the shuriken with precision to cut your opponent down.

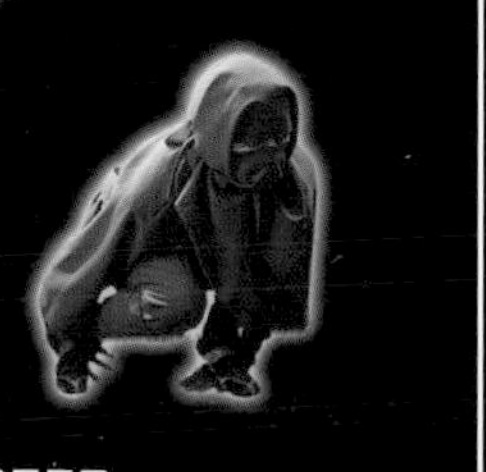

CREEP
Move silently with shinso usagi-aruki ("deep grass rabbit walking").

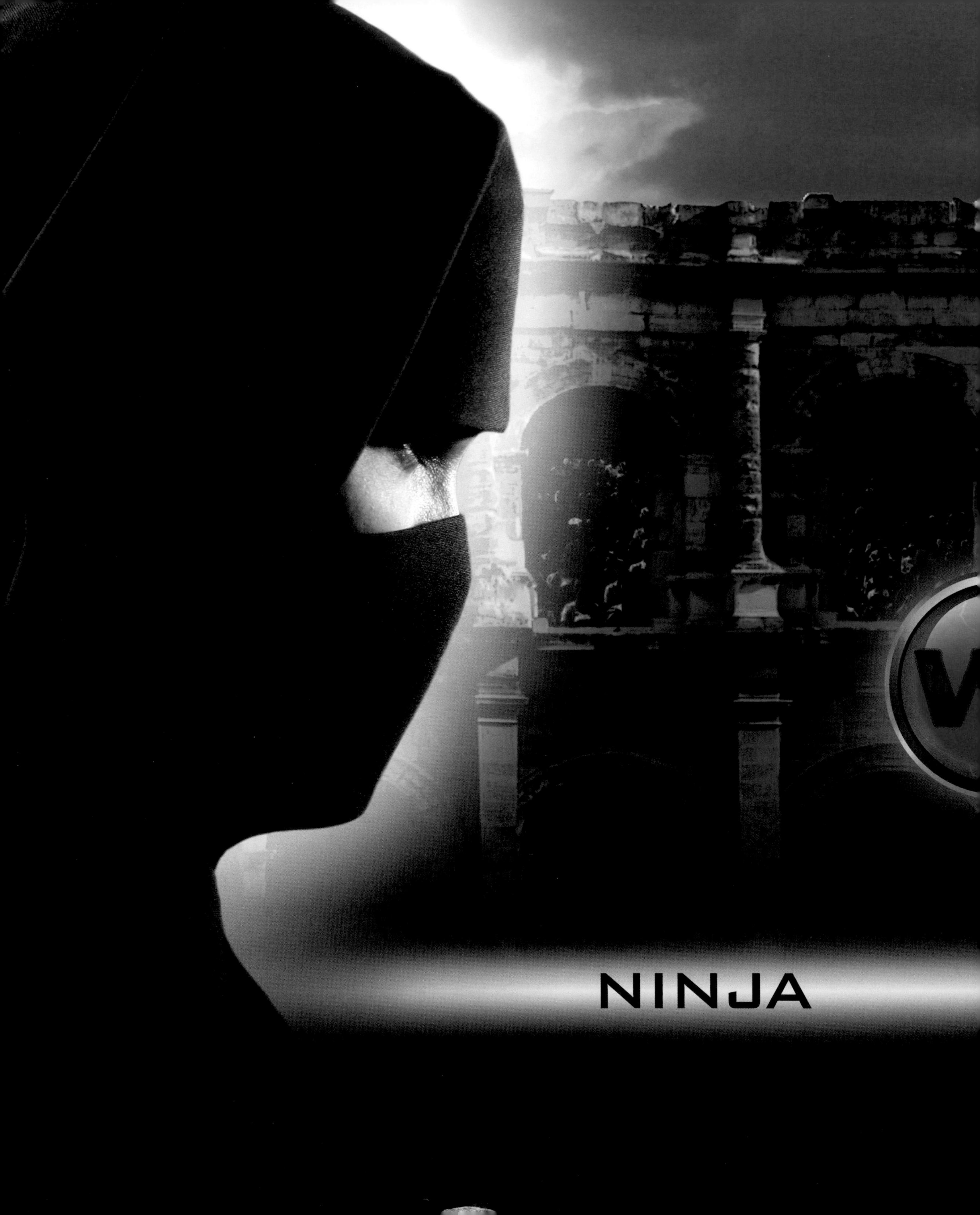
NINJA

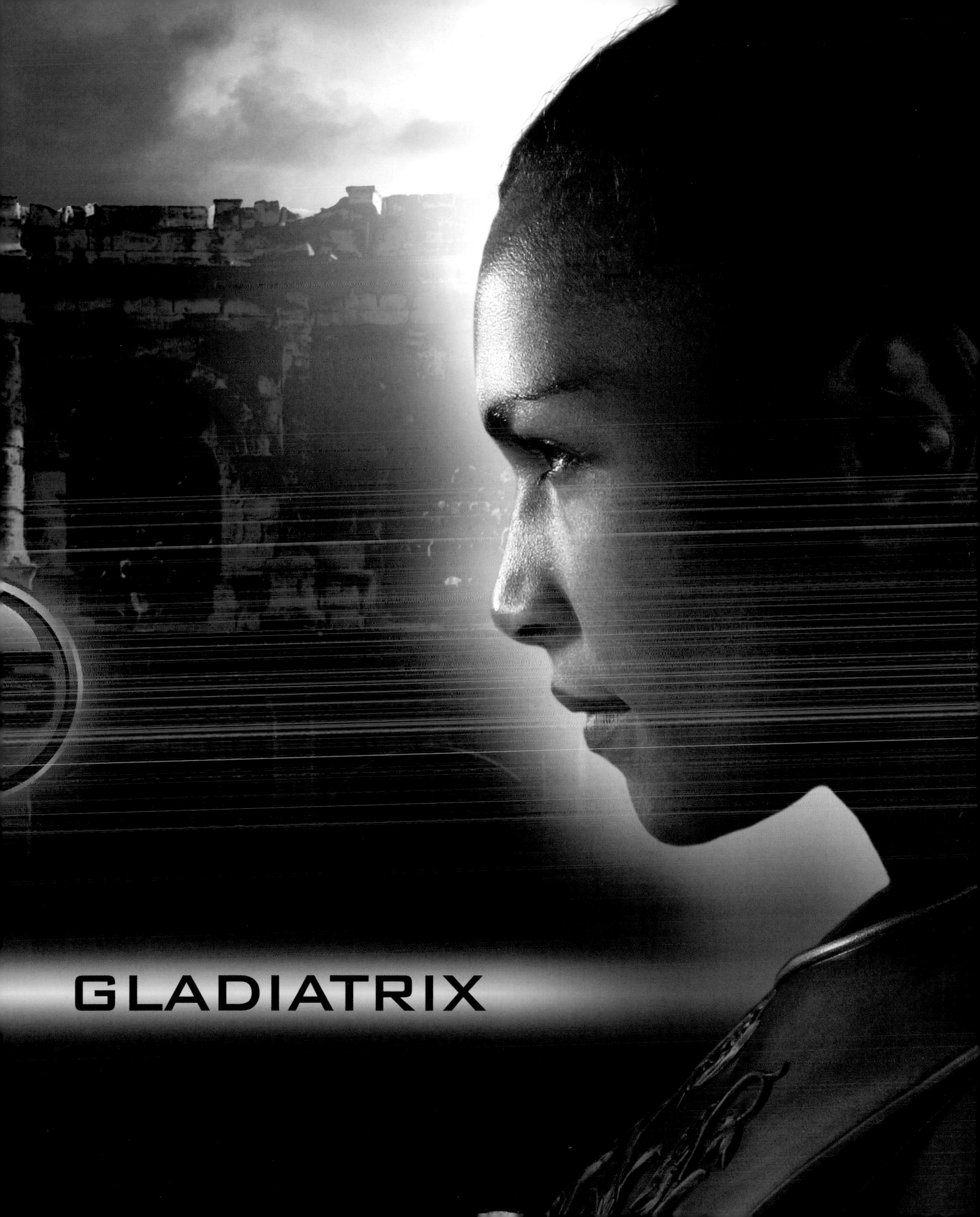
GLADIATRIX

GLADIATRIX

DATA FILE

ANCIENT ROMAN SOLDIERS SOMETIMES FACED FEMALE WARRIORS. FROM ABOUT 200 B.C. TO A.D. 200, WOMEN, INCLUDING CELTS FROM THE NORTH AND NUBIANS FROM AFRICA, TOOK TO THE ARENAS IN GLADIATORIAL CONTESTS. FEMALE FIGHTERS BOTH FASCINATED AND APPALLED THE ROMAN PUBLIC.

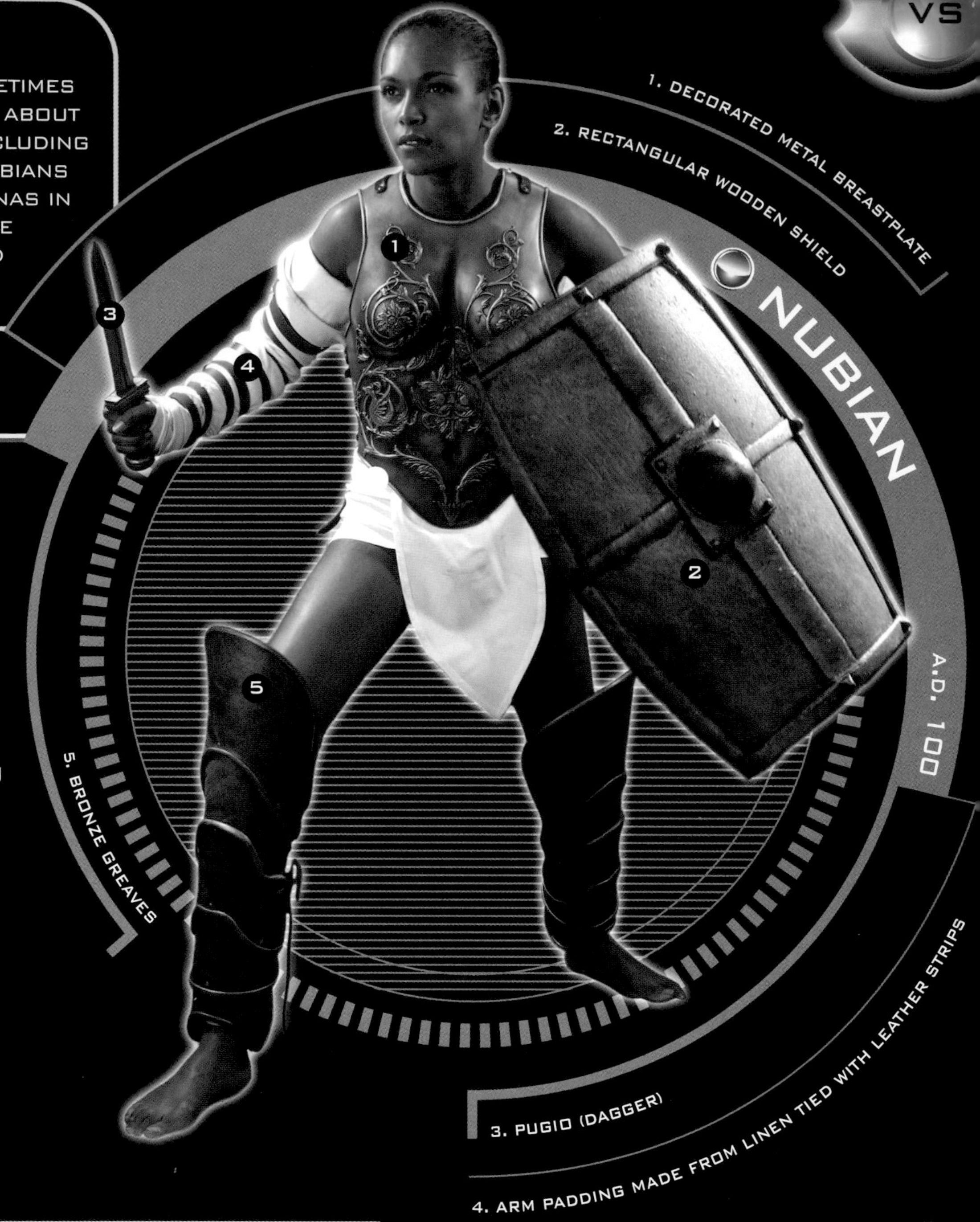
VS
1. DECORATED METAL BREASTPLATE
2. RECTANGULAR WOODEN SHIELD
NUBIAN
A.D. 100
5. BRONZE GREAVES
3. PUGIO (DAGGER)
4. ARM PADDING MADE FROM LINEN TIED WITH LEATHER STRIPS
1
2
3
4
5

PICK A WEAPON

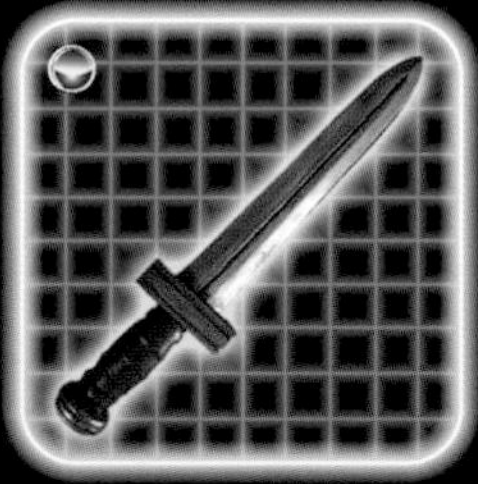

PUGIO
This broad-bladed dagger has a sharp point for stabbing with. It is a favorite gladiator weapon, good for close combat.

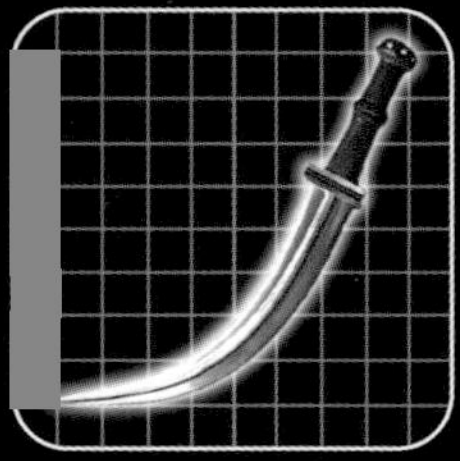

SICA
This 16-in (40-cm)-long curved dagger, also used by Thracian gladiators, should be aimed at the enemy's unarmored back.

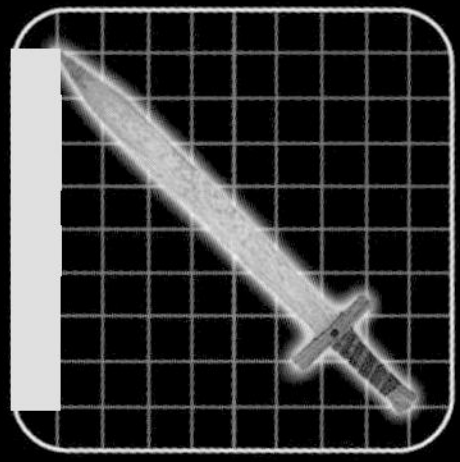

WOODEN SWORD
Use this wooden version of the gladius in training to practice your sword skills without getting hurt.

MAKE YOUR MOVE

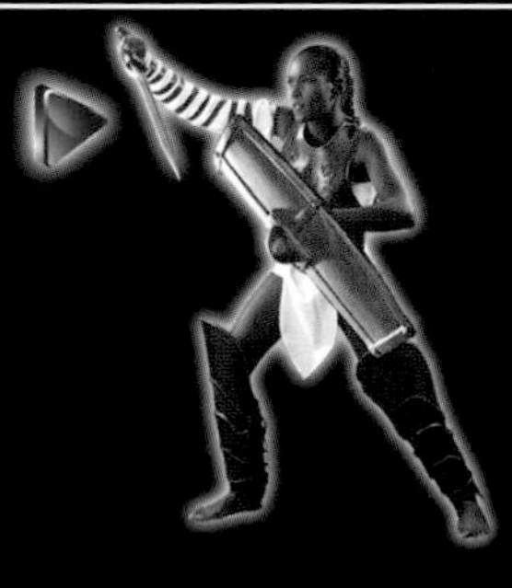

DEFEND
Keep the shield in front of you and the dagger raised away from your body.

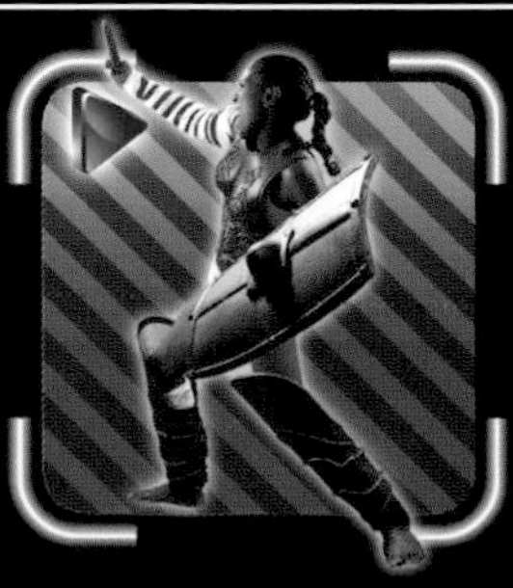

ATTACK
Move forward with your right arm raised, ready to stab sharply downward.

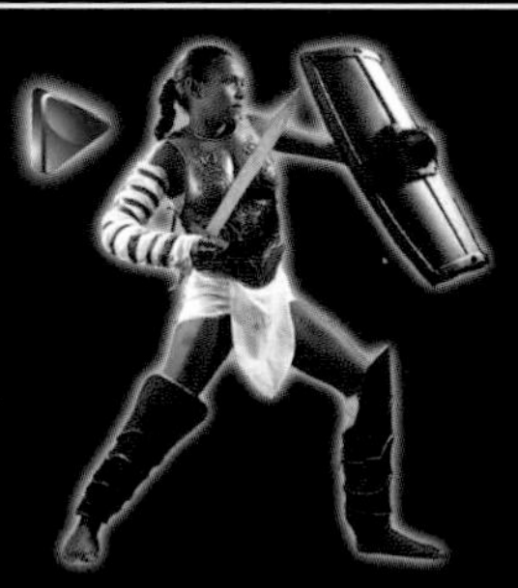

WARM UP
Get psyched up for a fight with a few quick practice moves before you clash.

ADD STAMINA

FOOD
Eat a handful of figs or dates just before you go into the arena—these high-energy foods will give you a much-needed boost.

ADVICE 1
Your daily weapon training should keep you strong and in good shape, building your stamina for a grueling fight and sharpening your reflexes.

ADVICE 2
Pray to Anubis, the Egyptian god who leads souls to the afterlife and who is also believed to look after fallen gladiators.

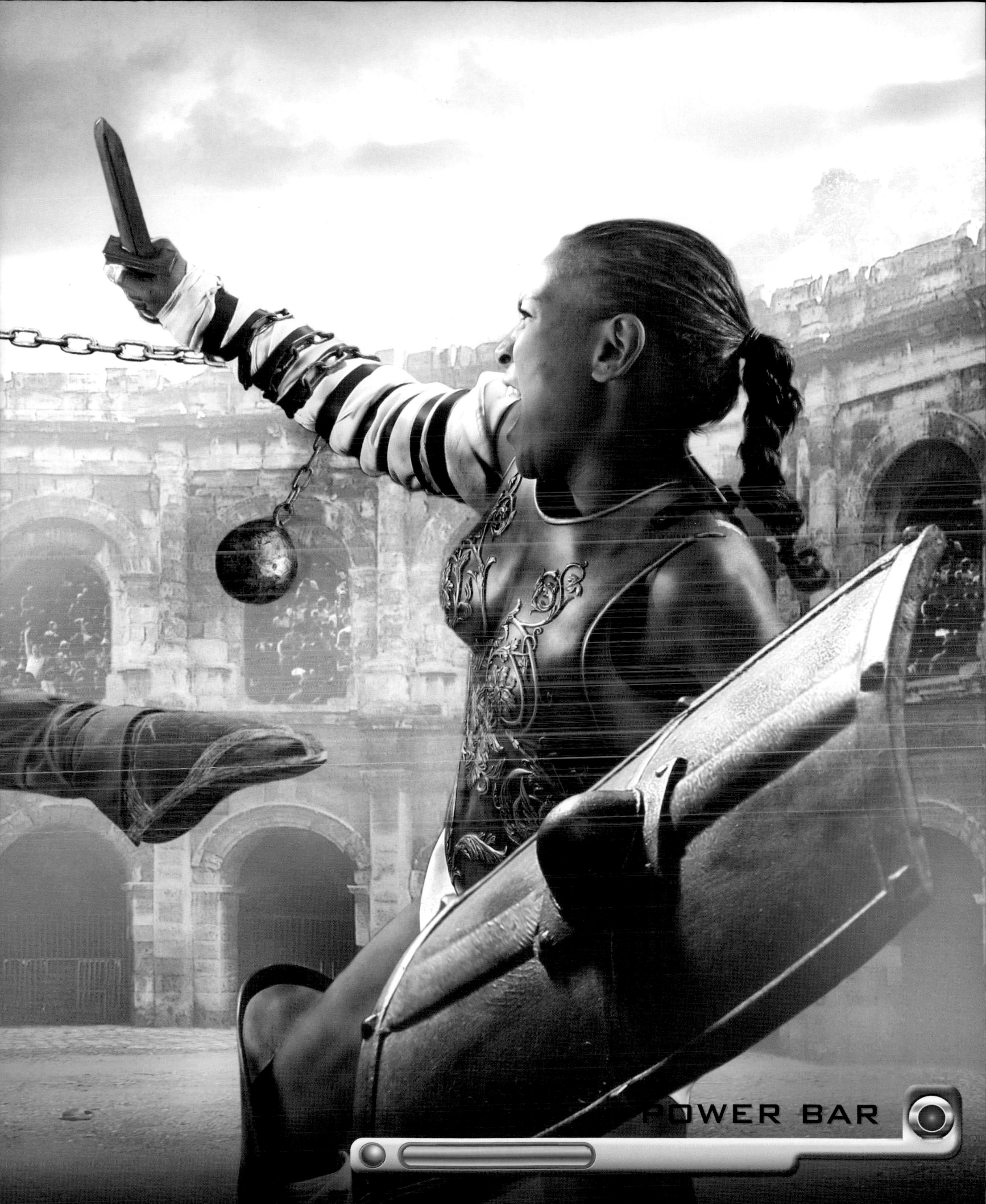
POWER BAR

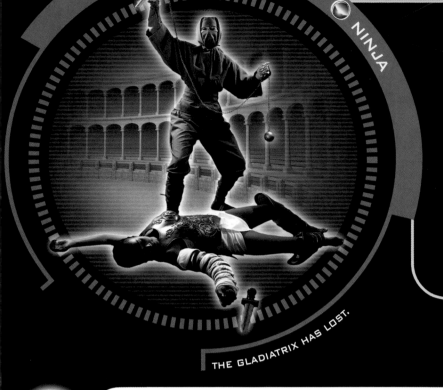

THE GLADIATRIX HAS LOST.

THE NINJA WINS

THE GLADIATRIX HAS BEEN TRAINED TO FIGHT IN PUBLIC AGAINST A FOE OF EQUAL STRENGTH. HER AGILITY AND BATTLE STAMINA ARE GOOD, AND HER WEAPONS ARE WELL SUITED TO THE DUEL. THE KUNOICHI USUALLY MURDERS BY STEALTH IN THE DEAD OF NIGHT BUT IS AN EXPERT SWORDSWOMAN WHO ADAPTS WELL TO OPEN HAND-TO-HAND FIGHTING. SHE CREATES AN ADVANTAGE BY FORCING THE GLADIATRIX OFF BALANCE BEFORE SHE HAS A CHANCE TO FOCUS. THE NINJA JUMPS HIGH IN THE AIR AND STRIKES WITHOUT HESITATION.

NINJA

A SHADOW SLIPS ACROSS A CASTLE WALL. A FIGURE LEAPS FROM A TOWER. BEFORE A JAPANESE WARLORD CAN EVEN REACH THE BATTLEFIELD, HE LIES MURDERED BY MYSTERIOUS ATTACKERS. JUST WHO ARE THESE NINJA?

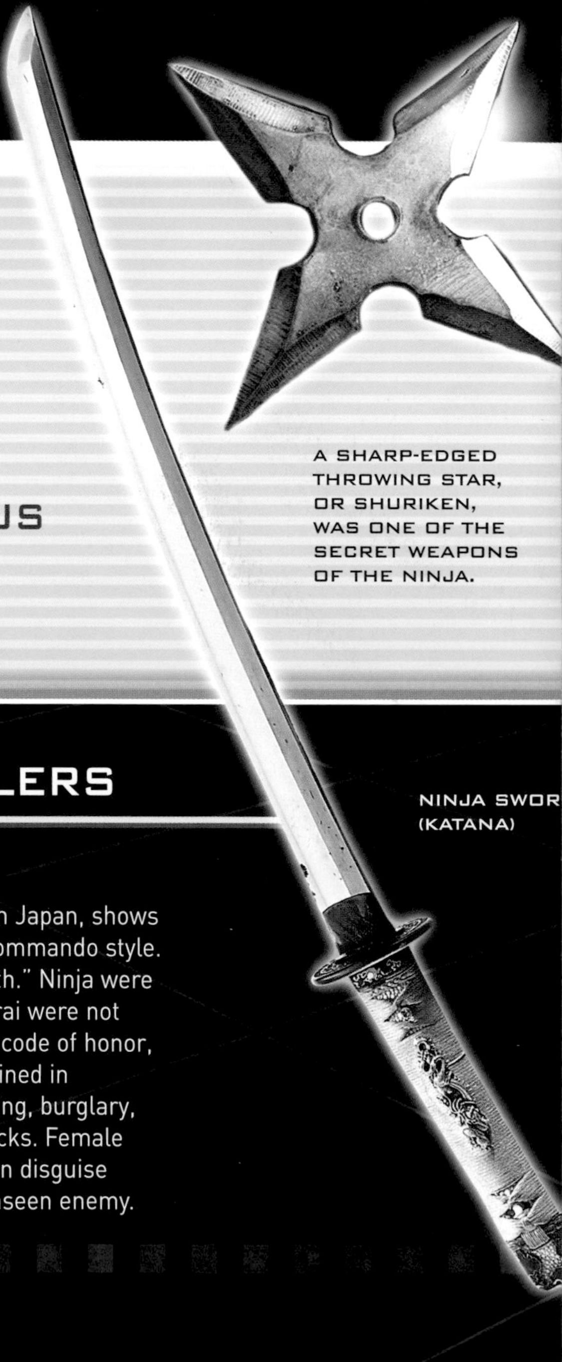

A SHARP-EDGED THROWING STAR, OR SHURIKEN, WAS ONE OF THE SECRET WEAPONS OF THE NINJA.

NINJA SWOR (KATANA)

THE SECRET KILLERS

NINJUTSU

A modern reenactment, staged in Japan, shows how ninja scaled a castle wall, commando style. *Ninjutsu* means "the art of stealth." Ninja were trained to do the jobs that samurai were not permitted to do because of their code of honor, the Bushido. Male ninja were trained in assassination, concealment, spying, burglary, diversionary tactics, and dirty tricks. Female ninja, or kunoichi, were experts in disguise and poisoning. Ninja were the unseen enemy.

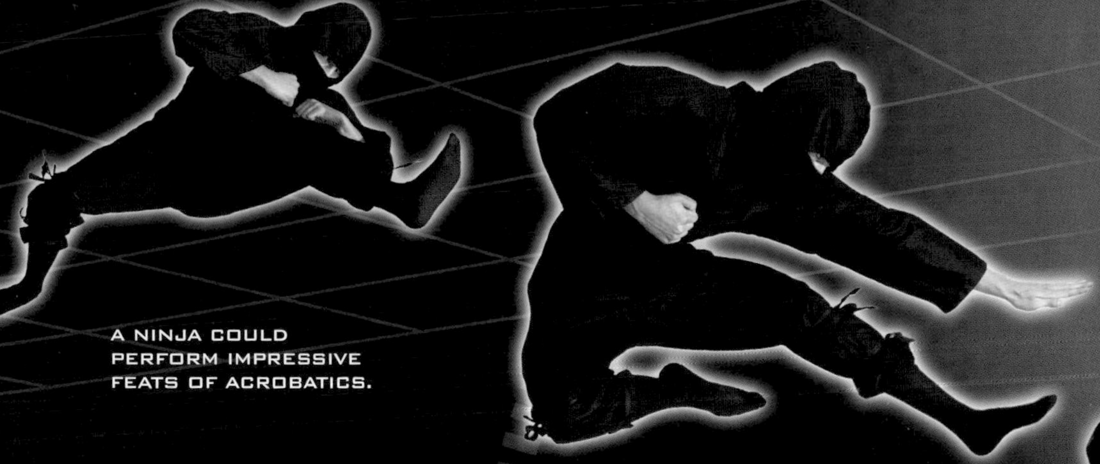

A NINJA COULD PERFORM IMPRESSIVE FEATS OF ACROBATICS.

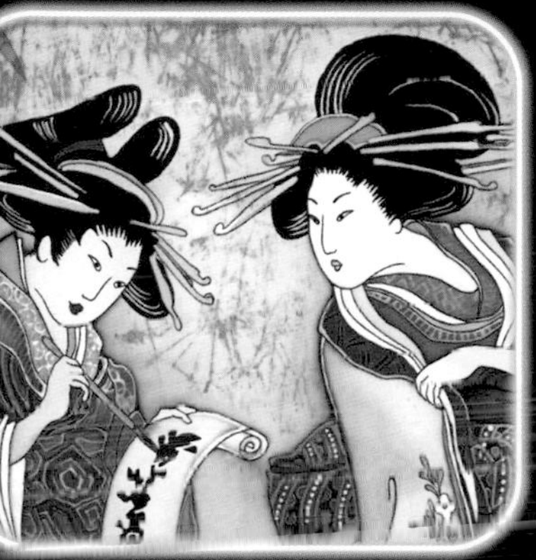

DANGEROUS LADIES

Often a kunoichi would disguise herself as a noblewoman, maidservant, or geisha and use feminine customs as a cover for murder. She might kill with poison in a guest's tea, blades concealed in her fan, or the extra-sharp point of a hairpin. Or she might simply listen and smile as a powerful lord discussed his battle plans—and memorize everything.

THE NINJA CULT

Today many people are fascinated by ninja. Male and female ninja feature in Japanese, Chinese, and international popular culture—in movies, comic books, and computer games. We don't know a great deal about these secretive fighters, so there is a lot of scope for fantasy and invention. These fighters wear bright scarlet, and we can see their graceful acrobatics, but ninja probably wore very dark clothes to help them hide.

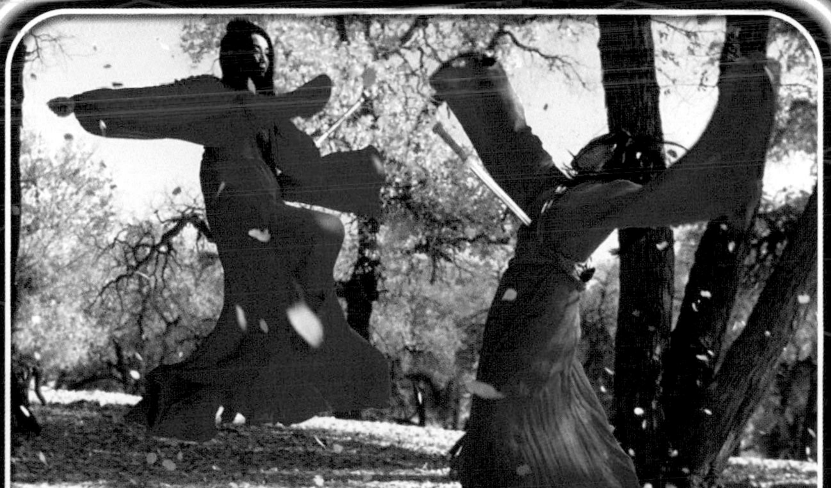

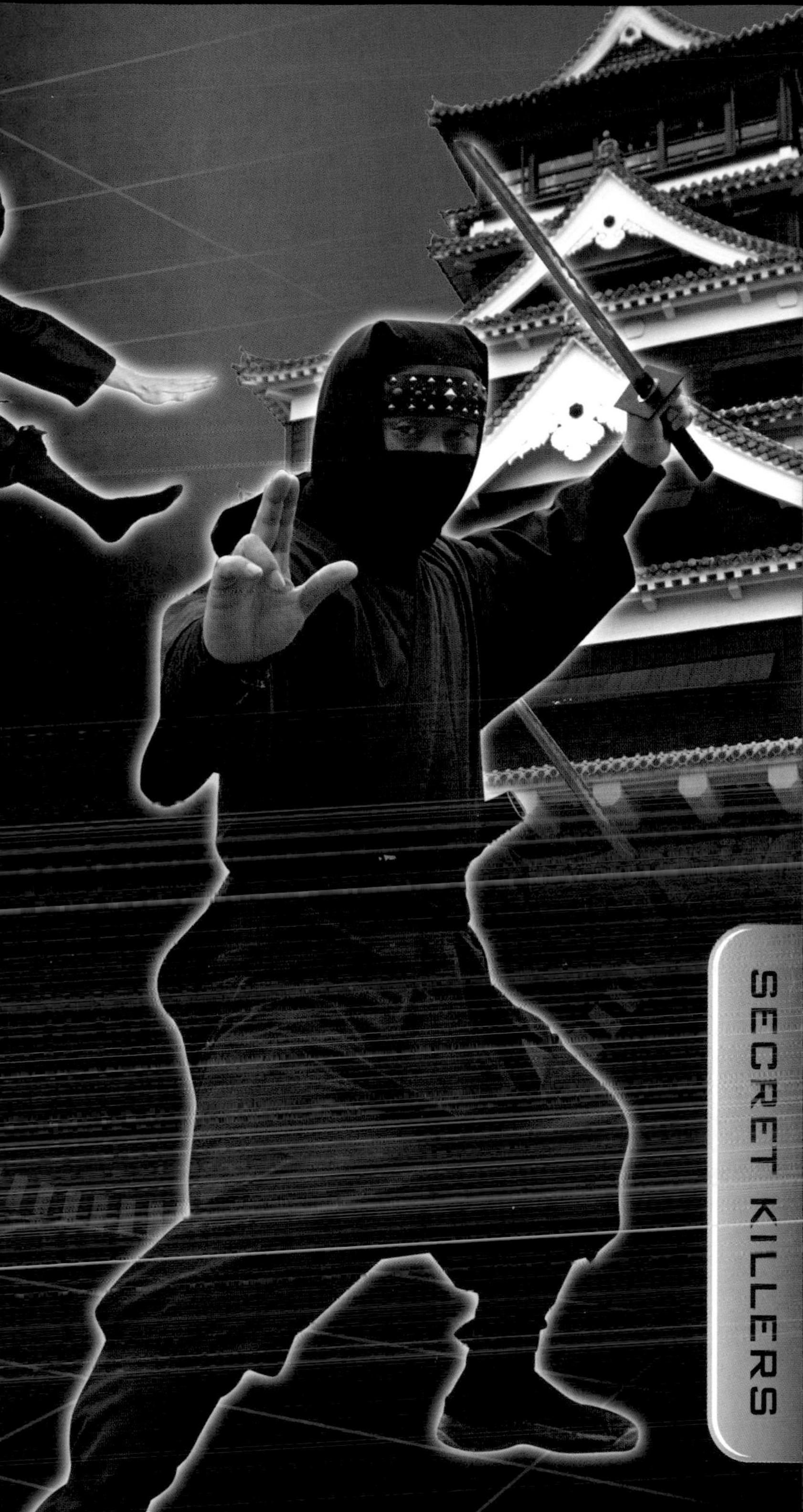

WHO WERE THE NINJA?

Much of the history of the ninja has been romanticized. However, ninja warriors, also known as shinobi, and female spies and assassins really did exist. They were probably active in Japan from the mid-1400s until the 1800s. The Iga and Koga provinces were the centers of activity. Ninja were widely feared as assassins, but their most useful skills were probably getting into castles during a siege or scouting behind enemy lines.

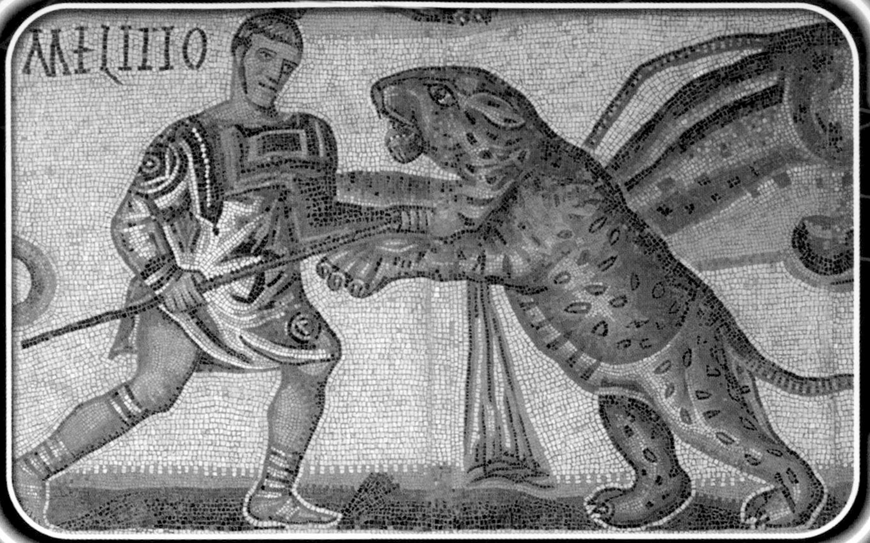

A VENATOR SPEARS A SNARLING LEOPARD.

WHAT NEXT?

As well as the standard gladiator shows, Roman arenas staged mock sea battles, the baiting and slaughter of wild animals, and the execution of prisoners. Organizers were always looking for a new act or spectacle to shock and thrill the public. From A.D. 63 onward, women were sometimes taken on as gladiators—to fight from chariots, to face each other in single combat, or as venatores (who fought wild animals). Many people thought that female gladiator shows were scandalous. Even though they were banned by law in A.D. 200, the events continued.

GLADIATRIX

BOTH MEN AND WOMEN LOVED TO WATCH GLADIATOR SHOWS IN ANCIENT ROME. SOMETIMES A FEMALE GLADIATOR (OR GLADIATRIX) COULD EVEN BE SEEN IN COMBAT, FIGHTING FROM A CHARIOT OR WIELDING A SWORD IN THE ARENA.

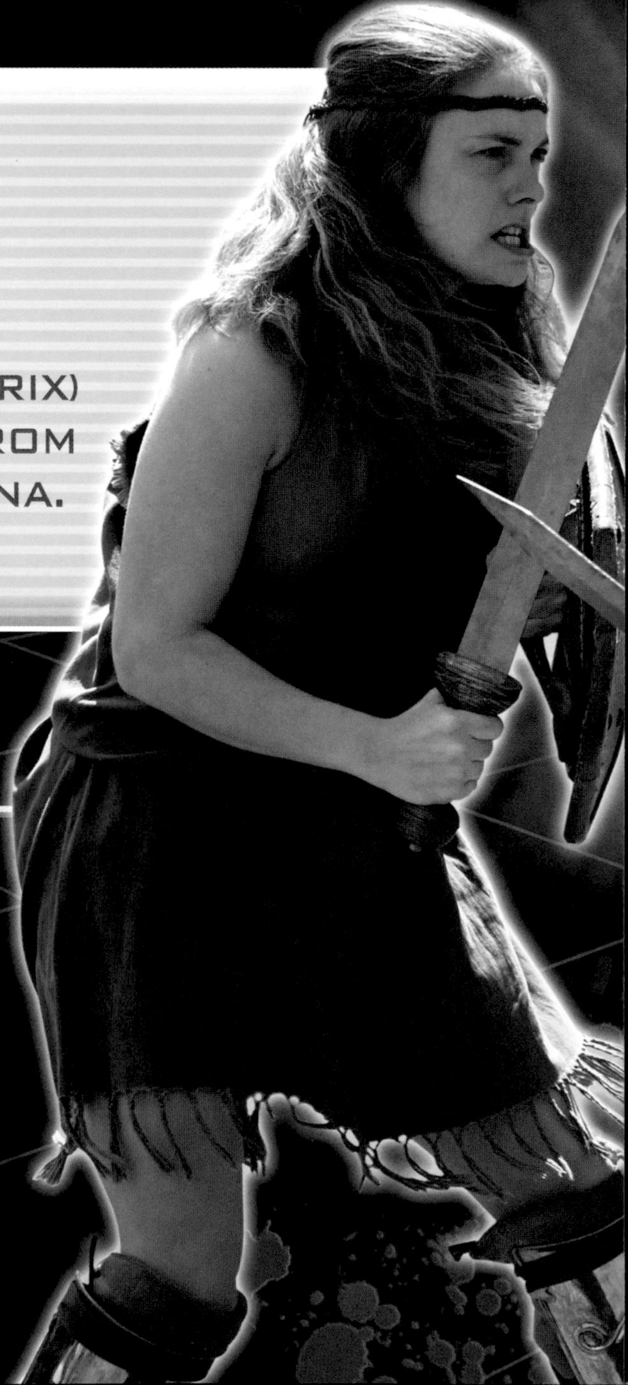

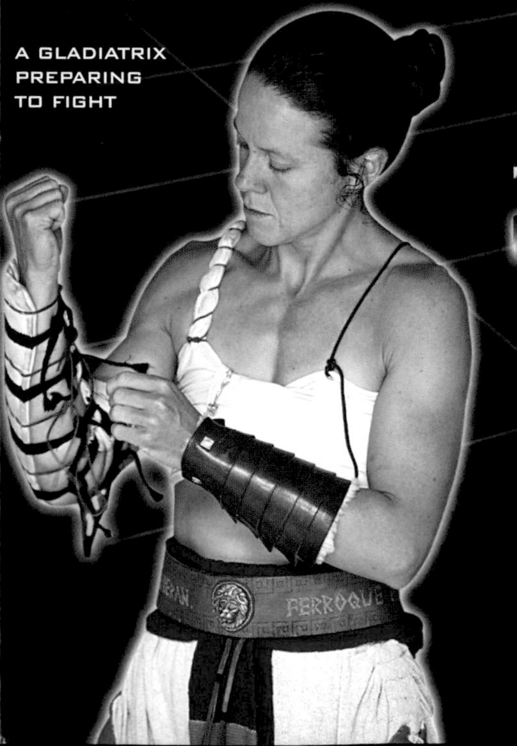

A GLADIATRIX PREPARING TO FIGHT

KILLER WOMEN

READY FOR COMBAT

Many Roman men ridiculed the idea of women being able to fight. One of these was a famous poet named Juvenal. His writings might be sarcastic, but they do tell us how a would-be gladiatrix might train—essentially in the same way as her male colleagues. He describes how she would learn to use weapons, slashing at wooden dummies and practicing her moves. She would prepare for combat by padding and bandaging herself before putting on her armor and perhaps a helmet.

OMEN GET STRONG

ctures found in Sicily, Italy, show at about 1,700 years ago some oman women did hard physical ercise. The mosaics show a group ten women training as athletes. he two shown here are jumping hile holding weights and acticing throwing the discus. nother picture shows one of em winning a contest.

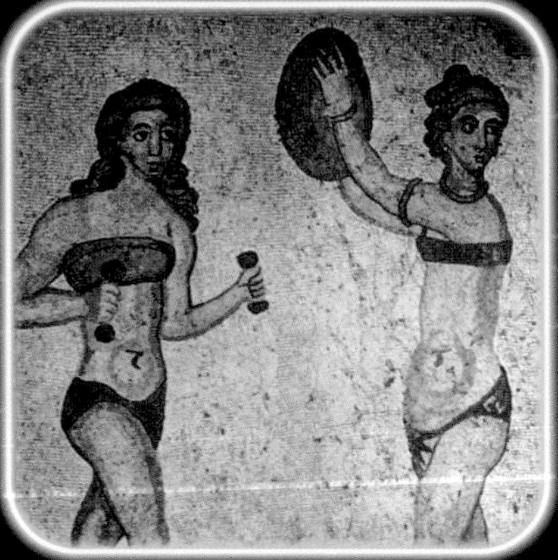

AMAZONS

This carving from Halicarnassus, now in Turkey, is the only piece of historical evidence that actually shows female gladiators in action. The stone records that these particular women were granted their freedom. One is named Amazon—a reference to the Amazons, a feared nation of female warriors from Greek legend.

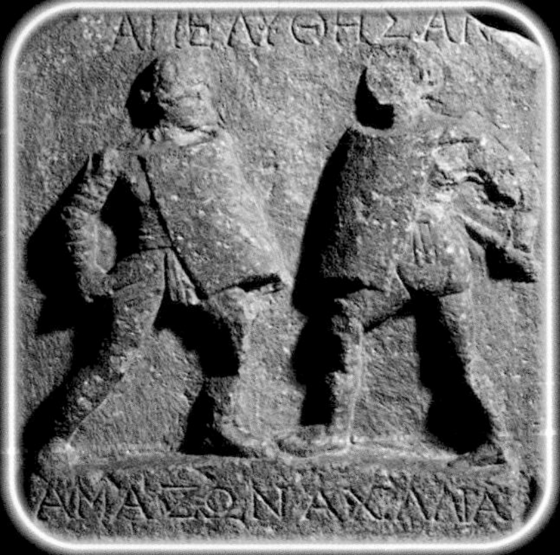

"In this contest, women took part most fiercely, and rude comments were made about other, refined women as well. So it was forbidden for any woman to fight in single combat."

Historian Dio Cassius

FEMALE GLADIATORS IN ACTION

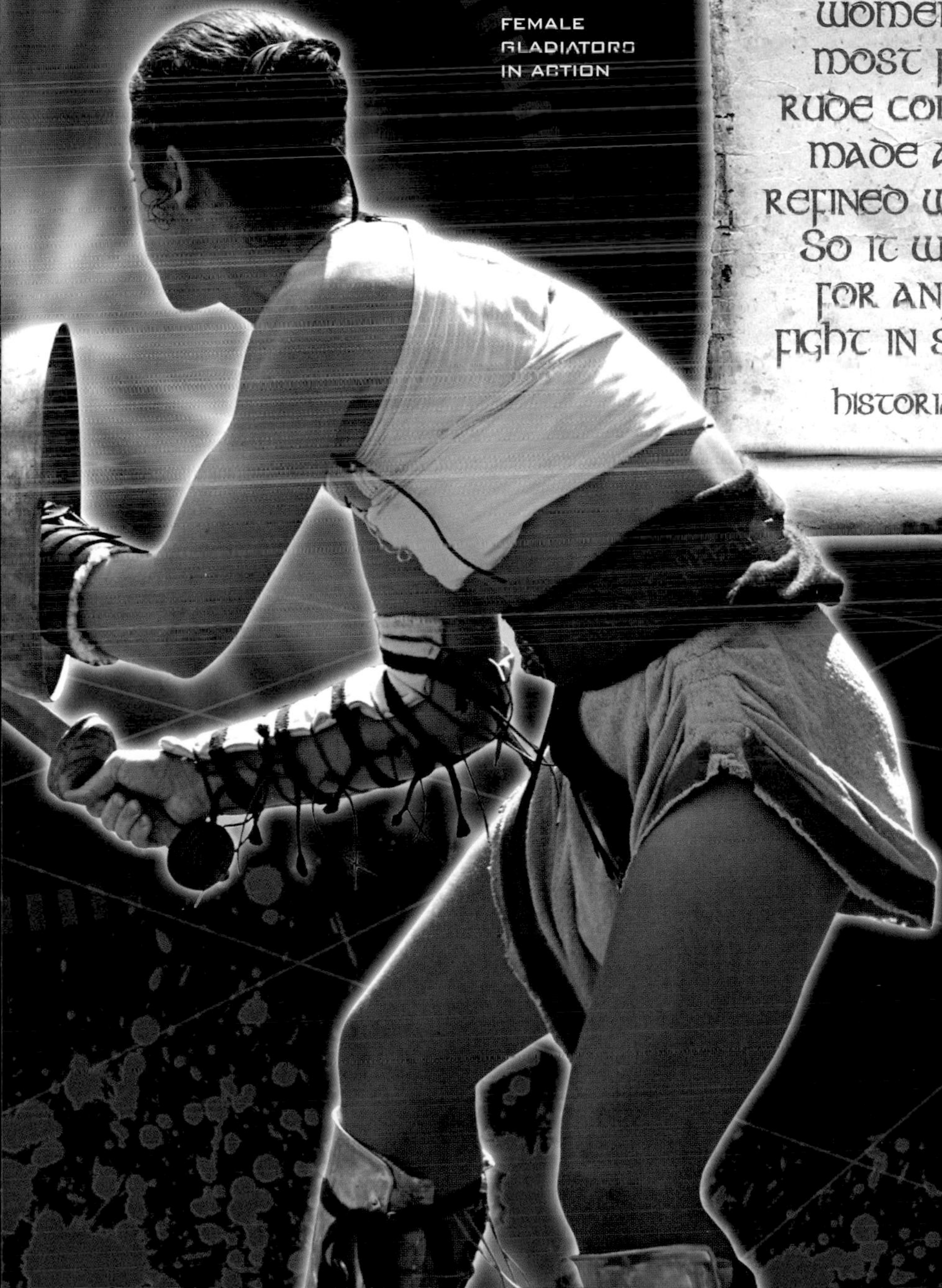

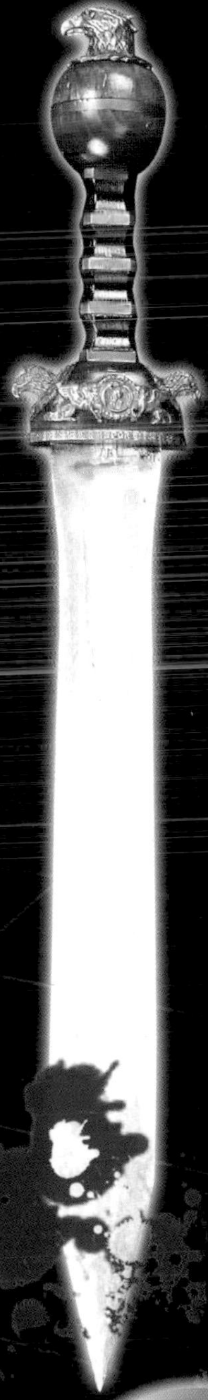

THE GLADIUS

This short sword was the main weapon used by Roman soldiers and also by many of the combatants in the arena, whether male or female. Its Latin name was gladius, which is where the words *gladiator* and *gladiatrix* come from. The steel blade of the sword was about 25 in. (65cm) long. It had two cutting edges, so it could be used for both slashing and stabbing.

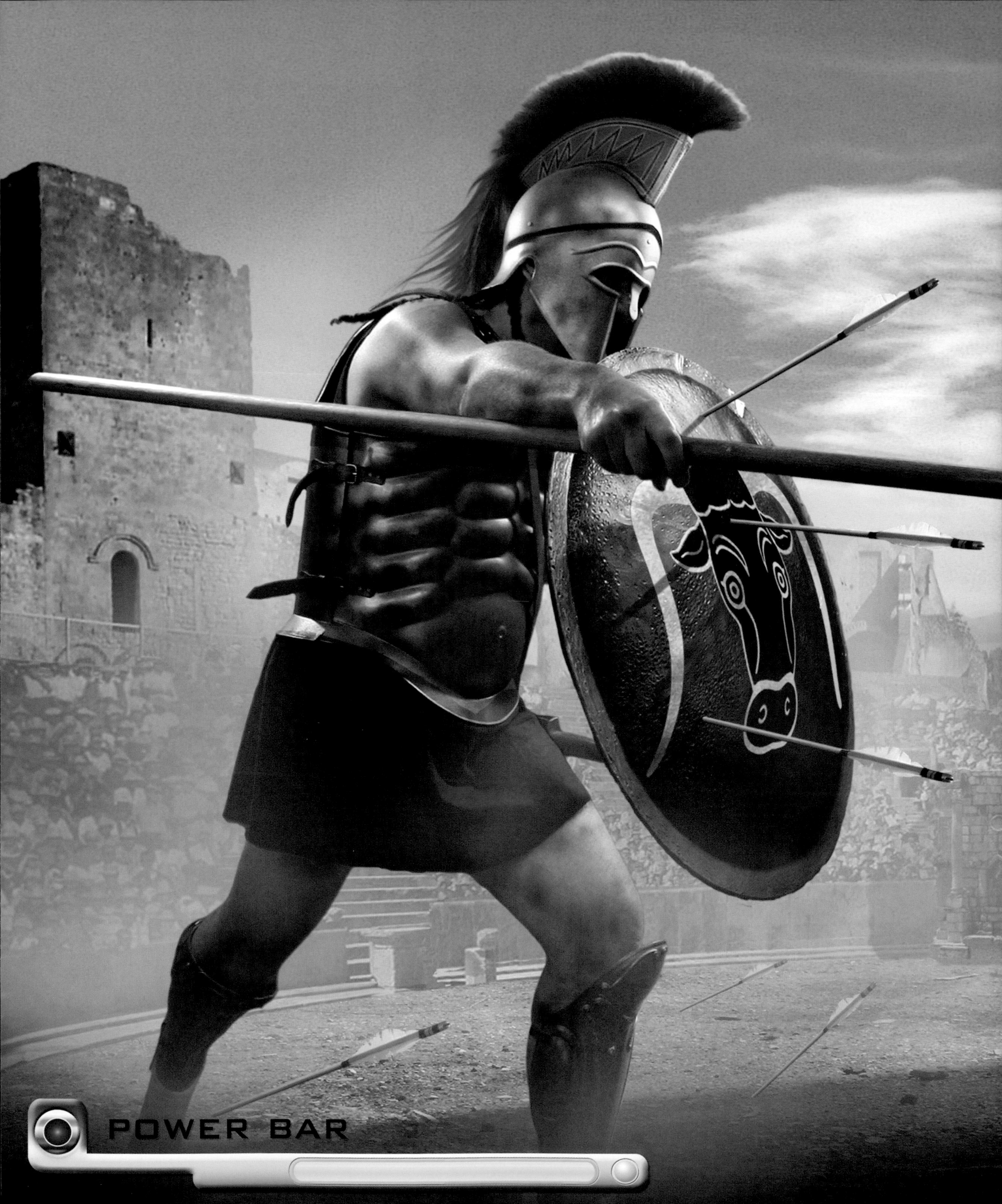
POWER BAR

SPARTAN

HOPLITE

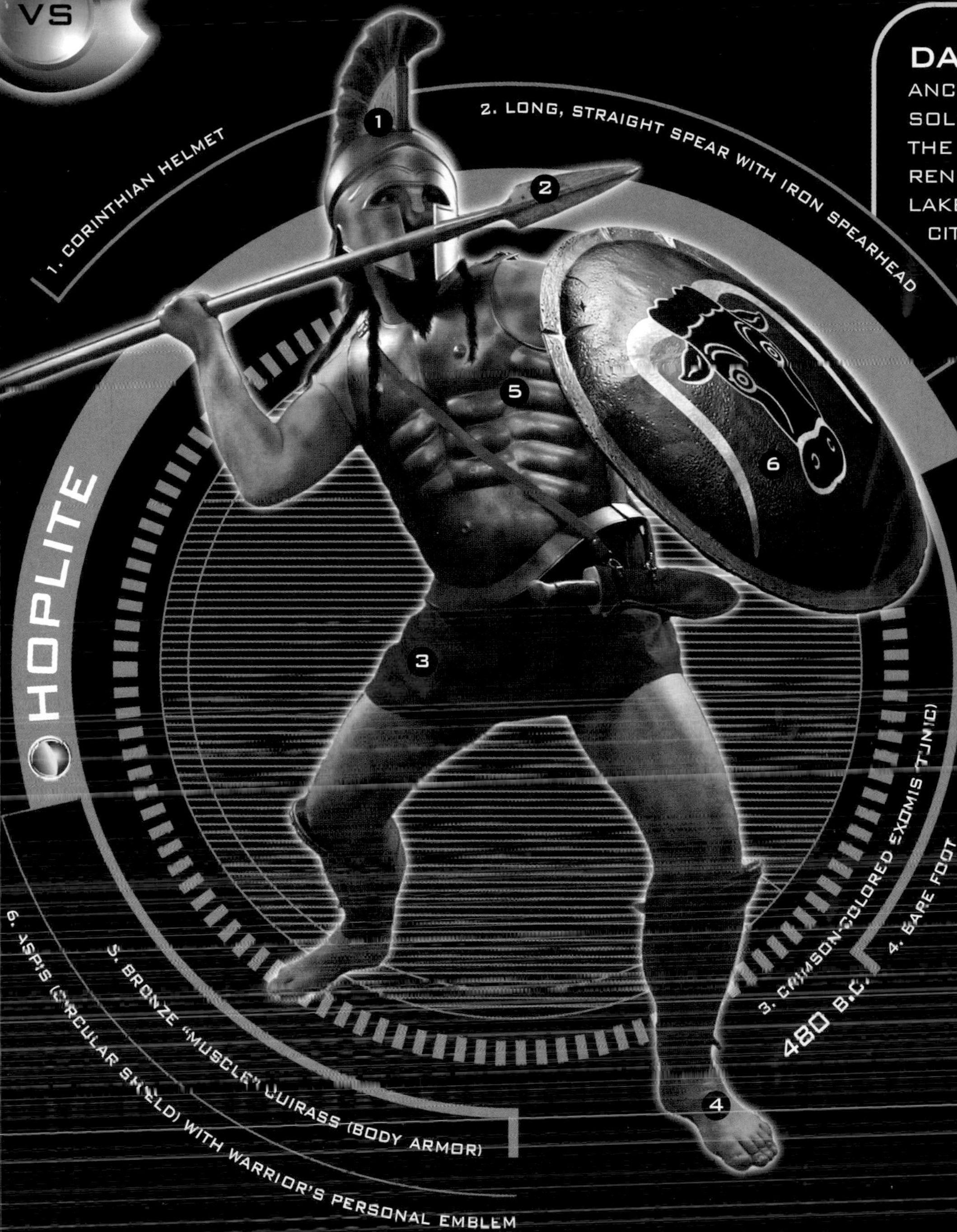
VS
1
2
3
4
5
6
1. CORINTHIAN HELMET
2. LONG, STRAIGHT SPEAR WITH IRON SPEARHEAD
3. CRIMSON-COLORED EXOMIS (TUNIC)
4. BARE FOOT
5. BRONZE "MUSCLE" CUIRASS (BODY ARMOR)
6. ASPIS (CIRCULAR SHIELD) WITH WARRIOR'S PERSONAL EMBLEM
480 B.C.

DATA FILE

ANCIENT GREEK HOPLITES, OR FOOT SOLDIERS, WENT INTO BATTLE FROM THE SIXTH TO THE FIRST CENTURY B.C. RENOWNED AS THE TOUGHEST WERE THE LAKEDAIMONIANS, FROM THE WARLIKE CITY-STATE OF SPARTA. FIGHTING WITH SPEAR AND SHIELD, THEY WERE THE PREMIER WARRIORS OF THEIR AGE.

PICK A WEAPON

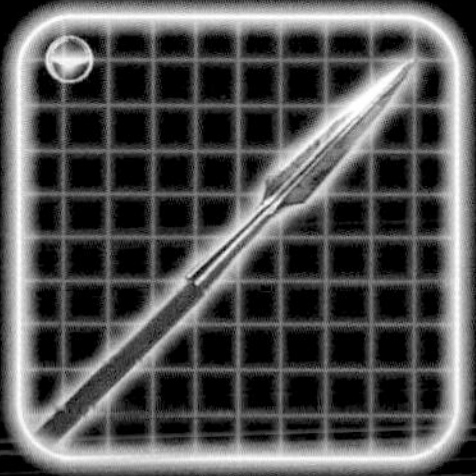

SPEAR
The 8-ft. (2.5-m)-long Lakedaimonian spear is a formidable weapon. Light and strong, it can be thrust at an enemy with great force.

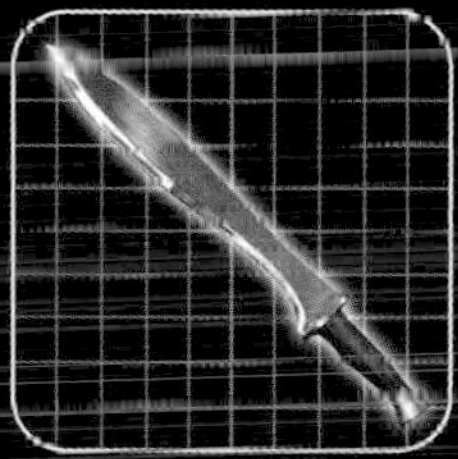

SWORD
Use the short sword to stab at your opponent's groin or torso. If you break your spear, this is perfect for scrappy close-range fighting.

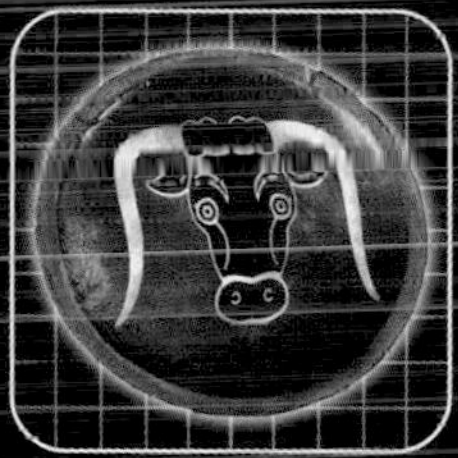

SHIELD
WARNING! Hoplites who lose their shield will be punished! At home, store it with the bronze armhole removed as a guard against theft.

ADD STAMINA

FOOD
Spartan hoplites are trained to work on an empty stomach—get used to a lean diet of thin broth and you'll never be too weak to fight.

FIRST AID
Get your wound rinsed and sewn up with thread soaked in hot olive oil and take a drug made from the herb dittany as pain relief.

ADVICE
Keep in shape while on campaign by practicing athletic exercises to battle music in the morning and evening.

MAKE YOUR MOVE

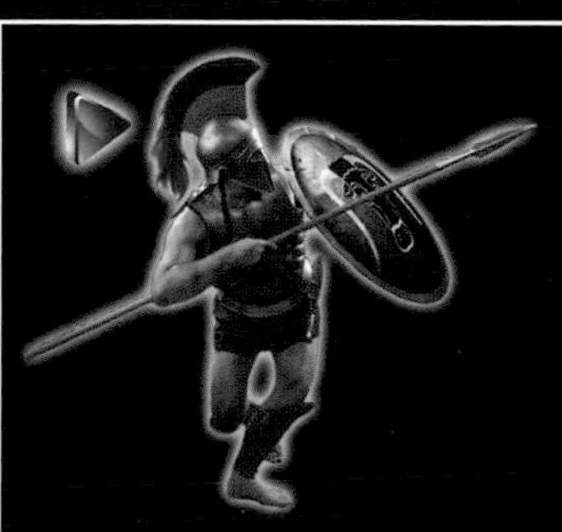

ADVANCE
Move in any direction and thrust quickly, guarded by your shield.

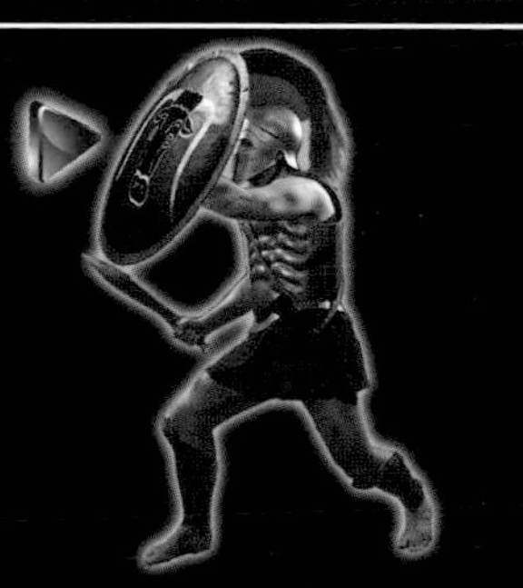

COUNTERSTRIKE
Cut from behind your shield while using it to deflect opposing blows.

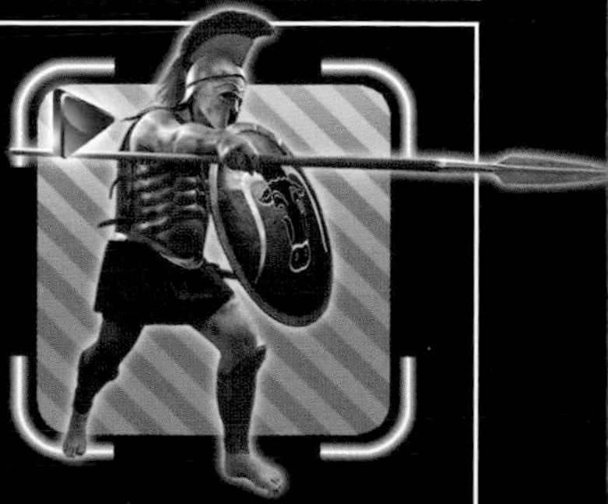

THRUST
Step onto the rear foot to make a strong, long-reaching defensive stab.

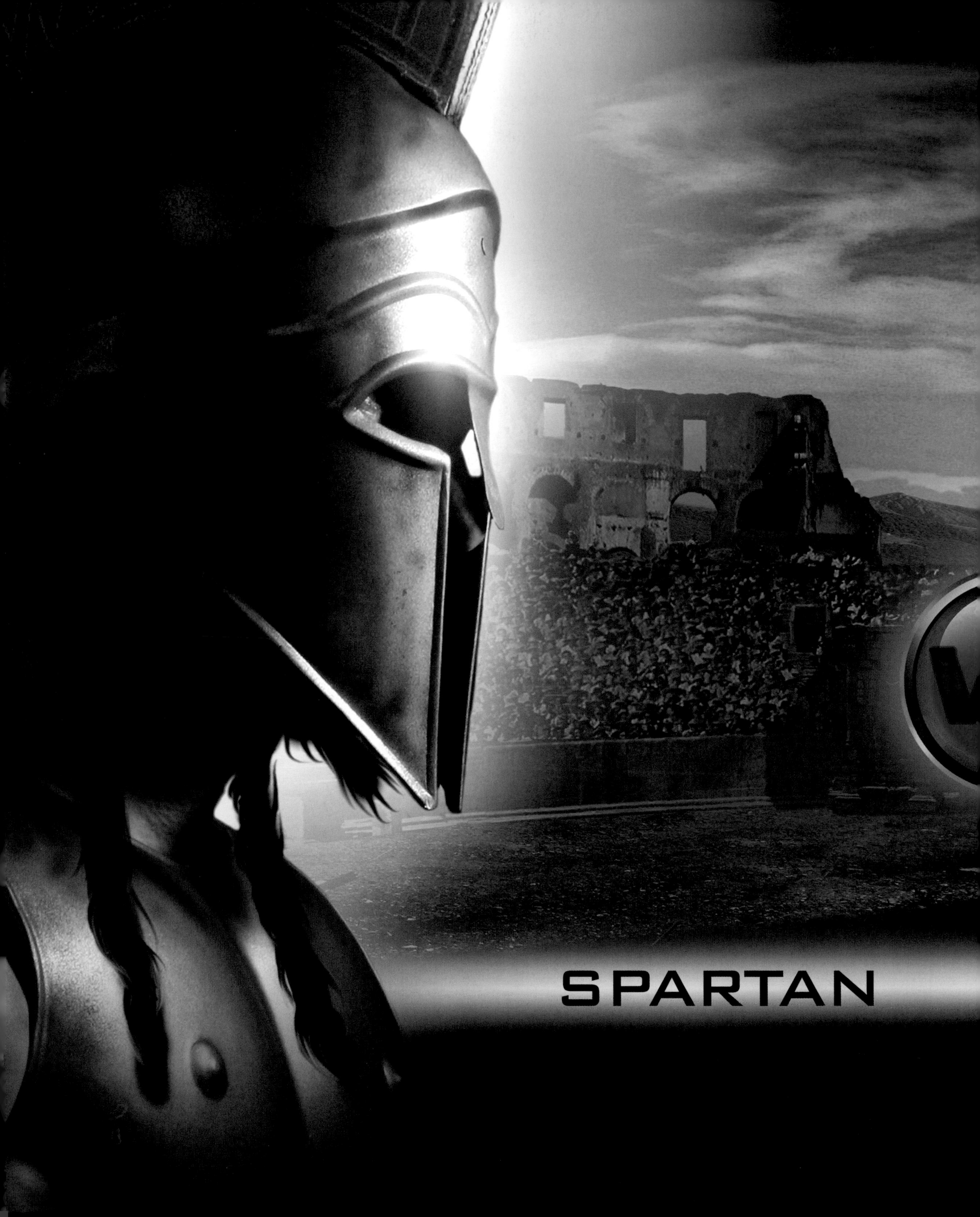
SPARTAN

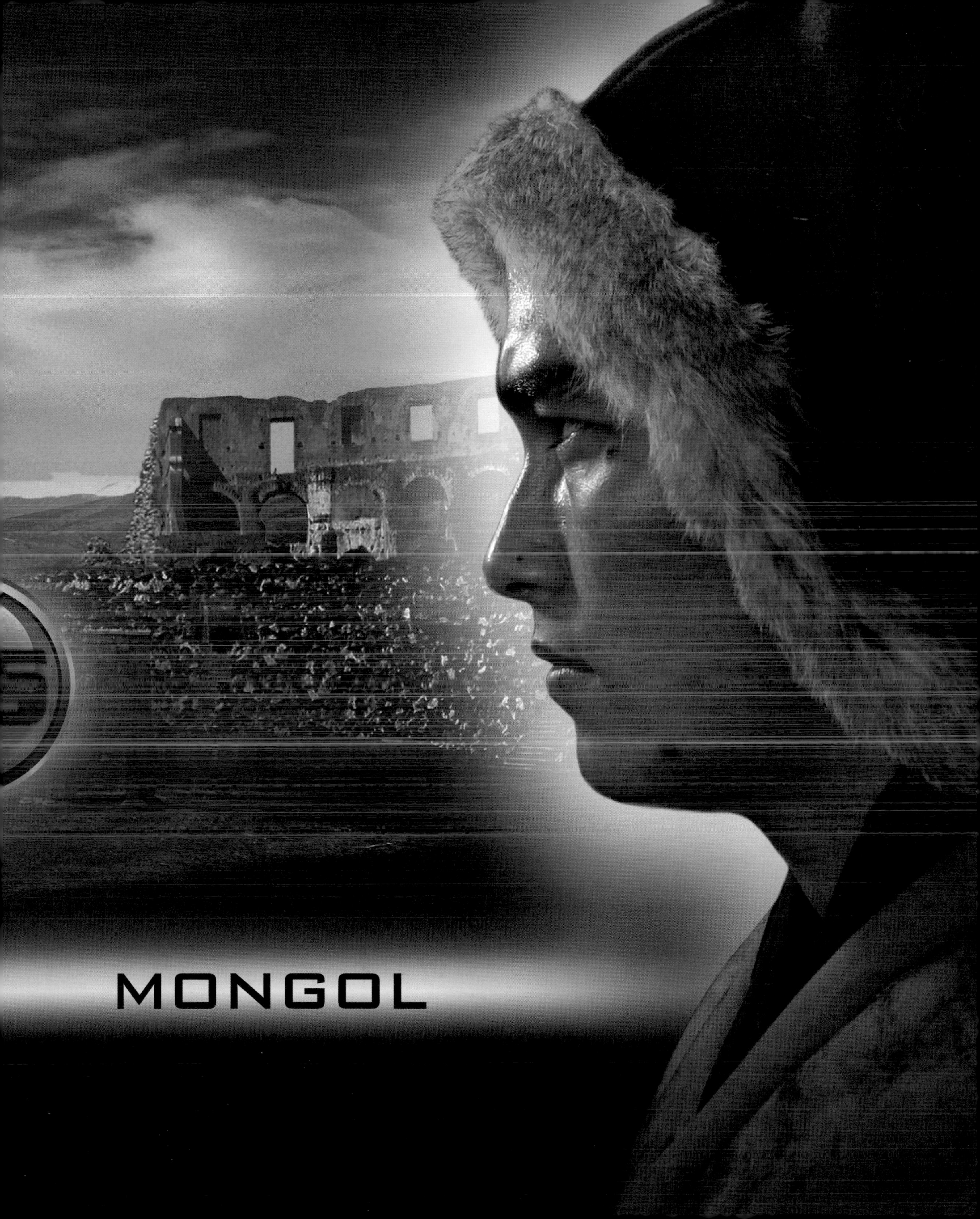
MONGOL

MONGOL

DATA FILE

MONGOL HORSEMEN RODE ACROSS ASIA IN THE 1200S AND 1300S, STRIKING FEAR INTO THE HEARTS OF ALL THEY APPROACHED. AMONG THESE HARDY, STRONG, AND HIGHLY SKILLED ARCHERS WERE THE KESHIKS, FIRING THEIR ARROWS IN AN AWESOME ONSLAUGHT.

PICK A WEAPON

SABER
A good choice if you're on horseback or on foot. The 24-in. (60-cm)-long curved sword is used one handed for cutting and slashing.

ARROWS
Pick large ones with broad arrowheads for close fighting so that you can deliver deep, piercing wounds to your enemy's face and arms.

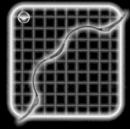

BOW
Use your bow to shoot arrows a long way, with power and deadly accuracy. Keep a spare bow or two in protective cases.

KESHIK

A.D. 1250

1. BOW MADE OF YAK HORN, SINEW, AND BAMBOO
2. THICK, FUR-[...]
3. ARROWS—30 SMALL AND 30 LARGER ONES
4. THICK SHEEPSKIN COAT WITH SIL[...] SHIRT UNDERNEATH
5. STURDY LEATHER BOOTS
6. SABER (SLIGHTLY CURVED SWORD)

MAKE YOUR MOVE

PARTING SHOT
Run away from a close opponent so that you can increase your bow range.

HIGH WARD
Lift the saber high to allow strong attacking slashes, and keep the shield close.

STEADY SHOT
Take time to line up an expertly aimed shot at the most vulnerable area.

FOOD

Hunt a wild marmot, fox, or hare to eat with some of the hard paste made from dried mare's milk that you keep with you at all times.

FIRST AID
Mongol camps follow close behind the front line, so if you are injured, you'll soon be given treatment and can rest, looked after by your family.

ADVICE

In daylight watch with the vigilance of a wolf, at night with the eyes of a raven—and in battle fall upon the enemy like a falcon.

ADD STAMINA

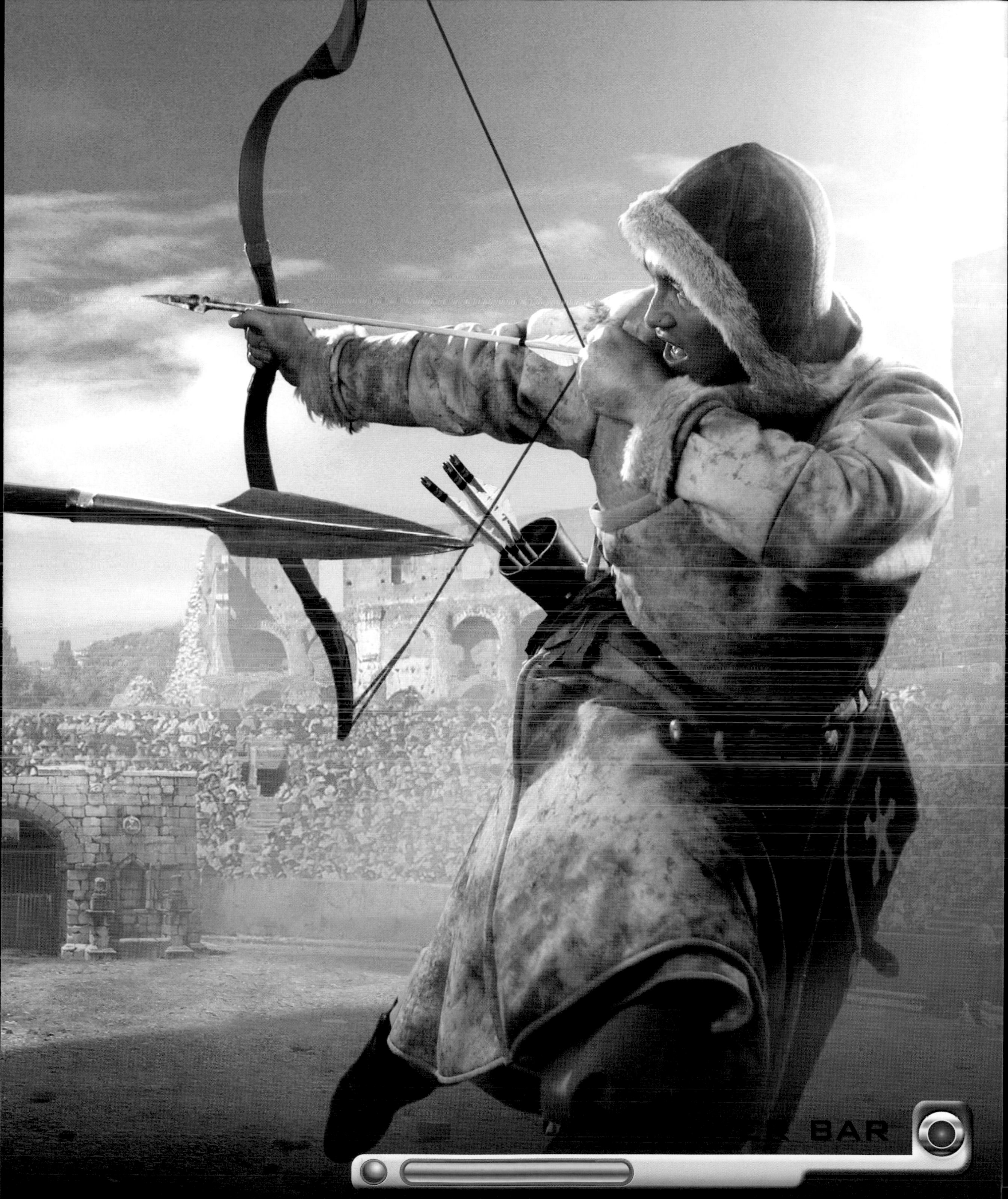
BAR

SPARTAN

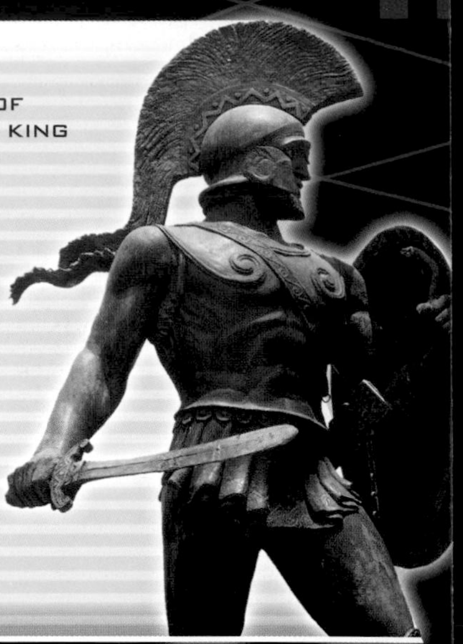

A STATUE OF LEONIDAS, KING OF SPARTA

GROWING UP IN THE GREEK STATE OF SPARTA WAS AS TOUGH AS IT COMES. CHILDREN LEARNED THAT THE FIRST DUTY OF EVERY ADULT CITIZEN WAS TO FIGHT SPARTA'S ENEMIES—AND SHOW NO FEAR. THE HOPLITE WAS THE SUPREME WARRIOR OF THE AGE.

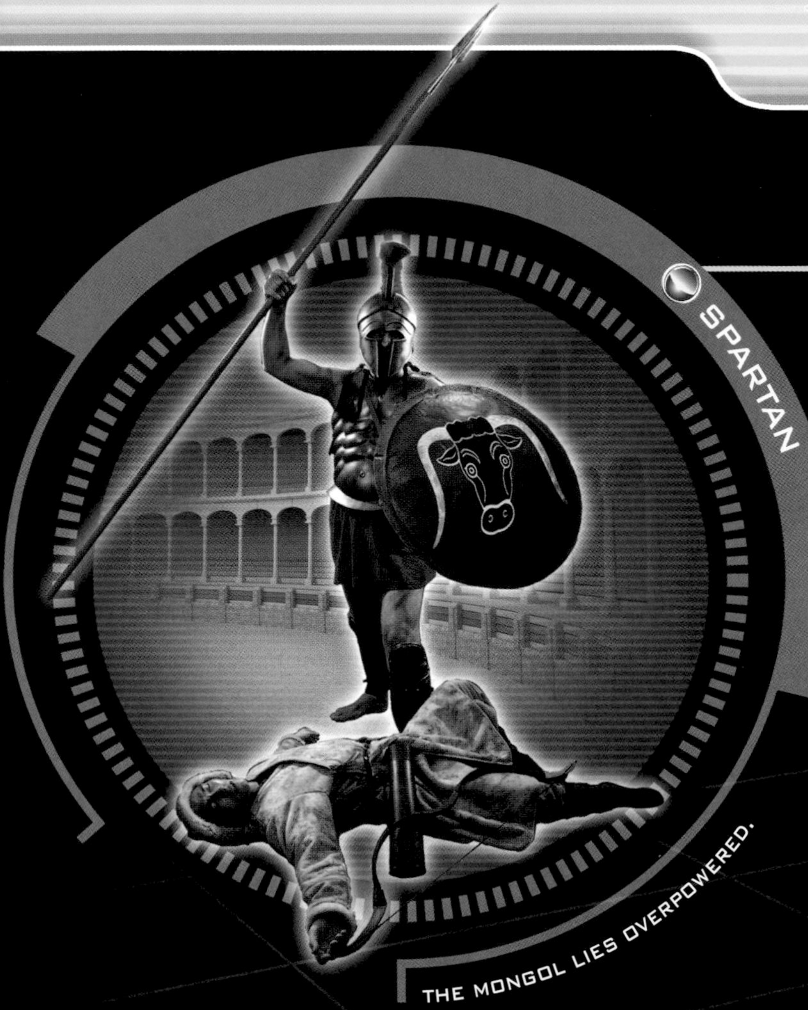
SPARTAN

THE MONGOL LIES OVERPOWERED.

THE SPARTAN WINS

THE MONGOL FIGHTS BEST WHEN GALLOPING ON HORSEBACK, HIS MANY ARROWS FLYING RELENTLESSLY AT THE ENEMY. THE SPARTAN IS BEST ON FIRM GROUND AS PART OF THE PHALANX, A CHARGING WALL OF SHIELDS AND SPEARS. ON FOOT, IN HAND-TO-HAND FIGHTING, THE SPARTAN HAS NO EQUAL IN THE MONGOL. EVEN ON HIS OWN, OUT OF THE PHALANX, HE IS FAST AND POWERFUL, AND HE BEARS DOWN FEARLESSLY ON HIS OPPONENT WITH HIS HEAVY SPEAR. AFTER ALL, HE HAS BEEN TRAINING FOR THIS MOMENT FOR MOST OF HIS LIFE.

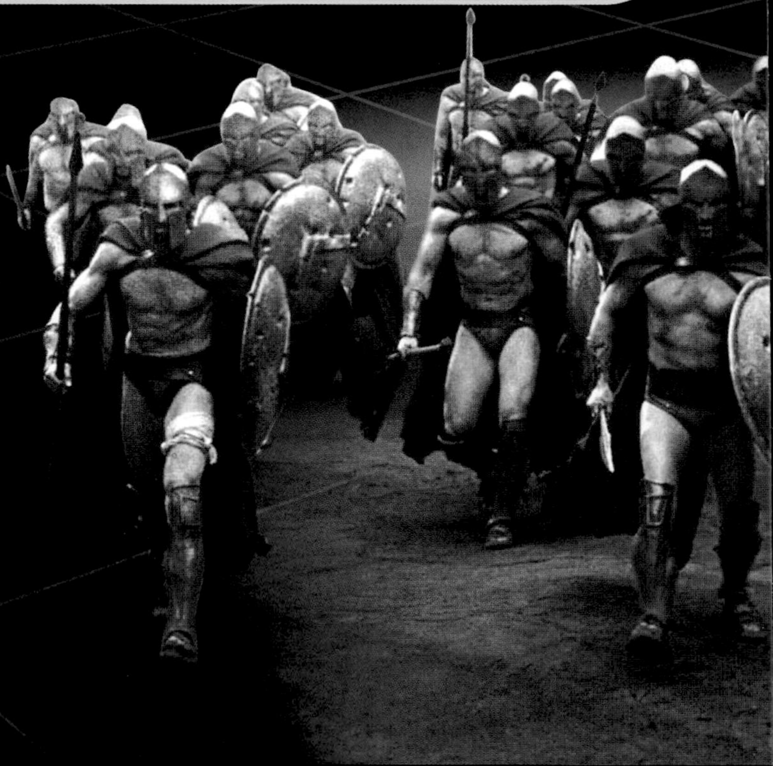

HOPLITES IN ACTION

THERMOPYLAE

One of the most famous battles in history took place at Thermopylae, Greece, in 480 B.C. For three days a small Greek army commanded by the Spartan king, Leonidas, held back one of the biggest armies the world had ever seen, assembled by the Persian king, Xerxes. A last stand was made by 300 Spartan hoplites, who fought to the bitter end. The Persians won the battle—but lost the war.

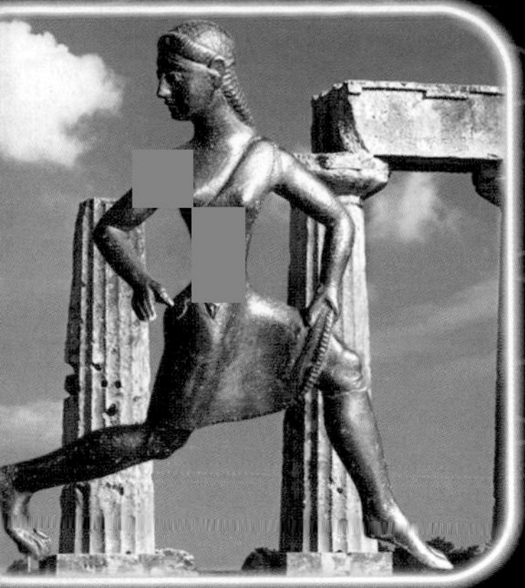

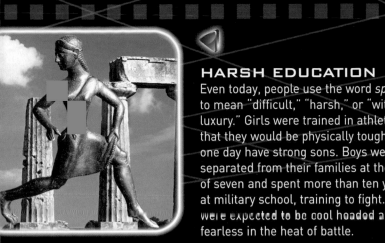

HARSH EDUCATION

Even today, people use the word *spartan* to mean "difficult," "harsh," or "without luxury." Girls were trained in athletics so that they would be physically tough and one day have strong sons. Boys were separated from their families at the age of seven and spent more than ten years at military school, training to fight. They were expected to be cool headed and fearless in the heat of battle.

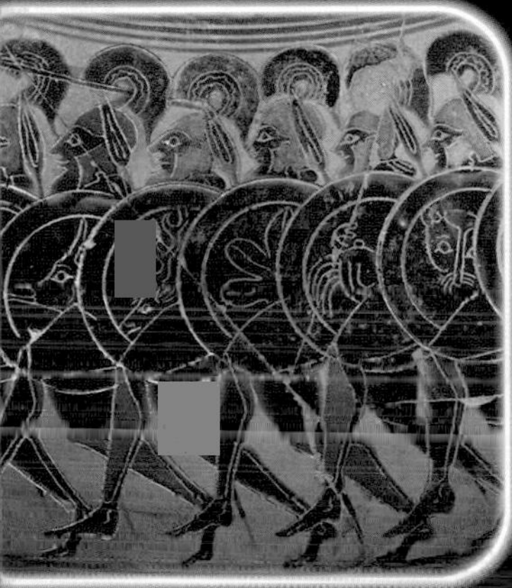

THE PHALANX

In battle, hoplites closed ranks in a formation called the phalanx. Their shields overlapped one another, making a solid barrier. Their spears bristled forward, preventing the enemy from fighting at close range. Rows of men advanced, with musicians playing to keep them in time. If the formation broke, the hoplites slashed at the enemy with their swords.

"Stranger, tell them in Sparta that we lie here, obedient to their commands."

Greek poet Simonides on the fallen Spartan heroes buried at Thermopylae

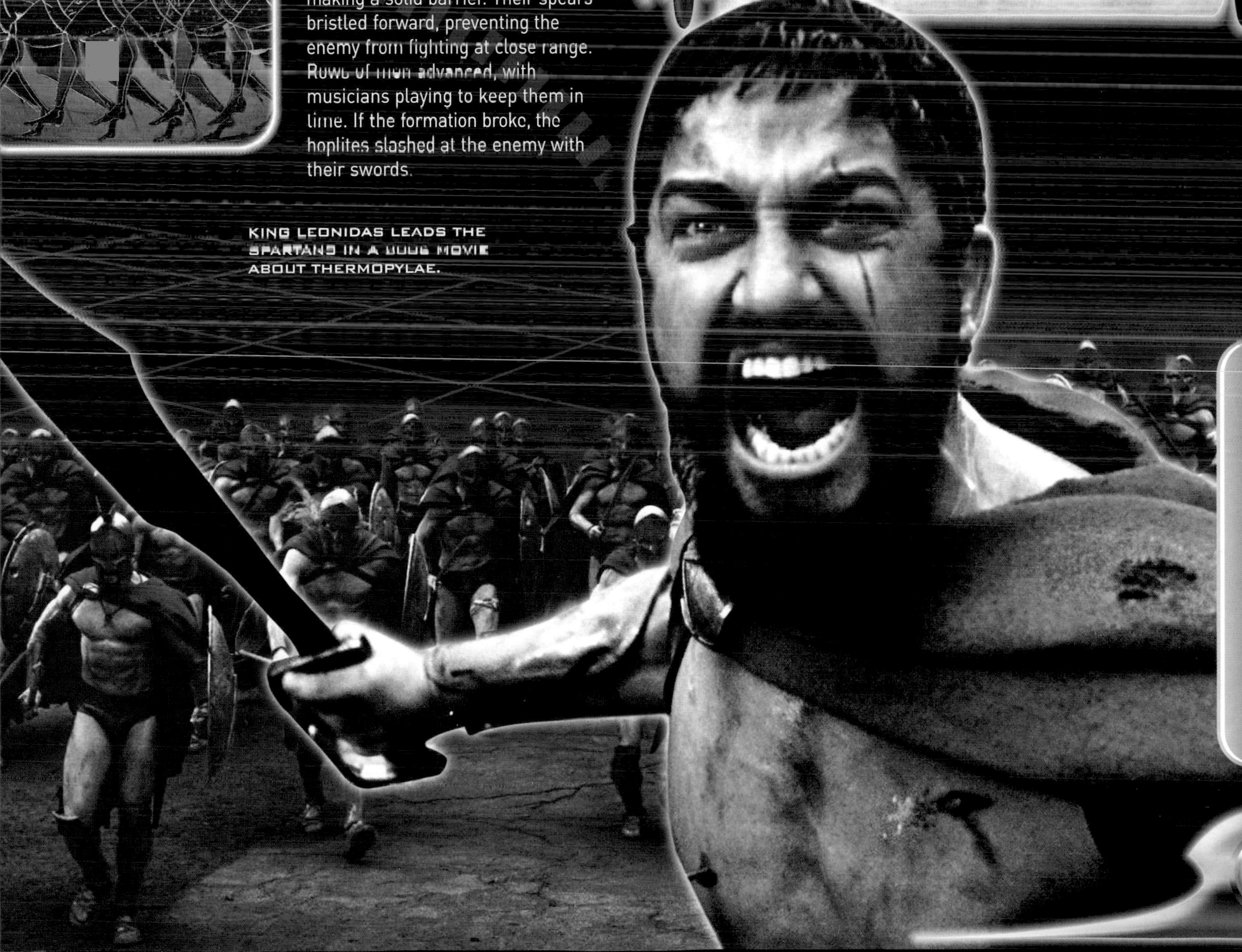

KING LEONIDAS LEADS THE SPARTANS IN A [illegible] MOVIE ABOUT THERMOPYLAE.

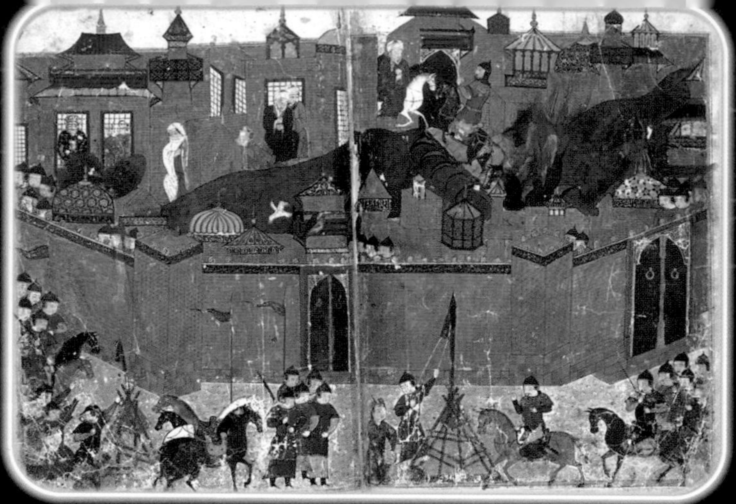

THE BURNING OF BAGHDAD

In 1258, the biggest army in Mongol history surrounded the magnificent city of Baghdad, in what is now Iraq. The war leader of the Mongol hordes was Hulagu, grandson of Gengl Khan. The city walls were soon breached, and hundreds of thousands of citizens were slaughtered as they fled. Mosque palaces, and libraries of priceless books were burned to the ground. The caliph, or ruler, of Baghdad was rolled up in a carpet and trampled to death by the hooves of the Mongol horses. Such was the price of resisting the Mongol advance.

MONGOL

THE MONGOLS WERE SUPERLATIVE HORSEBACK RIDERS AND DEADLY ARCHERS FROM THE STEPPES OF ASIA. THEIR ARMIES SWEPT INTO CHINA, INDIA, THE MIDDLE EAST, AND RUSSIA. THEY SEEMED SUPERHUMAN AND INVINCIBLE.

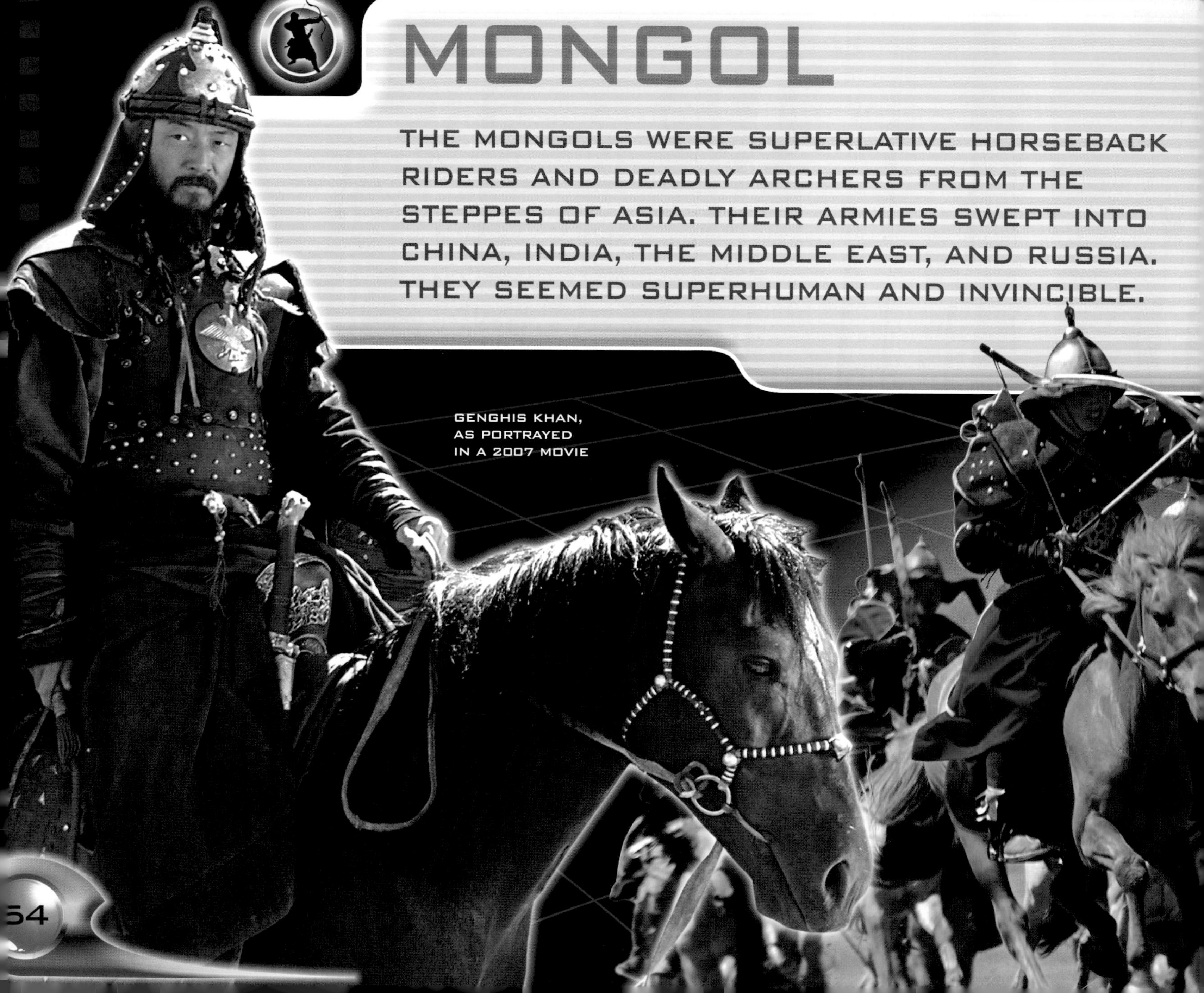

GENGHIS KHAN, AS PORTRAYED IN A 2007 MOVIE

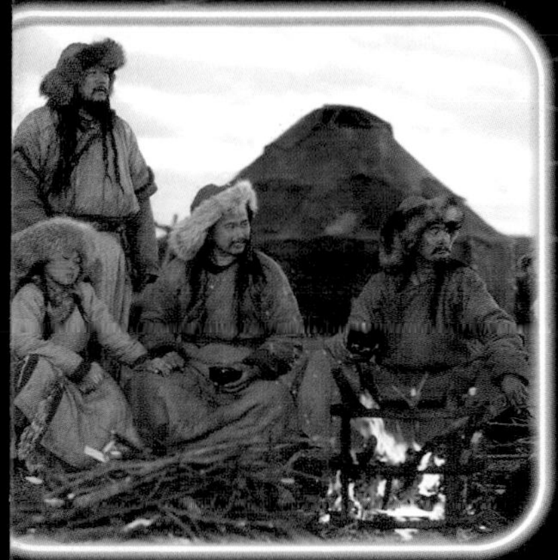

IFE ON THE STEPPES

c Mongols were nomads who traveled
th their sheep, goats, camels, and
ttle across the vast deserts and the
asslands, or steppes, of East and
ntral Asia. Mongol bands kept horses
herds numbering 10,000 or more and
lied heavily on mare's milk for their
od and drink. They camped in large felt
nts called gers. When on campaign,
hole Mongol communities followed
d supported the frontline soldiers.

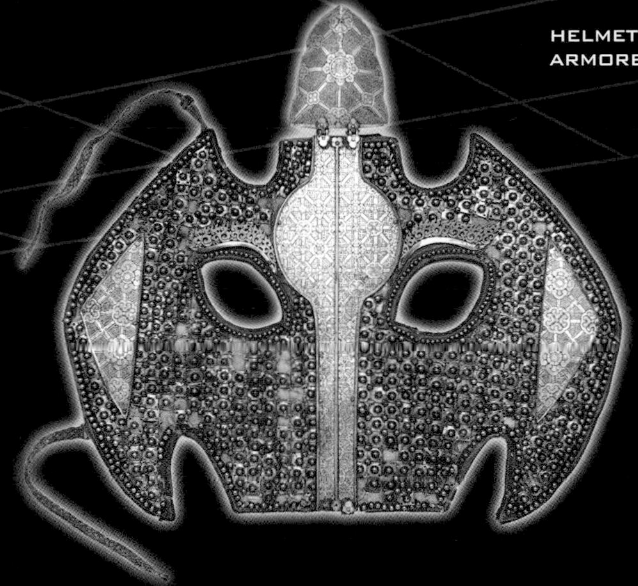

ARMOR TO PROTECT A HORSE'S HEAD

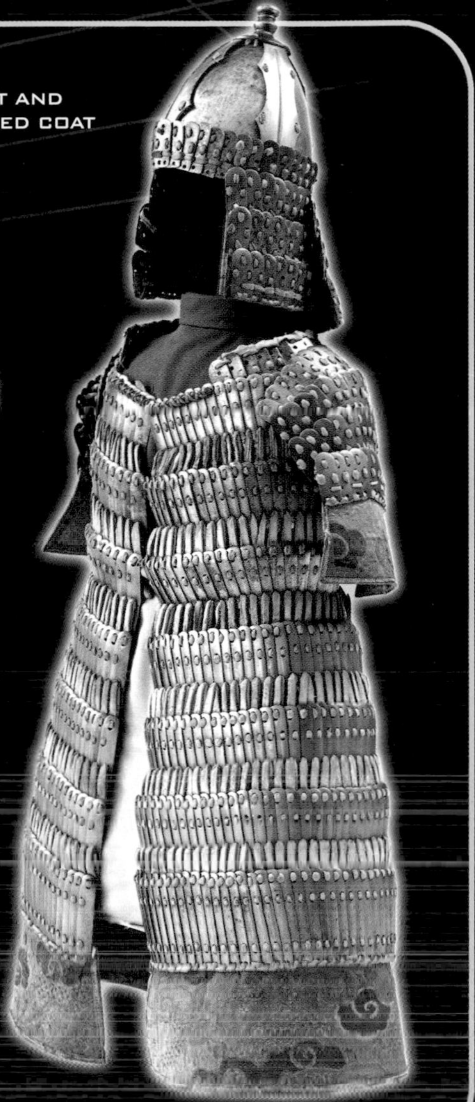

HELMET AND ARMORED COAT

ARMORED RIDERS

ELITE MONGOL CAVALRYMEN AND THEIR HORSES WORE ARMOR OF SMALL PLATES OR SCALES MADE OF METAL OR HARDENED LEATHER, ATTACHED TO A BACKING OF SILK OR OTHER CLOTH. IT NEEDED TO BE LIGHT ENOUGH TO WEAR ON LONG AND EXHAUSTING MANEUVERS AND TOUGH ENOUGH TO REPEL ENEMY ARROWS.

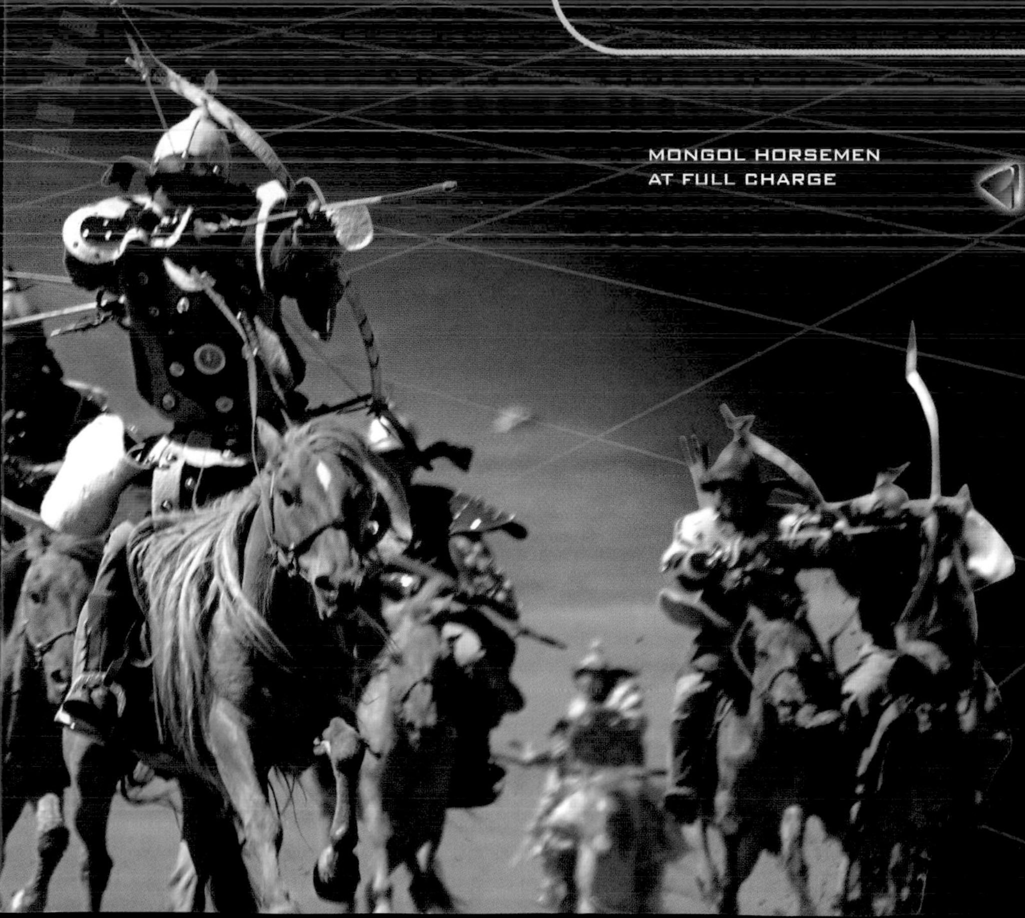

MONGOL HORSEMEN AT FULL CHARGE

GENGHIS KHAN

Mobility and endurance were the keys to the Mongols' success in battle. Their tough, stocky horses could gallop at speed, wheeling around, withdrawing, and then regrouping to charge once more. Weapons included the saber, the hooked lance, and a powerful bow. A hail of arrows would devastate enemy troops before a charge. In 1206, the Mongols united under a brilliant war leader named Temujin (1162–1227). He became known as Genghis Khan ("ruler of all"). His capital was at Karakorum in Mongolia, but his armies fanned out to attack China, Central Asia, Persia, and Russia.

FIVE VICTORS

OUR PAIRS OF WARRIORS, SEPARATED BY CENTURIES AND VAST DISTANCES, NEVER MET IN REAL LIFE. SO HOW DO WE KNOW WHO HAS WON? EACH IS SHAPED BY TRAINING, FIGHTING STYLE, WEAPONS, IDEALS, AND MENTAL AND PHYSICAL STRENGTH. IN HISTORY, MANY FACTORS INFLUENCED THEIR SUCCESSES: ARMY SIZE AND ORGANIZATION, TACTICS, TECHNOLOGY, AND EVEN WEATHER. IN OUR CONTESTS, EACH IS ON FOOT, IN SINGLE COMBAT, IN AN ARENA. WE CAN FIGURE OUT WHAT IS LIKELY TO HAVE HAPPENED, BUT EACH WARRIOR IS AN INDIVIDUAL. WHATEVER THE WEAPONS AND FIGHTING STYLE, INDIVIDUAL SKILL IS CRUCIAL TO THE OUTCOME.

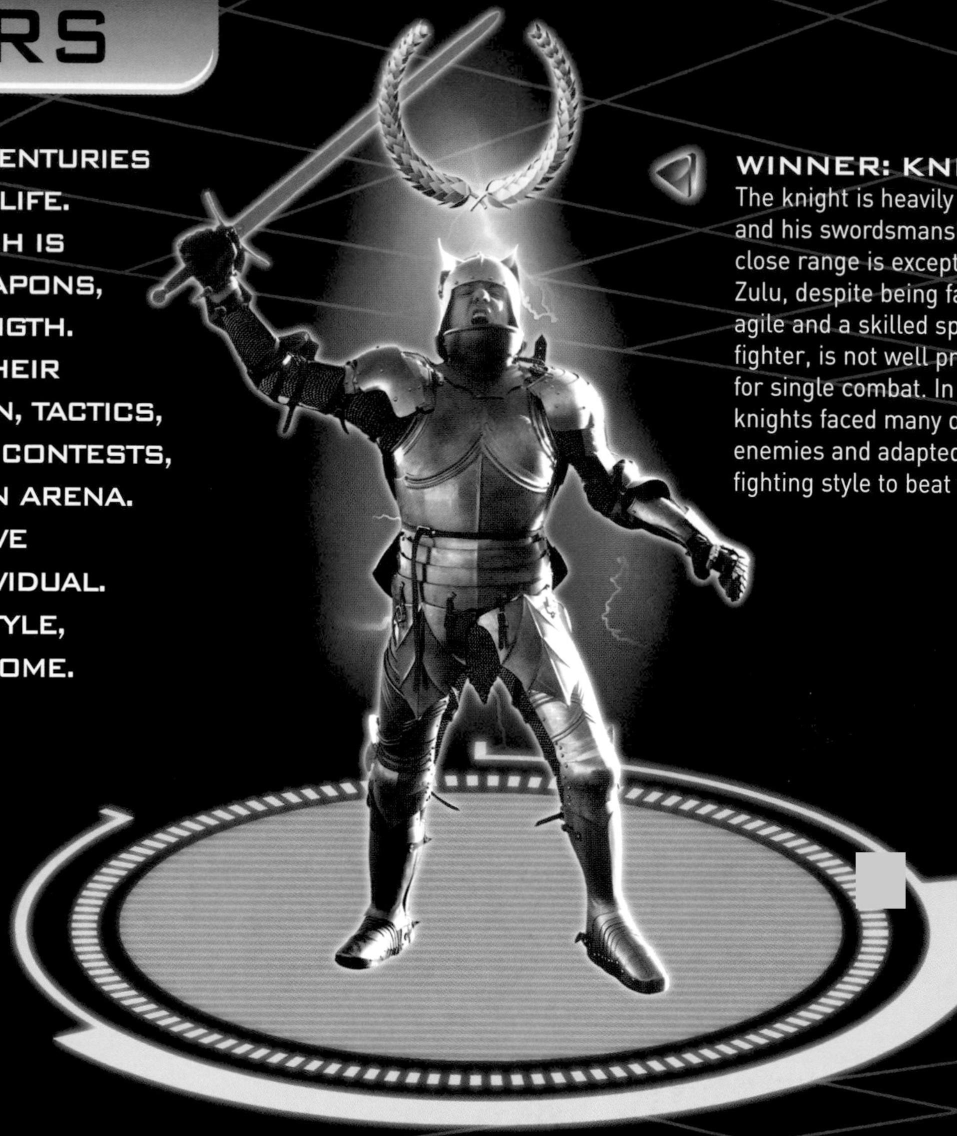

WINNER: KNIGH

The knight is heavily armec and his swordsmanship at close range is exceptional. Zulu, despite being fast an agile and a skilled spear fighter, is not well prepare for single combat. In histor knights faced many differer enemies and adapted their fighting style to beat them.

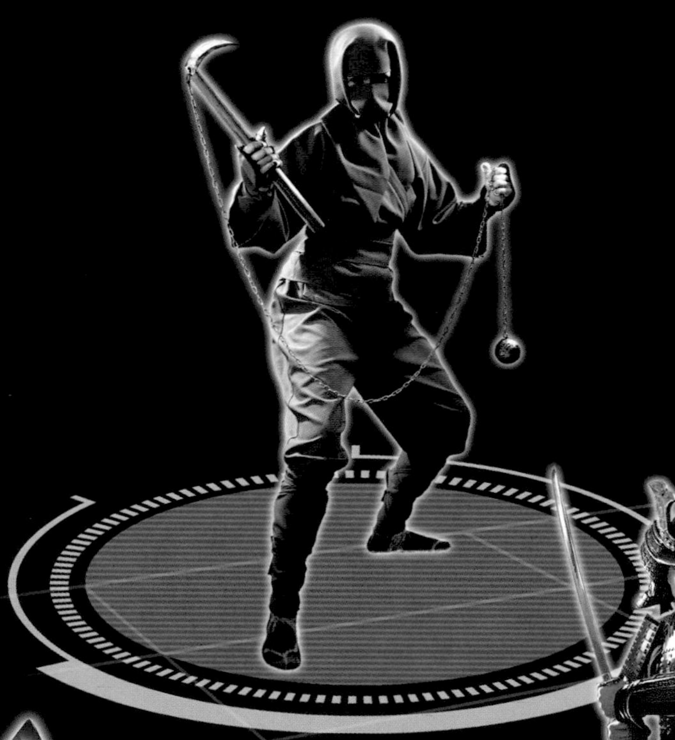

WINNER: NINJA

The ninja beats the gladiatrix. Unlike gladiators, ninja were not trained for prolonged combat. They were tough, skilled with many weapons, used cunning and surprise, and always intended to kill.

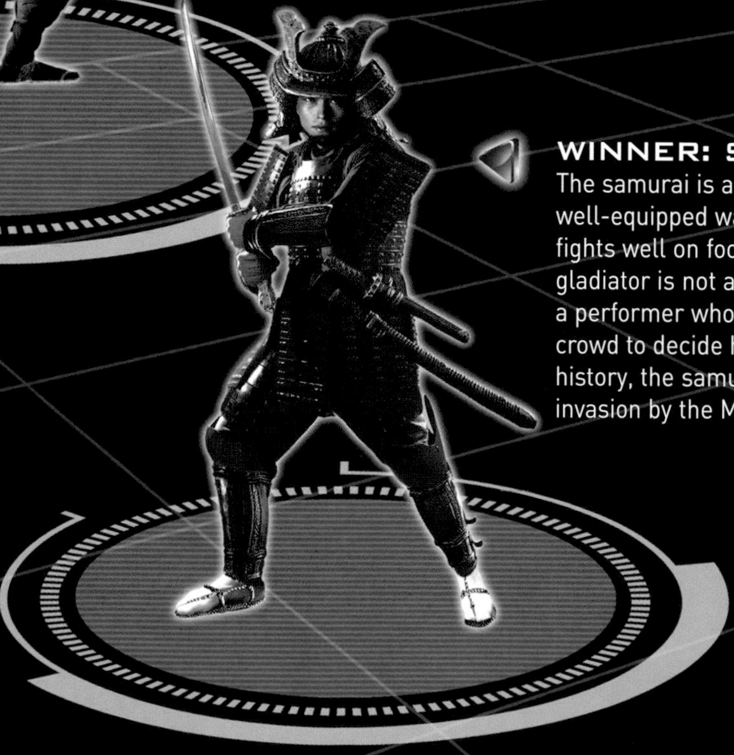

WINNER: SAMURAI

The samurai is a disciplined, well-equipped warrior who fights well on foot. The gladiator is not a soldier but a performer who looks to the crowd to decide his fate. In history, the samurai resisted invasion by the Mongols.

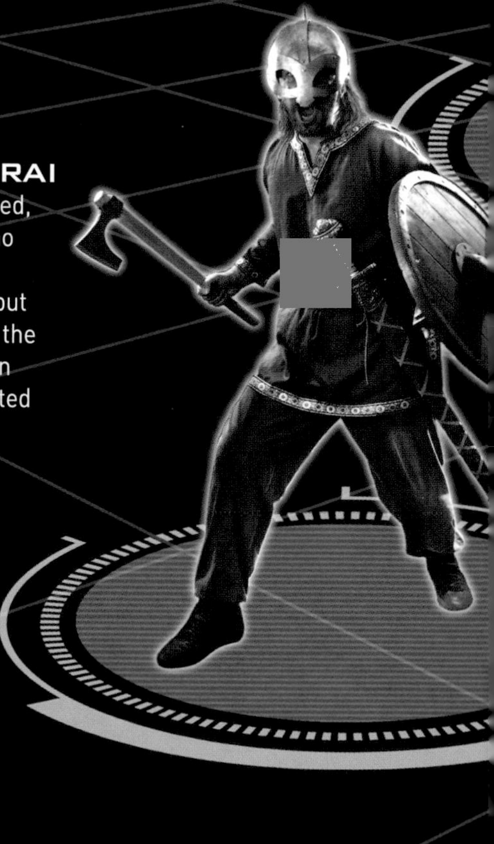

THE KNIGHT

THE KNIGHT IS STRONGER THAN THE OTHER VICTORS. E HAS THE WIDEST VARIETY OF DUELING KILLS AND WEAPONS. HIS LIFELONG RAINING, WARLIKE MENTALITY, AND WARRIOR ODE GIVE HIM THE EDGE OVER ANYONE. E HAS LEARNED FROM OTHER KNIGHTS' XPERIENCE IN FACING DIVERSE ENEMIES. E IS OUR ULTIMATE WINNER.

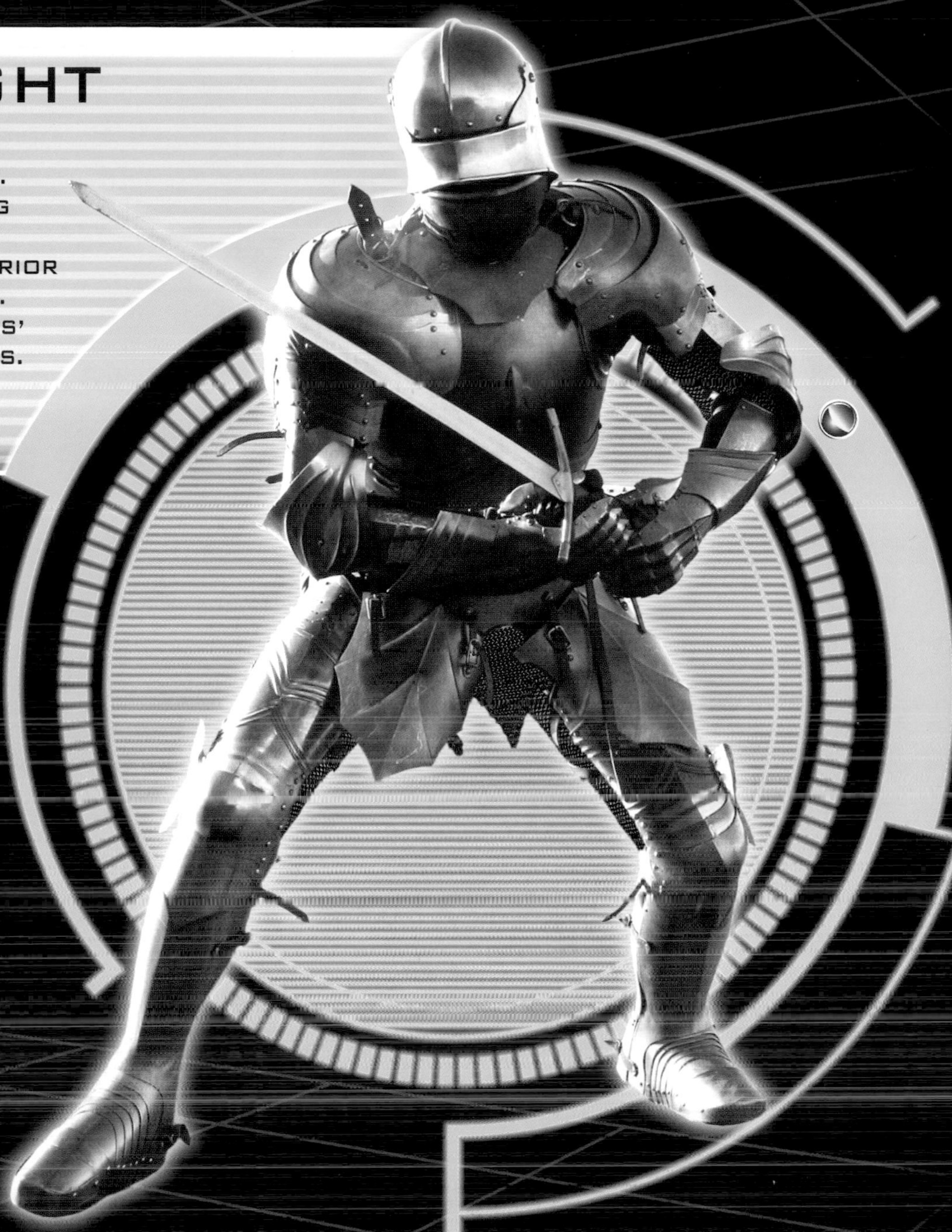

WINNER: SPARTAN

The Spartan is in his element in foot combat and is used to facing light archer opponents. He is fast and powerful. The Mongol is part of a formidable army, but on his own, on foot, he is not strong or fast enough to compete and is too close to fire his arrows effectively.

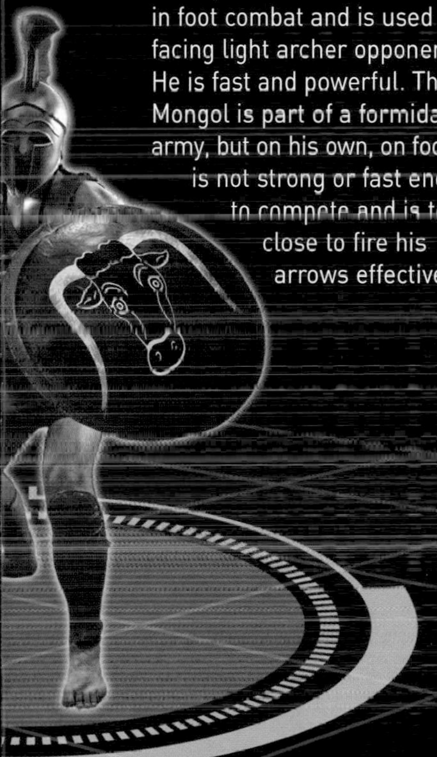

WINNER: VIKING

The Viking wins glory by slaying opponents. Aztecs win honor by capturing an enemy ready for sacrifice later—so the jaguar warrior is hampered by his approach. In history, the Aztecs were defeated altogether because their code of war was so different from that of their European conquerors.

WINNER FROM HEAD TO TOE

HELMET—other helmets give good protection, but the knight's hinged visor allows good visibility, too.

WEAPON—the knight's personal weaponry, evolved over hundreds of years, is excellent for dueling. His sword is his best weapon.

ARMOR—the knight's armor is better even than that of the samurai, Aztec, Spartan, and Mongol.

MIND—the knight trains to think quickly and respond strongly in any fight.

SPIRIT—all warriors have fighting spirit, but the knight's is a deadly combination of skills, equipment, ideals, and experience.

REMATCHES

WE'VE FOUND OUR FIVE VICTORS AND OUR ULTIMATE WINNER. BUT WOULD THINGS HAVE BEEN DIFFERENT IF THE CONTESTS HAD BEEN BETWEEN DIFFERENT PAIRS? WHAT DO YOU THINK? WHOSE WEAPONS ARE BEST? WHO IS MOST SKILLED? WHO HAS THE MENTAL EDGE?

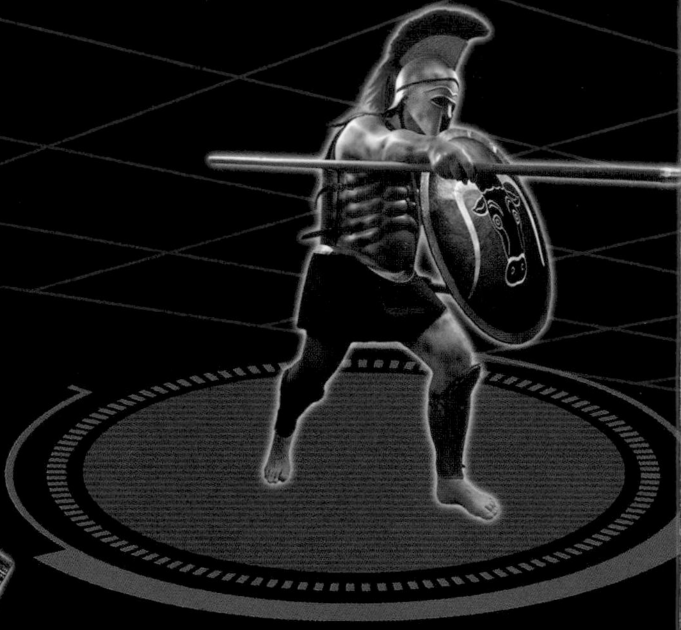

AZTEC VS SAMURAI

The Aztec swings his vicious macuahuitl at the samurai's limbs. His shield and cotton armor give him good protection, but can he really compete with the weapons and swordsmanship of the samurai? The samurai will win honor from killing or dying. The Aztec is prepared to die but is not hungry to kill.

WINNER: YOU DECIDE . . .

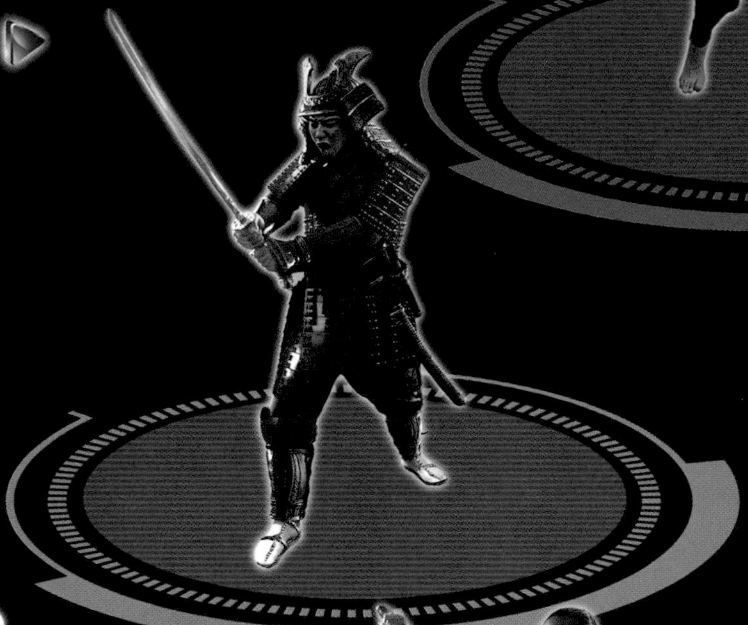

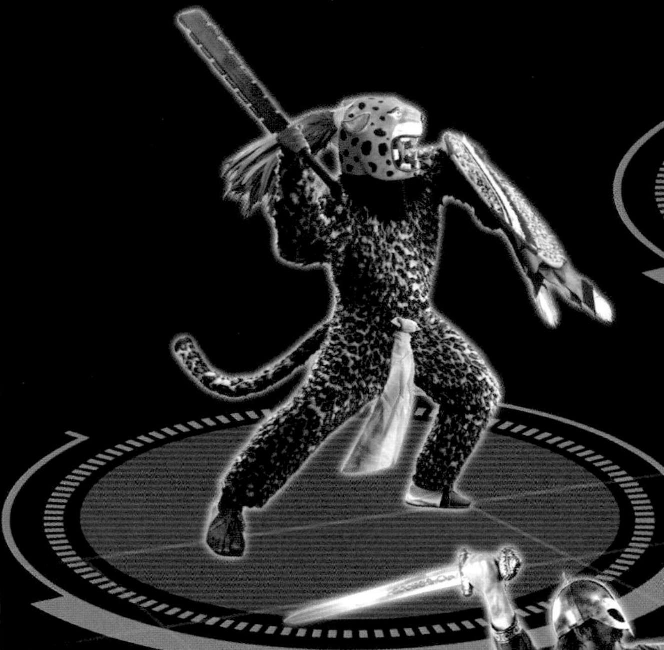

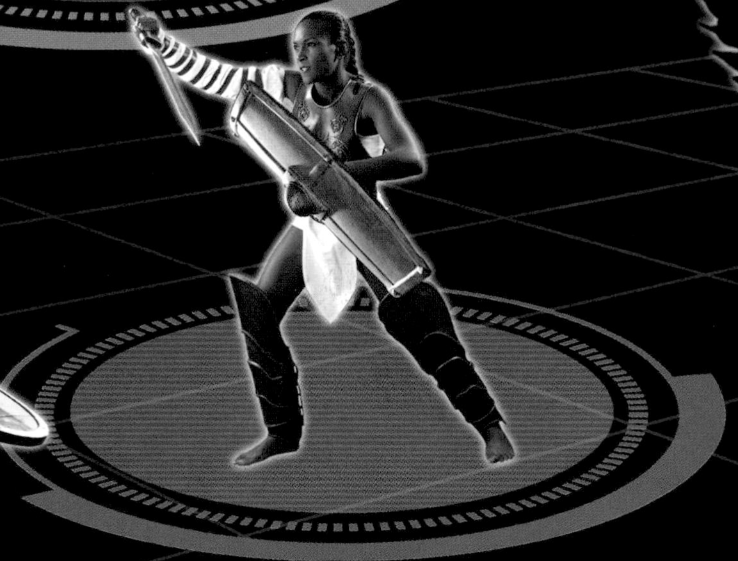

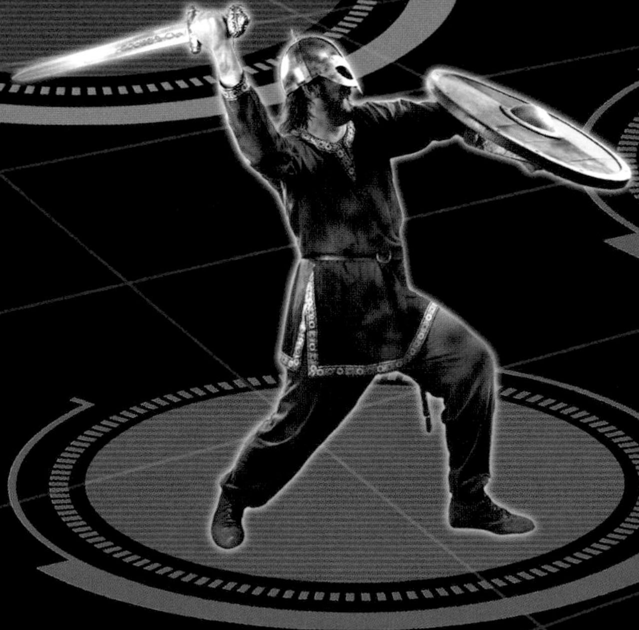

VIKING VS GLADIATRIX

The gladiatrix punches forward with her shield whi readying her dagger to strike. But she is used to ar opponent of equal strength and a fixed-length fight not a battle to the death against a beefy, ferocious warrior who has killed many enemies before. Her head is unprotected. Who will triumph?

WINNER: YOU DECIDE . . .

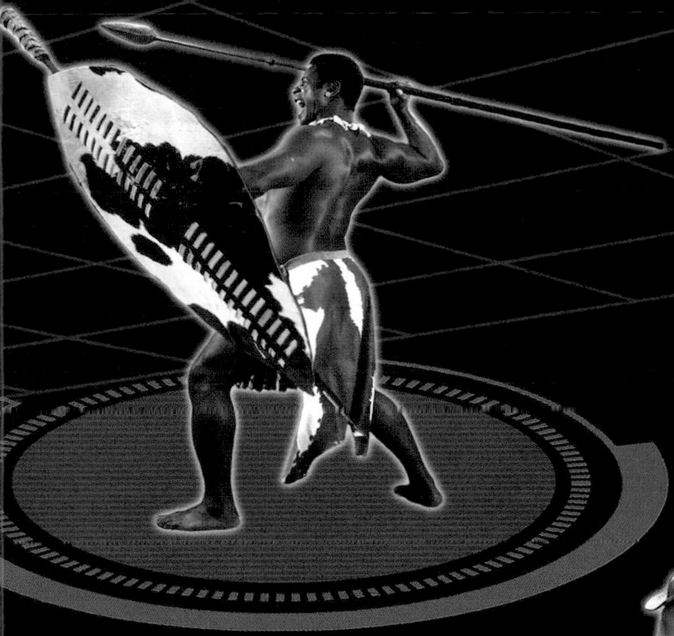

SPARTAN VS ZULU

Both warriors fight with shield and spear—ancient yet effective weapons adapted for their own fighting styles. Both have trained from boyhood, and in both cultures, to be a man is to be a warrior. But who has the tougher training regime and the better physical condition, the deadlier focus and the better armor?

WINNER: YOU DECIDE . . .

GLADIATOR VS KNIGHT

The gladiator is strong and heavy, his shield is large, and his helmet gives good protection, so he can defend himself well. But can he hope to find a chink in his opponent's armor or compete with the knight's array of precise and deadly dueling moves? Surely it's just a matter of time before the game is up?

WINNER: YOU DECIDE . . .

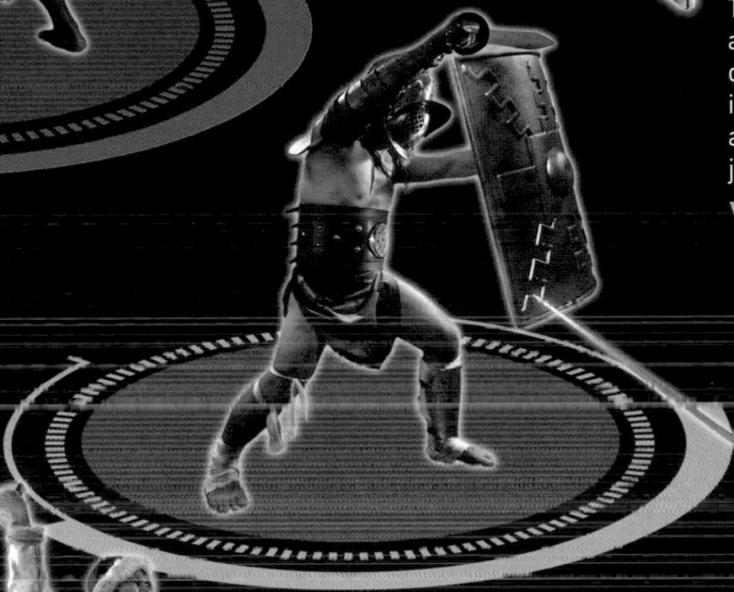

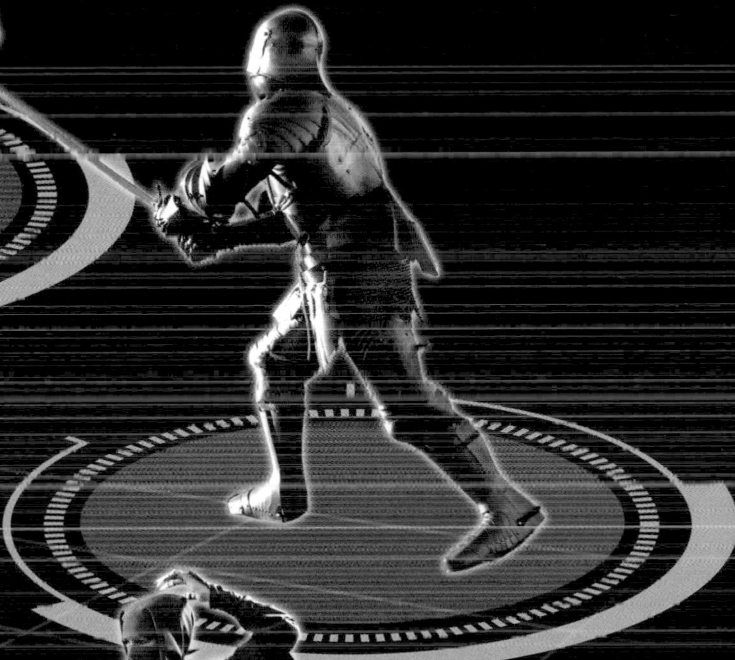

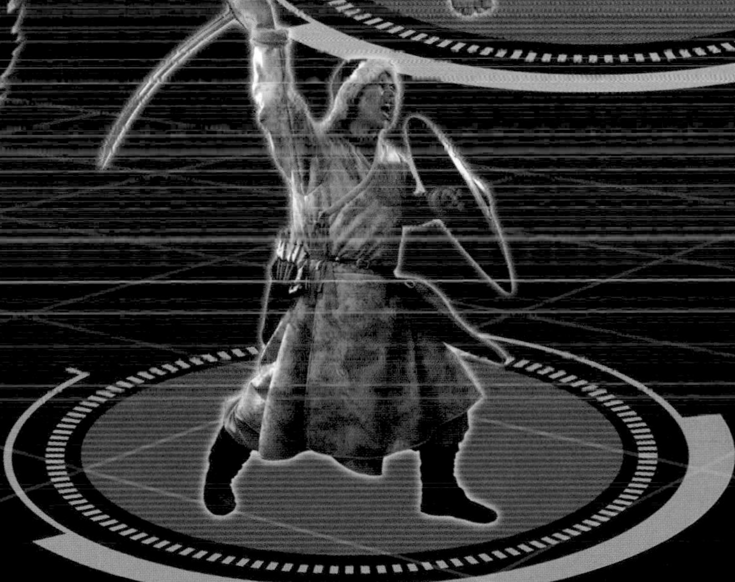

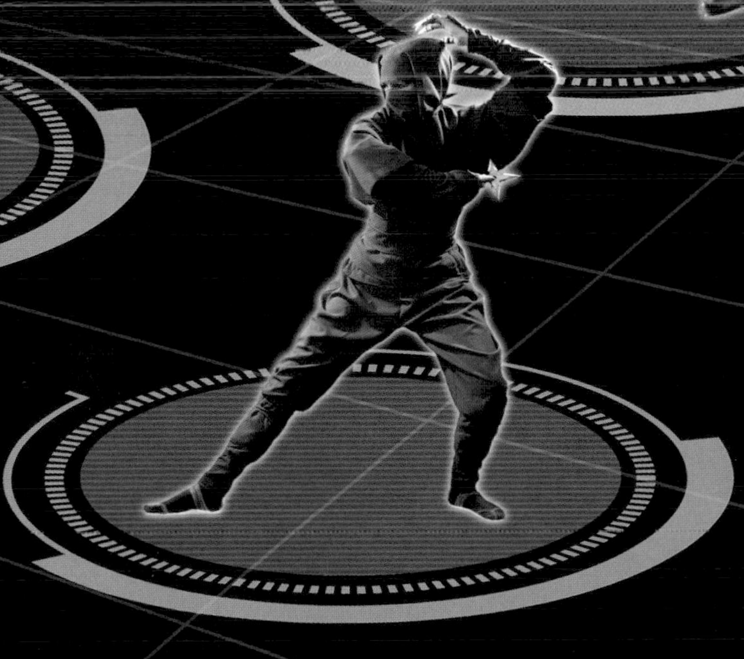

MONGOL VS NINJA

Both have terrifying reputations. The Mongol is clumsy on foot, but his saber is a good choice for close combat. The ninja is mentally agile and moves with strength and speed. But she has no armor, whereas his thick coat and silk shirt can stop and hold a piercing blade. Who will manage to deliver the fatal blow?

WINNER: YOU DECIDE . . .

WARRIOR WORDS

AZTEC

ATLATL (ot-lot-l) A spear thrower consisting of a stick carved with special loops for the fingers that is used to launch darts or spears.

CONQUISTADORS The Spanish forces who invaded and conquered several Native American peoples, including the Aztecs.

ELITE The most powerful, talented, successful, or richest members of a society. Elite warriors are those who have achieved high status through success in battle.

EMPIRE A group of lands and nations governed by a single ruler.

FLOWER WAR A battle waged by the Aztecs to train soldiers and to capture prisoners for sacrifice. It was a young soldier's first battle.

MACUAHUITL (ma-kwa-wheat) A saw sword.

OBSIDIAN A glasslike volcanic substance that occurs naturally in Mexico.

PARRY A move to block or deflect an attack.

SACRIFICE The killing of a living thing as an offering to the gods.

TEMPLE A building dedicated to a god or goddess and used for rituals, festivals, or offerings.

VIKING

BERSERKER A particular type of Viking warrior who was especially fierce and violent.

BOSS A round metal knob that covers the hand grip of a shield.

CULT A system of religious belief, often an extreme version of a more widespread religion, with particular beliefs and customs. An example is the berserker cult.

FRENZIED In a state of violent excitement.

JARL (yarl) A Scandinavian regional ruler or chieftain, usually one level below a king.

LETHAL Deadly.

LITHSMAN An ordinary freeborn Viking warrior.

MEAD An alcoholic drink made from honey.

PLUNDER To steal people's goods and possessions by force in a raid or attack.

PROW The front part of a ship.

SCABBARD The piece of equipment in which a sword is stored when not in use.

SCANDINAVIA The geographical region that includes modern-day Norway, Sweden, Denmark, and Iceland.

GLADIATOR

AMPHITHEATER An oval or circular stadium where Roman audiences watched gladiator fights and other sporting events.

ARENA The central, sand-covered part of an amphitheater where fights were staged.

BARRACKS A complex of buildings where soldiers—or gladiators—lived and trained.

GLADIUS The ancient Roman short sword, used by soldiers and by gladiators.

LANISTA The head and owner of a school of gladiators.

LUDUS A gladiator school.

MURMILLO A type of gladiator who wore a crested helmet.

RETIARIUS A type of gladiator who fought with a trident (three-pointed spear), net, and dagger.

SECUTOR A type of gladiator specially equipped to fight a retiarius.

SLAVE A person who is deprived of freedom and rights, can be bought and sold, and is forced to work for no reward.

VISOR The movable part of a helmet that covers the face.

SAMURAI

BUSHIDO The samurai code of honor, or "way of the warrior." It included the principles of justice and honesty, contempt for death, self-control, politeness, loyalty to superiors, and a duty to defend the honor of one's name.

DAIMYO (dye-myow) A samurai leader or warlord.

DO Samurai body armor, made of leather straps or scales joined together with silk or leather cord.

HARA-KIRI A method of ritual suicide carried out by samurai warriors. It means "stomach cutting."

KATANA The long samurai sword.

MEDIEVAL Belonging to a period of history from approximately A.D. 500 to 1500.

NOBLE Belonging to the nobility, a high level of society.

SHOGUN A Japanese military leader.

TANTO A samurai dagger.

TORSO The top part of a person's body—the chest, stomach, and back.

YARI A spear used by samurai and by Japanese foot soldiers.

KNIGHT

CHIVALRY The knight's code of honor.

COAT OF ARMS A badge worn by a knight on his shield or clothing to identify him in battle.

COURTEOUS Polite, considerate, and respectful.

CRUSADES The series of "holy" wars, from A.D. 1095 to 1291, launched by Christian Europe for control of the parts of the Middle East known as the Holy Land.

DUEL A fight between two people (also called single combat).

EARL A type of knight—rich, a large landowner, and a minor royal.

MACE A heavy, spiked club.

MAIL Armor made from many small, interlinked iron rings.

POLEAX A type of battle-ax with a hammerhead and spike as its head.

SIEGE An attempt to force a castle or town to surrender or be captured by cutting off its supplies and communications and attacking its defenses.

TOURNAMENT A pageant where knights fought mock battles to practice and show off their fighting skills.

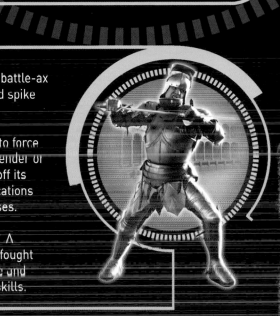

BATTLE-AXES
Warriors have used versions of this ancient tool in battle for thousands of years. Cheaper than swords, battle-axes can be swung or thrown. Look out for the variety in ax heads.

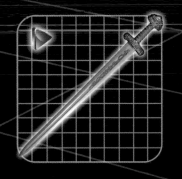

SWORDS
A sword is a long metal blade with a sharpened edge or edges and a point. Design and technique vary, but for many cultures this is the weapon that is most highly prized.

DAGGERS
These weapons developed from prehistoric tools. Shorter than swords and easier to conceal, they are useful stabbing weapons for use in close combat.

ZULU

AFRIKANER A South African person descended from Dutch settlers.

IBUTHO (plural: ambutho) A regiment of 1,000 Zulu warriors. Each had its own shield colors, and often it contained warriors who were all the same age and had trained together since boyhood.

IKLWA A Zulu stabbing spear.

IMPI The Zulu word for any group of armed fighters—for example, an army—made up of many ambutho.

INYANGA (plural: isinyanga) A Zulu healer or traditional herbal doctor.

IQAWE A great hero renowned among Zulu warriors.

ISIJULA A throwing spear used for hunting as well as in battle.

IWISA A club (sometimes called a knobkerrie) used for delivering heavy blows to the head.

RATIONS The amount of food issued to soldiers when they are on active duty.

RITUAL A formal action performed in a particular and usually solemn way, sometimes for a religious purpose.

NINJA

ASSASSIN Someone who kills secretly or by surprise.

GEISHA A traditional Japanese female entertainer who dances and plays music to please men.

HOKODE Hand claws used for climbing walls and fighting.

KUNOICHI A female ninja.

KUSARIGAMA A ninja weapon consisting of a long chain linking a sickle to a heavy ball.

MARTIAL ARTS Any of a group of styles of fighting and self-defense. Japanese examples include kendo, jujitsu, judo, and karate.

NINJUTSU The "art of stealth," or of being a ninja. Its 18 disciplines included unarmed combat, sword fighting, disguise and impersonation, espionage (spying), and geography.

SHURIKEN A throwing star—a star-shaped arrangement of blades used as a missile.

SICKLE A curve-bladed implement used in farming for cutting crops that also makes a dangerous weapon.

TESSEN A fan concealing blades among its folds.

YAM A sweet potato.

GLADIATRIX

AMAZON A member of a tribe of female warriors from ancient Greek legend.

ANUBIS The ancient Egyptian god of burial and funerals, thought to protect the dead and lead their souls to the afterlife. In ancient Rome, Anubis and Mercury (in some ways a Roman equivalent) were associated with gladiators. People dressed as Mercury would carry fallen gladiators from the arena.

CELT A member of a group of peoples who lived in Central Europe some time before 800 B.C. The Celts were some of the Romans' most hated and feared enemies.

CHARIOT A horse-drawn two-wheeled cart used in ancient warfare or for racing.

MOSAIC A picture or design made from small pieces of colored glass or stone. Many surviving Roman mosaics include pictures of gladiators.

NUBIAN A person from the ancient kingdom of Nubia (now part of Egypt and Sudan), which lay just beyond the Roman Empire.

VENATOR A type of gladiator who fought against wild beasts such as big cats. He or she fought with a spear.

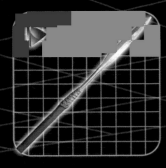

SPEARS
A spear is a simple but effective weapon. Made from a wooden shaft and a sharp metal head, it can be short or long, thrown like a javelin, or used at close range to thrust.

SHIELDS
These hand-held weapons are used offensively, hitting hard with the edge or center, and defensively to deflect and block enemy blows. Look for the variety in shape and design.

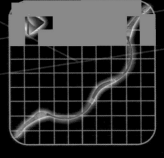

BOWS
A bow is a spring for firing arrows. The archer draws (pulls back on) the string of the bow, storing energy that powers the arrow forward, far and fast.

SPARTAN

CITIZEN A member of a city.

CITY-STATE A city that is also an independent state. Ancient Greece was made up of city-states including Athens, Corinth, Sparta, and Thebes.

CUIRASS Body armor, often made of bronze, worn by Greek soldiers to protect the torso.

EMBLEM A picture, design, or badge worn by a warrior.

EXOMIS A particular type of tunic worn by Spartan hoplites. Spartans usually wore crimson tunics in battle—for them, crimson was a manly, warlike color and an honorable choice because the dye was expensive.

HOPLITE An ancient Greek foot soldier armed with spear and shield. Named after the Greek word for shield, *hoplon*.

LAKEDAIMONIAN Another word for Spartan. Originally Sparta was the capital city of a state called Lakedaimonia, but the state itself became known as Sparta, too.

PHALANX A battle formation used by Greek hoplites. It consisted of eight ranks of men, each lined up with their shields locked together to form a wall. The front three lines held their spears ready for attack.

MONGOL

ARCHER A person who shoots with a bow and arrows.

CAVALRY Soldiers who fight on horseback.

GER A Mongol portable house (often called by its Turkish name, yurt). It is a circular tent made of a wooden framework covered in felt.

HORDE A Mongol field army.

INVINCIBLE Unbeatable.

KESHIK A Mongol light archer. About six out of every ten Mongol troops were keshiks.

LANCE A type of spear.

MANEUVER A large-scale military movement such as an attack by an army.

NOMAD One of a group of people who have no fixed home or town but live in temporary camps and move from place to place.

PERSIANS The people of the vast Persian Empire, centered on modern-day Iran.

QUIVER The container in which an archer stores his arrows.

STEPPE A vast area of grassland stretching from Eastern Europe across Central Asia.

In this index, "data page" refers to the page of information about each warrior that folds out from each combat scene.

ABC

DEF

GHI

JKL

MNO

PQR

STU

VWXYZ

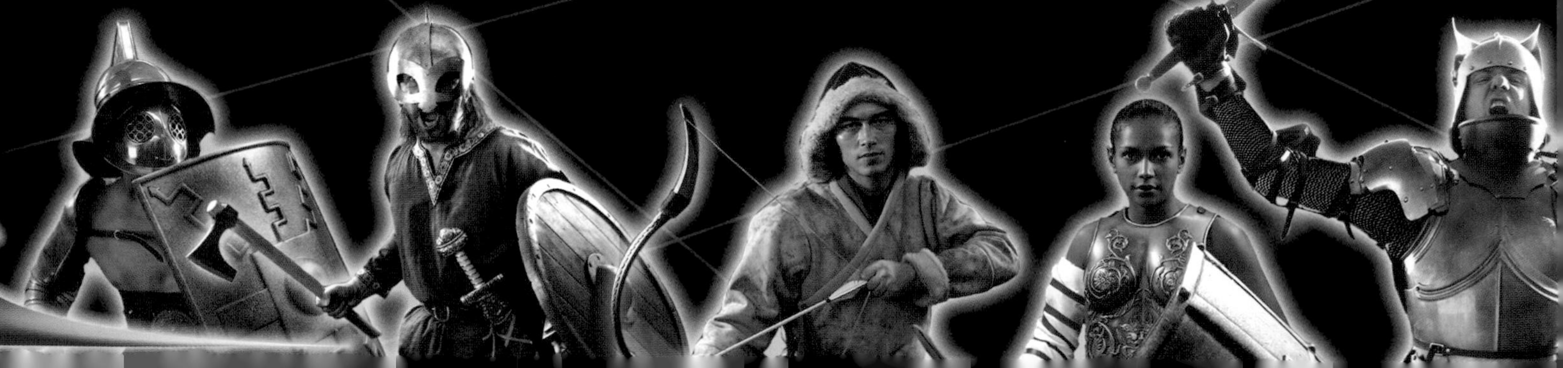

KINGFISHER
LONDON & NEW YORK

CONCEPT BY Hannah Wilson
WRITTEN BY Catherine Brereton, Philip Steele, Hannah Wilson
ILLUSTRATION BY Steve Stone, represented by Artist Partners Ltd.
DESIGN BY Jo Connor

CONSULTANTS: Dr. Hugh Bowden, King's College London; John Clements, Association for Renaissance Martial Arts; Professor Peter Heather, King's College London; Ian Knight; Dr. John M. D. Pohl, UCLA; Dr. Stephen Turnbull, Leeds University

Published in the United States by Kingfisher,
175 Fifth Ave., New York, NY 10010
Kingfisher is an imprint of Macmillan Children's Books, London.

Distributed in the U.S. by Macmillan, 175 Fifth Ave., New York, NY 10010
Distributed in Canada by H.B. Fenn and Company Ltd., 34 Nixon Road, Bolton, Ontario L7E 1W2

Library of Congress Cataloging-in-Publication data
has been applied for.

ISBN: 978-0-7534-1916-8

Kingfisher books are available for special promotions and premiums. For details contact:
Special Markets Department, Macmillan, 175 Fifth Avenue, New York, NY 10010.

For more information, please visit www.kingfisherpublications.com

First American Edition October 2009
Printed in China
1 3 5 7 9 8 6 4 2
1TR/0609/SC/LFA/157MA/C

CREDITS

THE PUBLISHER WOULD LIKE TO THANK THE FOLLOWING FOR PERMISSION TO REPRODUCE THEIR MATERIAL:

Every care has been taken to trace copyright holders. However, if there have been unintentional omissions or failure to trace copyright holders, we apologize and will, if informed, endeavor to make corrections in any future edition.
(t = top, b = bottom, c = center l = left, r = right)

Pages 4bl Shutterstock/Kateryna Potrokova; 12tl Shutterstock/LoopAll; 12bl National Geographic Society/Ted Spiegel; 12br with the kind permission of the British Museum Board of Trustees; 13tc with the kind permission of the British Museum Board of Trustees; 13tr Alamy/Homer Sykes; 13c Alamy/Troy GD Images, 13b S.H.E Production, Canada; 15tl Art Archive/National History Museum, Mexico City; 15tr Art Archive/Museum fur Volkerkunde, Vienna; 15cr with the kind permission of the British Museum Board of Trustees; 15bl Getty/Moritz Steiger; 15br Corbis/Lake County Museum; 22 Alamy/Japan Art Collection; 23tr Alamy/Malcolm Fairman; 23bl Alamy/Photos12; 24l Getty/DK; 24cl Scala/National Museum, Naples; 24br Alamy/Jochen Tack; 25t Corbis/Roger Wood, 25bl Alamy/Content Mine International; 25cr Shutterstock/PixAchi; 25 Rex Features; 32bl Photolibrary/Stephan Goerlich; 32–33 Arena Artists Partners; 33ct Getty/Robert Harding; 33c Art Archive/Musée Condé Chantilly; 33br Heritage Images/The Board of Trustees of the Armouries, Leeds; 34cl Bridgeman Art Library (BAL)/Heini Schneebeli; 34bl BAL/Heini Schneebeli; 34bl BAL/Heini Schneebeli; 34bl Alamy/Interfoto; 34bl BAL/Heini Schneebeli; 34r Art Archive; 35tl Alamy/Dennis Cox; 35b Alamy/Zute Lightfoot; 42bl Stephen Turnbull; 42cb Alamy/Interfoto; 43t Getty/Aurora Images; 43c Getty/Aurora Images, 43tr Alamy/Iain Masterton; 43cl Shutterstock/Lilun; 43bl Rex Features; 44tl Corbis/Alinari; 44bl Alamy/Nick Turner; 44r Alamy/Nick Turner; 45tc Alamy/Photos12; 45tr with the kind permission of the British Museum Board of Trustees; 45bl Alamy/Nick Turner; 45r Rex Features/Solent News; 52tr Alamy/Rolf Richardson; 53tl Shutterstock/Petros Tsonis; 53tl Alamy/The London Art Archive; 53cl Art Archive/Archaeological Museum, Naples/Dagli Orti; 53b Ronald Grant Archive; 53br Kobal/Warner Bros.; 54tl Art Archive/Bibliothèque National, Paris; 54bl Rex Features/Picturehouse/Everett; 55tl Kobal/Igor Vereschagin; 55tc Scala/Metropolitan Museum, New York; 55tr The Board of Trustees of the Armouries, Leeds; 55br Corbis/Hamid Sardar

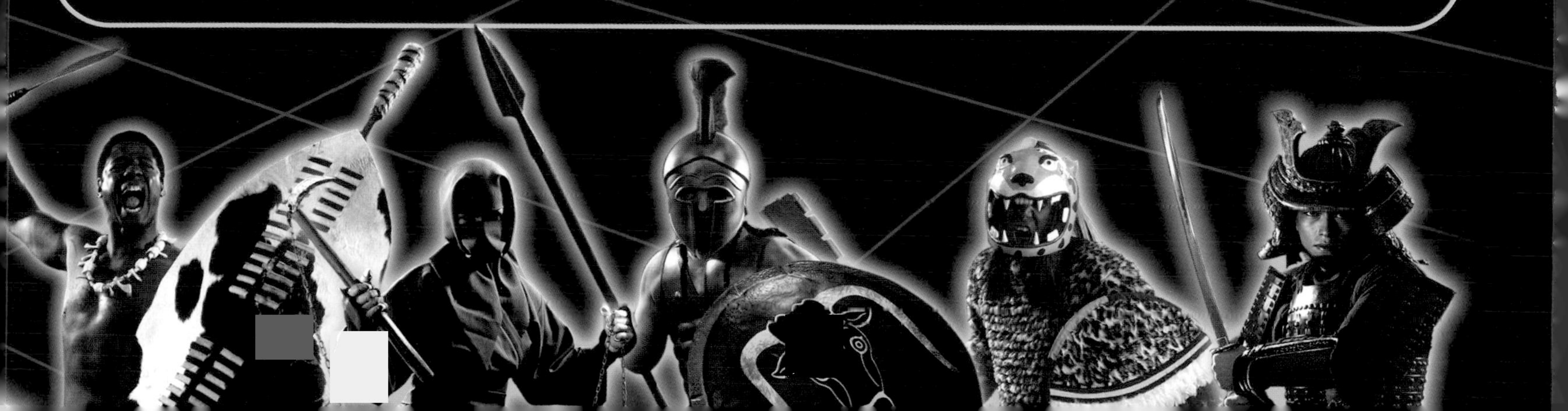

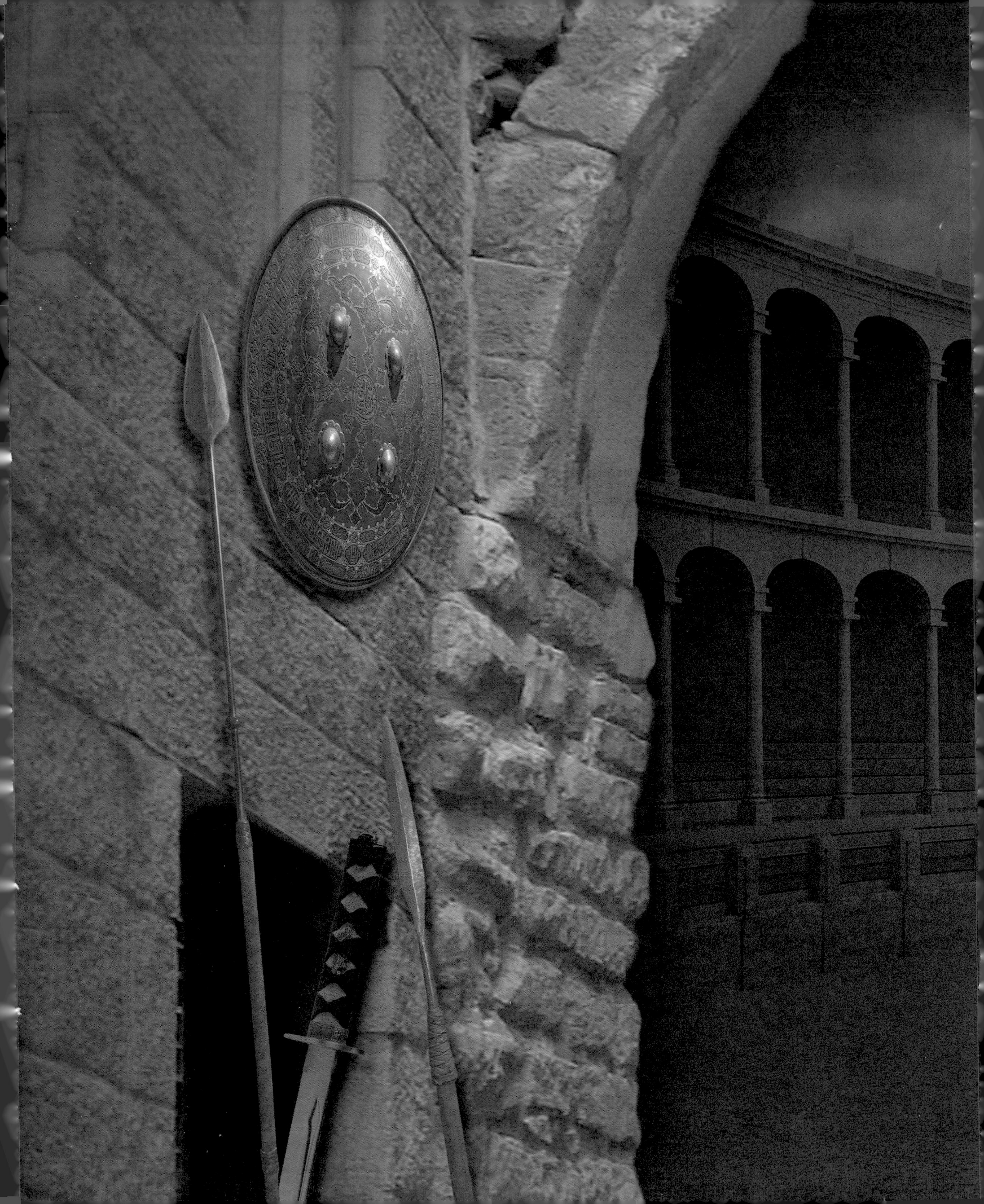